"Normally, I don't tackle strange men in elevators."

When Ethan didn't say anything, she leaned back against the polished wood, crossing her arms under her breasts, drawing his attention there like a homing beacon. She tilted her head, and sent him the prettiest smile he'd ever seen.

"Do you accept my apology?"

Maybe it was the husky quality of her voice, but something struck him hard, square in the chest, dead center, like a shot from a crossbow.

He nodded. Diverted his attention to the elevator doors.

Who *was* she? What kind of allure did she have that he was practically brain-dead just from hearing her voice, looking into her eyes, holding her briefly in his arms?

In a red rose scooped-top thing, white skirt, and pink shoes, she looked fresh and luscious.

It seemed like gilding the lily that her mouth was the same shade as her blouse, or that, when she smiled, she had glamour-girl dimples.

D0050293

By Marianne Stillings

SATISFACTION
AROUSING SUSPICIONS
SIGHS MATTER
MIDNIGHT IN THE GARDEN OF GOOD AND EVIE
THE DAMSEL IN THIS DRESS

ATTENTION: ORGANIZATIONS AND CORPORATIONS
Most Avon Books paperbacks are available at special quantity discounts for bulk purchases for sales promotions, premiums, or fund-raising. For information, please call or write:

Special Markets Department, HarperCollins Publishers, 10 East 53rd Street, New York, New York 10022-5299. Telephone: (212) 207-7528.   Fax: (212) 207-7222.

MARIANNE STILLINGS

Satisfaction

AVON
An Imprint of HarperCollinsPublishers

This is a work of fiction. Names, characters, places, and incidents are products of the author's imagination or are used fictitiously and are not to be construed as real. Any resemblance to actual events, locales, organizations, or persons, living or dead, is entirely coincidental.

AVON BOOKS
An Imprint of HarperCollins*Publishers*
10 East 53rd Street
New York, New York 10022-5299

Copyright © 2007 by Marianne Stillings
ISBN: 978-0-06-085066-1
ISBN-10: 0-06-085066-3
www.avonromance.com

All rights reserved. No part of this book may be used or reproduced in any manner whatsoever without written permission, except in the case of brief quotations embodied in critical articles and reviews. For information address Avon Books, an Imprint of HarperCollins Publishers.

First Avon Books paperback printing: December 2007

Avon Trademark Reg. U.S. Pat. Off. and in Other Countries, Marca Registrada, Hecho en U.S.A.
HarperCollins® is a registered trademark of HarperCollins Publishers.

Printed in the U.S.A.

10 9 8 7 6 5 4 3 2 1

If you purchased this book without a cover, you should be aware that this book is stolen property. It was reported as "unsold and destroyed" to the publisher, and neither the author nor the publisher has received any payment for this "stripped book."

For my agent, Pam Hopkins.
Thank you for your representation,
your professionalism,
your insights, suggestions, love,
support, and weather reports.
This book is for you
with my gratitude and deepest regard.

Chapter One

Sleeping single in a double bed? Then think pink, the color of love and romance! Wear pink to attract your Mr. Right—shell-pink, rose, magenta, any hue will do. Snuggle between pink sheets, nosh on pink foods, and splash the doorway over your bedroom with passionate pink paint. When you're "in the pink" you won't need to go looking for love, honey; it'll smack right into you!

Georgiana Mundy's Feng Shui for Lovers

A bell pinged, and the set of double doors slid open. Stepping inside the empty elevator, Ethan Darling thumbed the button for the thirty-first floor, then crossed his arms and leaned his shoulder against the cherrywood paneling, watching as the polished steel panels began to glide quietly together.

"Wait, wait, wait!"

Fingers fluttered between the closing doors like a frantic butterfly.

Without thinking, Ethan thrust his hand through the narrow gap, curling his fingers around the edge of the cool metal door at the exact moment a pink blur shot into the car and slammed into his chest, knocking him back a few steps. A forehead conked him on the nose, causing sharp pain between his eyes, and momentarily blurring his vision.

The woman was either a klutz or a clever assassin. Before he could decide which, her heel crunched down on his right foot, and he clenched his jaw to keep from calling her a very ungentlemanly name. Her abrupt movements gave her gigantic shoulder bag the momentum of a wrecking ball, and as it headed directly for his nuts, he jerked his hips back just in time to salvage his manhood.

Somewhere along the line, he'd grabbed her shoulders and pulled her against his body to keep them both from falling. Through the fabric of his suit jacket and shirt, he felt firm muscle, solid bone, and warm feminine flesh where her boobs and belly met his torso.

Her head lowered, she was panting hard, and had looped her arms around his neck to steady herself. Anybody entering the elevator would have sworn they were lovers locked in a passionate embrace—unless they happened to notice the look of agony mixed with the ecstasy on his face.

For a moment, the compartment grew quiet while he stared down at the top of her head. Finally, he murmured thinly, "You hurt?"

She kept her head down as she disentangled

her arms from around his neck and pushed herself off him. In a husky voice, she whispered, "I'm embarrassed."

He dropped his arms to his sides, suddenly not knowing what to do with them. Her body had fit him so perfectly, felt so good, he was almost sorry their little skirmish was over.

Running her fingers through her glorious tumble of long brown hair, she apparently tried to smooth the tangled mass, but only succeeded in galvanizing his attention. Ms. Smackdown was really a knockout.

Finally she raised her face, their eyes locked, hers widened, and she rushed, "I hurt you! Oh, God, I'm so sorry!" She lifted her hand as if to touch his cheek, but seemed to think better of it, curled her fingers in, and lowered her arm.

"I'm fine," he bit out, realizing as he did so that the pain in his side had flared again. Maybe his abrupt movements had irritated the scarring, but suddenly the wound burned like hell, and it was all he could do to keep from snapping at her to leave him the hell alone.

She examined him more closely. "But I see pain there, in your eyes. Are you sure I didn't—"

"Positive." He wanted to clutch his ribs, but didn't make a move.

A warning bell sounded, and he realized her purse had dropped into the open doorway, preventing the doors from closing. He reached past her to pick it up, the bell ceased ringing, the doors slid together, and the elevator began to rise.

Finally, he thought with relief as he handed her the bag.

She smiled sheepishly up at him. "I, um, I hope I didn't cause any damage when my purse hit you."

He shrugged, noticing the brown of her irises, sort of like melty bits of chocolate toffee. Her lashes were dark, too, and sooty, making her eyes appear languid and mesmerizing. For a couple of seconds, he totally forgot how to breathe. If his heartbeat wasn't set on automatic, he'd've needed jumper cables to get it going again.

"I'm running late this morning," she explained with a flirty little grin. "Normally, I don't tackle strange men in elevators."

When he didn't say anything, she leaned back against the polished wood, crossing her arms under her breasts, drawing his attention there like a homing beacon. She tilted her head, and sent him the prettiest smile he'd ever seen. He got the impression she looked at injured puppies in exactly the same way.

Squaring his shoulders, straightening his stance, he strengthened his defenses. She was too womanly or something. Too feminine. A real girly-girl. He hated that.

"You're not exactly a chatterbox," she observed. "Do you accept my apology?"

Maybe it was the husky quality of her voice, maybe it was the sincerity he read in her eyes, maybe it was the scent of her floral perfume, but something struck him hard, square in the chest, dead center, like a shot from a crossbow.

Normally, he was smooth with women, sophisticated, but standing next to Ms. Knockout made him feel totally out of his element, as though he'd never spoken to a girl before in his life. Good thing he wasn't the talkative type, otherwise he might blurt out something he'd really regret, such as, *When can I see you again?*

Unwilling to answer her question and give away how she affected him, he only nodded.

He diverted his attention to the elevator doors. Just how the hell long did it take to go up thirty-one floors? he wondered, turning his anger on the elevator buttons. He thumbed the lighted 31 five or six times in rapid succession. Yeah, it was stupid, but at least it gave him something to do that didn't involve thoughts of his elevator companion.

Who *was* she? What kind of allure did she have, that he was practically brain-dead just from hearing her voice, looking into her eyes, holding her briefly in his arms?

In a red rose scooped-top thing, white skirt, and pink shoes, she looked fresh and luscious. It seemed like gilding the lily that her plump mouth was the same shade as her blouse, or that, when she smiled, she had glamour-girl dimples.

She was damned cute, and if he'd been some hormonal college kid, he'd be going for it right about now, but he was thirty-seven and at this point in his life, he liked his women cool and angular, quiet, smart, classy—and in a cab headed for home before midnight.

This woman was warm and curvy, and just the type to talk a man's ear off during sex. The cuddling, mold-herself-to-you, let-me-cook-you-breakfast, do-you-like-kids? kind of woman.

He eyed the seam in the elevator doors, willing it to open.

"That's a beautiful suit you're wearing," she said, giving him an appraising look. "Expensive silk, and well tailored, too. Armani? You have excellent taste. Too bad it's the wrong color for you."

If this elevator ride wasn't over in about five seconds, he thought, he was climbing out through the ceiling. Shoving his hands in his pockets, he stabbed her with his deadliest glare.

She lowered her head a little and smiled up at him. "All I meant was, your suit is the wrong color blue. For *you*. With your dark hair and hazel eyes, you need to stay away from navy. Charcoal would be much better, with a deep gold silk tie, to bring out the flecks in your eyes."

Flecks? "My eyes don't have flecks—"

"Sure they do." She gazed up at him for a moment and her eyes went all soft and sad again. Reaching into her handbag, she rummaged around in it for a moment. With a small flourish, she brought out a kind of handkerchief-looking thing. "Please take this," she said, holding it out to him. "It'll help."

"Help what?"

"Green is for healing."

"I don't need healing." Under his arm, the wound across his ribs shouted a dissenting opinion.

Before he could stop her, she took his hand and pressed the silky fabric into his palm, curling his fingers over it. The material was warm and soft and smelled faintly of her perfume. Her hand still cupped under his, she said, "Keep this scarf in your aura."

He scowled down at the fabric. "The urge for a suggestive comeback is burning my tongue."

"Resist," she whispered, sliding her fingers from under his hand, leaving a trail of heat in their wake. "Keep the scarf with you, and look at it often," she instructed, apparently unaware of the effect her touch had on him. "Any injuries you have will heal much faster. I promise."

Before he could tell her she was full of it, a bell pinged. The doors rumbled wide to reveal the thirty-first floor. Stepping out onto the thickly carpeted hallway, he held the door for her as she followed him out.

"Thanks, Mr. . . ." She arched her brows expectantly, letting her voice trail off.

He hated this part. Every female he'd ever met thought she was being cute and original, and this woman would undoubtedly be no exception. On hearing his name, she'd blink those big brown eyes, smile adorably, and coo, *Really? Your name is Darling? Why, that's just . . . darling!* Then she'd giggle or wrinkle her nose or say something coy.

When he'd been younger, he'd used it to get girls into bed. Now it was just plain annoying.

"The name's Ethan Darling."

She said nothing, but slowly moved her gaze

down his body and back up. He felt every inch of her perusal as if she were running her fingers over his naked flesh.

Nibbling thoughtfully on her bottom lip, she said, "Really. Your name is *Darling*." Abruptly, she burst out laughing like she'd just heard the funniest joke in the world. It was a deep throaty sound, rich and full and sexy as hell, and it affected his body in ways he really didn't want to think about right now. Catching her breath, she choked, "I can only imagine what you did in a past life to deserve *that* kind of karma!"

She gestured at the green silk he still clutched in his hand, and her eyes grew serious. "Please remember to keep it close. It'll help with the pain."

"I told you, I'm not in—"

But before he could finish the lie, she spun on her heel and took off down the hall, leaving him to watch her walk away.

He glared down at the fabric for a moment, then slid the damned thing into his pocket. A second later, he curled his fingers around it, letting it fill the palm of his hand. He rubbed his thumb against the cloth, enjoying its seductive warmth, imagining for a moment he was touching the curve of her cheek.

Everyone he'd ever met in his life had wanted something from him, from his time to his money to his very soul. Yet this woman had taken one look at him and decided he needed to be given something, and she'd given it. Instead of snarling at her, he should have thanked her.

Swallowing a curse for being the stupid jackass he was, he put the encounter behind him and headed for the KALM-TV offices at the far end of the hall, where, a few minutes later, a bubbly blond receptionist escorted him into the private offices of Osgood Horton.

"Welcome, Inspector Darling," Horton said, rising from behind his desk to offer Ethan his hand. "Please have a seat."

Osgood Horton, the manager of KALM-TV, looked exactly the way Ethan had supposed a man named Osgood Horton would look: forty-ish, baldish, shortish, plumpish. But the guy had a firm, sincere handshake, reminding Ethan once more that looks could be deceiving.

"You can forgo the Inspector part, Mr. Horton," Ethan said as he settled into the deeply cushioned leather chair across the desk from the station manager. "I haven't been a detective with the SFPD for six years."

Horton gave him a too-white grin. "Don't private detectives have some kind of official title?"

"Just call me Ethan. What can I do for you, sir?"

Horton pursed his lips and gave a quick nod. "Not much for small talk, eh? *Right* to the point. I like that, Ethan. I *like* that." He smacked his open palm on the edge of his desk so hard, everything bounced, including several small framed photos of what appeared to be his family. Settling back into his chair, Horton eyed Ethan over the top of rimless half-moon glasses. "I'm told Paladin Private Investigations is the best."

"Thank you."

"And I want the best."

"Then KALM-TV has come to the right place. Are you looking for surveillance equipment, personal security, the services of a private investigator, or perhaps risk analysis and management—"

"Yes!" Horton barked, raising a finger as if to punctuate the decision.

"Yes, which?"

"Personal security *and* private investigation." His brow lowered, and so did his voice. "You watch TV, Ethan?"

"Not if I can help it."

"Never?" he whispered, as though the gods might smite him for even contemplating such a thing. "News broadcasts? Sports? Stock market reports?" He glanced nervously around as if looking for hidden microphones. Under his breath, he mumbled, *"American Idol?"*

"I don't have a lot of free time," Ethan said. Why bother telling the man he hated most television shows and would only watch if somebody literally held a gun to his head?

Horton took in a long, deep breath and seemed to consider Ethan's remarks. "So you've probably never seen *Fetching Feng Shui* or *CaliforniYum*, the two highest-rated shows on the West Coast?"

Ethan stared at the man. *"Californi . . . Yum?"*

Horton beamed. "Cute, right? My brainchild. She wanted to call it *Cooking with Georgie* or *Georgie's Kitchen*, or some such thing. Too vanilla, too white-bread, no snap, no mass appeal! In this business, you've got to think high concept. Grab the audience by the balls, you know?" Grinning with enthusiasm, he curled his chubby fingers into a fist as if to demonstrate what grabbing an audience by its nether regions might look like.

"Who's Georgie?"

Horton's eyes widened. "Who's *Georgie*? Why, why, why, she's Georgiana Mundy, Ethan. Certainly you've *heard* of her?" He whipped off his glasses and tossed them onto his desk. Blinking several times in obvious astonishment, he said, "Miss Mundy's our *star*. *Every*body knows who Georgiana Mundy is. She's written three cookbooks, two lifestyle guides, has two top-rated TV shows of her own, has appeared on *Today* and *Good Morning, America*, and has been interviewed by some of the top names in journalism. Why, why, why . . . she's Julia Child, Martha Stewart, and Emeril Lagasse all rolled into one!"

A mental picture formed inside Ethan's head of Georgiana Mundy, a six-foot-tall middle-aged felon with a Boston accent and a five o'clock shadow. Fighting down a cringe, he said, "Is Miss Mundy in some kind of trouble?"

Horton nodded, his battleship gray eyes earnest, wary. "I don't know. But something, yes, something is going on."

"Can you be more specific?"

"About two years ago," Horton said thoughtfully, "just a little under two years ago, Georgie canceled all her speaking engagements and took a sort of sabbatical, you might say. Her best friend was quite ill, and Georgie found it too stressful to work. She was gone for about two months."

"This friend have a name?"

"Snow something . . . no, wait. Uh, Sunny? No. That's not it. Oh, I remember. *Raine*. Raine Preston. They've been friends since they were kids, I guess."

"Miss Mundy ever talk about what was wrong?"

Horton shook his head and rubbed his jaw with his knuckles. "Only to say that everything had turned out okay, and that her friend had gone into remission or something. But since then, she's been, I don't know, *stressed* in some way she wasn't before. Nervous. Distracted. Oh, she's still the same old Georgie, but different. I've asked her about it, and she just smiles and brushes me off, but I'm worried, Ethan. Yes, I am, I'm *worried*."

Ethan gave Horton an appraising look. "What do you think's wrong?"

"Don't know. That's why I called Paladin."

"Do you want Miss Mundy protected, or investigated?"

Horton sucked on his bottom lip. Then, "Well, I'm not sure. Because, you see, there's more. Somebody's been playing pranks on the set. Switching the labels on some of Georgie's spices so that the chili powder's labeled cinnamon, and the basil's labeled parsley, that kind of thing. If she hadn't caught it in time, well, have you any idea the culinary havoc that could have created, Ethan?"

"I'm a salt-and-pepper man, myself."

The station manager eyed him, shaking his

head. "Yes. Yes, I can see that you are. Hmm. Unfortunate. Well, the fact remains, Georgie usually cooks for a studio audience. As part of the show, her guests sample the dishes she prepares. They're supposed to close their eyes in ecstasy and whimper, *Mmmm, yes, oh, God, yes!* like they've just experienced their first orgasm, not gag, wince, choke, and spit up into their napkins!"

Well, there are orgasms, and then there are orgasms.

"Does Miss Mundy have any enemies that you're aware of?"

"None!" Horton insisted, his eyes wide with astonishment and sincerity. "Everybody adores Georgie. Why, why, why, she's sweet and kind and generous, beautiful, funny, charming—"

"Nobody's that perfect," he interrupted, before Horton got to the part where Georgie Mundy walked on water. "As to everyone adoring her, the fact is, the more popular someone is, the more likely there's somebody who's jealous or angry about it. So, bottom line, what do you want me to do?"

"Well, first off, I guess I want you to find out who's behind these tricks on the set. You know, before they get out of hand and somebody gets hurt."

"For which the station would be liable."

"A litigious nightmare, to be sure!"

"And you also want to know what's going on in her life off the set. This whatever-it-is that's caused her so much stress?"

"Yes. I want to know if her behavior has anything to do with—"

Horton's words were abruptly halted when the blond receptionist flung his door open. "Ozzie!" she squeaked, her eyes wild with panic. "Come quickly. It's Georgie!"

Simultaneously, Ethan and Horton jumped to their feet.

"What's wrong?" Ethan asked as the three of them headed out the door and down the hall.

"I don't know," the girl said breathlessly. "Sh-she was inside her dressing room when somebody heard her scream. When they opened her door, they found her on the floor. Somebody said she was dead!"

Chapter Two

Affirmations carry a megaton of power. To get Mr. Right knocking on your door, chant the following every day: *I now let into my life a man I truly desire. I am involved in a perfect, loving, intimate relationship.* The trick here is, when you say it, honey, *you gotta believe it!*

Georgiana Mundy's *Feng Shui for Lovers*

Georgie lay perfectly still, her eyes tightly closed as she listened to the hubbub going on around her. Guilt nibbled at her conscience like a mouse consuming cheese. Okay, maybe gnawing would be a better word, since her conscience never cut her any slack.

Right now that overactive conscience was scolding her, reminding her it was cruel to let everyone believe something was wrong when it really wasn't. But she couldn't confess just yet. She needed to buy a little more time to come up with a reason for screaming and fainting—pretending to faint, anyway.

"Let me through! Is she all right? Did somebody call 911? Georgie, baby, speak to me!"

Ozzie, of course. Alarmed, worried. For her. So sweet. Such a dear man. She should let him know she was all right. Her conscience jabbed at her skull.

She was about to end the game when strong, warm fingers gently pressed her throat just under her jaw. Ozzie's fingers? No. He had soft, pudgy hands. Whoever owned these fingers would be strong and angular.

"Pulse is good," said a voice from close above her. The man with the fingers, no doubt. "She's just fainted."

His voice was familiarish, but she couldn't quite place it.

An arm slid under her knees, another under her shoulders, and she felt herself being lifted from the floor. As though she really were out cold, she let her arms dangle at her sides and her head loll against the man's shoulder.

And what a shoulder. *Certainly* not Ozzie's. And this guy smelled good, too. Clean and soapy, and, yes, there it was, that familiarishness feeling again . . .

"Where can I take her?" he said, the reverberation of his deep voice rumbling against her ear.

"Well, uh, uh," Ozzie rushed, his voice filled with panic. "There's a couch in the women's restroom! Take her there." Poor Ozzie. Georgie fought the urge to open her eyes and confess her deceit.

"Do you, uh, do you think we should call the paramedics?"

"No need, Mr. Horton. I have a feeling she'll be just fine."

Where *had* she heard that voice? He'd lifted her effortlessly, and she was no bantamweight, that's for sure, so he must be very manly. Desperately, she wanted to pinch open one eye to see if he was as good-looking as he sounded.

As he moved with her down the hall, she felt like she was in a canoe, gliding quietly along a river to some exotic landing known as the Women's Restroom. Soon they would dock, and she'd have to open her eyes and explain to the natives just what in the hell was going on.

The swinging door of the ladies' room sang its familiar squeak-swish song as her champion carried her in, easing her onto the soft corduroy couch everyone used on those days their menstrual cramps were too much to bear, they had a headache, or were pregnant and needed to pamper their swollen ankles for a little while. Somebody shoved a velvety pillow under her head.

"Mr. Horton," Manly Man said, with a very authoritative air, if Georgie was any judge. "You can stay. But send everyone else away and close the door."

"Shouldn't I call the—"

"She'll be fine. I promise."

Georgie knew she was fine, but how did this stranger know? And just why was Ozzie taking orders from him? Whoever this guy was, he was beginning to irritate her, and she hadn't even seen him yet.

"Everyone out, please," Georgie heard Ozzie order. "Hurry, people. Thank you. We've got it under control. Thank you . . ."

The sound of protests, concerned voices, and the scuffle of feet inched her guilt up another notch.

While Ozzie was apparently occupied at the door, Georgie felt her rescuer lean forward, putting his mouth close to her ear. "You can open your eyes now," he said. His breath caused little chills to dance down her spine. Her skin prickled with awareness, her heart skipped a beat—but she didn't budge.

He bent nearer, and she felt the heat from his body wrap around her like an embrace. Softly, so only she could hear, he whispered, "If green is for healing, what color is for faking?"

Her lids flew open. *Him!* Glaring down at her with a *gotcha* gleam in his eyes.

"You," she mouthed on no breath at all. She inhaled. "From the elevator . . . the Darling guy. How did you . . . why are you—"

"Georgie?" Ozzie scurried from the door to her side, crouching next to Scowling Manly Darling Man. "Georgie, honey, what happened? Was it something you ate? Are you having your period, sweet thing? Because I remember my sisters—"

"I'm fine, Oz," she assured him, taking his hand between hers, patting it as though he were a small child in need of comfort. "I just fainted, and—"

"No, you didn't." The Darling guy set his jaw, looking down at her, daring her to challenge him.

"What makes you think so?"

He seemed to assess her for a moment, and she realized that by not denying it, she'd tacitly confessed.

"When people faint," he said slowly, a triumphant glint in his hazel eyes, "their head drops forward and they fall flat on their faces. Given the small size of your dressing room and the furniture crammed into it—"

"I *beg* your pardon," she interrupted. "My dressing room is carefully arranged according to feng shui—"

"You managed," he continued, interrupting her, "to fall neatly into a little ball in the center of the room without smashing your beautiful face on your dressing table, bookcase, coffee table, or costume rack."

Beautiful? She tried to move her thoughts past that comment, but it was hard to do. He thought she was beautiful?

"Your pulse was strong, and too rapid for somebody who'd just passed out. You were scared," he said flatly. "Maybe even terrified. The question is, of what?"

She eased herself up onto one elbow and scowled. "Are you, like, a doctor or something?"

"No." His eyes met hers in an accusing stare. "Why'd you scream and then pretend to faint?"

"Pretend?" Ozzie said, his tone one of disbelief and worry. "Pretend? Georgie?"

There was no way she was going to explain a damn thing to either of the men, but most especially not to this stranger. He already knew way too much about her as it was. Besides, for all she knew, the Darling guy could be working for the Corcorans. Paul's father was a powerful man, influential, vindictive. She would have to guard against both of the Corcorans forever.

It was then she remembered her guilt, and her original lie. "I . . . saw a mouse." She widened her eyes as though still suffering from the trauma of the incident. Adding a dramatic tremble to her voice, she said, "I have an irrational fear of mice. Untreatable. Textbook case, I'm told. Incurable. You're lucky I didn't have a heart attack."

Darling pursed his lips and narrowed one eye. "You screamed and fainted because you saw a mouse."

More like a rat, she thought, but nodded anyway.

He grunted, obviously not buying it, but she didn't care. She only wanted to get back to her dressing room and look out the window one more time . . .

Movement behind the glass in the building next to the Golden Gate Towers had caused her to glance out her dressing room window . . . and there he'd stood.

Paul Corcoran. A mere few feet away, staring back at her, his hands in his pockets, his head slightly lowered, an unreadable expression on his way-too-pretty face. The shock of seeing him standing there had caused her to scream and recoil from the window. She'd tripped over her dressing-table chair and fallen to her knees. When she'd heard footsteps rapidly approaching her dressing room door, she'd curled into a ball on the floor and closed her eyes, trying to buy herself time . . . time to give her thundering heart a chance to slow, time for coherent thought to return to her brain, time to hope it had been a mirage she'd seen, and not her worst nightmare.

She looked at Ozzie, then back at Darling.

"It was a *mouse,*" she stated. "Looking at me. Evilly." Having created the stupid mouse myth, she now had to make it stick.

"A six-ounce mouse looked at you *evilly,* so you screamed and fainted." Darling was looking at her a little evilly at the moment, but he was a lot bigger than six ounces.

So what? Whether or not he believed her, she didn't care. Who was to say if she'd actually seen a mouse? The truth was too complicated to explain, and even if she found a way, the aftermath could be disastrous if she trusted the wrong person. She'd stopped trusting people decades ago, and even if she hadn't, Paul had struck the final blow when he'd done what he'd done. As a result, she had little faith in anyone except herself, and Raine.

"Thank you for coming to my aid," she said coolly, "but you can go on about your business now." She smiled dismissively.

Since he didn't buy her story—not that it mattered—the best thing would be to simply get rid of him. Whatever he was doing at KALM didn't involve her, so she never had to see him again.

"Oh!" Ozzie blurted out, as though he had suddenly awoken from a dream. "Georgie, I need to introduce you two. In all the commotion . . . well, anyway, this is Ethan Darling. He's a private investigator. I've hired him to try and find out who's been messing with your sets."

She flicked a look at Darling, whose unsmiling face gave nothing away. Her stomach churned and her knees went weak. Good thing she was already lying down.

With a casual lift of her shoulder, she said, "I—I don't think that's necessary, Oz. Just somebody playing a prank. A joke. There hasn't been any real harm done."

"I disagree, sweet thing. I believe these incidents need to be checked out." Averting his eyes, he said, "And, and, and, well, um, I've also hired Ethan to sort of watch over you, in a, um, in a bodyguard sort of—"

"No!" she blurted. In one movement, she sat up and swung her legs to the floor, glaring into the station manager's shocked face. *"No bodyguard.* That's ridiculous. Besides, I value my privacy, Ozzie, you know that."

"But Georgie, honey, it's just until—"

"Absolutely not." She pushed herself to her feet. Damn, that was all she needed, some guy following her around, watching her every move. No, it wouldn't do. It would *never* do.

She began pacing the carpeted area where the couch sat tucked against a wall. Placing her fingers at her temples, she said, "I'll simply envision my protective white light. Surround myself with it, immerse myself in it. I'll be fine. No bodyguard."

Ozzie stood, lifting his hands, palms up. "But I hired him—"

"Then fire him," she snapped, trying to overcome her panic. "No bodyguard!"

She walked over to the short bank of sinks that stood across from the stalls and turned a tap, splashing her face with lukewarm water.

Out of the corner of her eye, she saw Darling slowly rise to his feet. He was watching her now, thinking about everything. Ethan Darling seemed to be a very intelligent man and the last thing in the world she needed right now was a smart man in her life . . . one who could figure things out.

Turning off the tap, she reached for a paper towel from the dispenser to dab her flushed cheeks. "Mr. Darling, please don't take this personally—"

"It's Ethan."

She rolled her lips together, smiled condescendingly. "I don't need or want a bodyguard. I know you probably carry a gun, and I have an aversion to them."

"Kind of like mice?" he drawled.

"Much worse. I don't want them anywhere near my aura."

"Mice?"

"Guns."

"But Georgie—" Ozzie began.

"It's okay, Mr. Horton," Ethan interjected. "Let's leave Ms. Mundy to slip into her protective white light. You and I can go back to your office to discuss those set disturbances. If the lady doesn't want a bodyguard, then we wouldn't want to force the issue."

Too smooth, Georgie thought. He'd given up way too easily, and he didn't seem like the kind of man who'd give up at all, once he'd set his mind on something.

Dammit, she'd have to be doubly on guard now. What with Paul being around—and watching her—and the weird things that had been happening on the set, she already had her hands full.

As soon as Ozzie opened the restroom door, a rush of women pushed past the two men to crowd around her.

". . . in the world happened? Are you okay, honey?"

". . . eat this. It's chocolate. It'll help . . ."

". . . like, hee-hah. Who is that *man*?"

She smiled and assured them all she was perfectly fine, but her gaze never left Ethan as he walked toward the door. Just as he reached the threshold, he turned, and their eyes locked.

His glittering stare held a challenge: *I don't know what you're up to, but I'm going to find out.*

She raised her chin and stared back: *Take your best shot, pal.*

With a cool smile and a tilt of his head, he

sealed the bargain. Disappearing into the hall-way, he let the door swing closed behind him.

Georgie swallowed the lump of fear and appre-hension in her throat.

He'd tossed the gauntlet at her feet, and she had no choice but to pick it up. This was a game to him, and she had a feeling he was a very ac-complished player. But he had no idea how high the stakes were for her—and she was going to have to make damned sure he never found out.

"I'd like to take a look at Georgie's dressing room," Ethan said, as he and Horton returned to the sta-tion manager's office. "Can you keep her away from it for about a half an hour?"

Horton closed his office door behind them. "Sure. Sure, sure." He moved around behind his desk, dropped heavily into his chair, and rubbed the back of his neck.

"Do you think she's okay, Ethan? I mean, I *guess* a mouse could somehow have made it up to the thirty-first floor of this building without an oxy-gen mask or hemorrhaging its little brain."

"Or she could be lying."

"Georgie never lies, so she must have seen *something* that made her—"

"Everybody lies, Mr. Horton," Ethan said on a world-weary sigh as he settled into his chair. "It's *why* they lie that's important."

The alluring woman with the glorious brown hair and sexy little bod had lied through her pearly whites, and no doubt about it. As a police officer, he'd learned to read faces, gestures, listen to the tone of a person's voice, pay attention to the word choices made. Georgie Mundy had lied. What's more, she knew he knew it, and she didn't care.

Catch me if you can, her eyes taunted.

It'll be my pleasure, he'd promised.

"I'm going to assign a man to keep an eye on Miss Mundy," he said to Horton, "but that will just be our little secret, okay?"

The station manager's eyes brightened. "Ah? Aha, yes. Good, good, good. I get it. Our little secret. Reading you loud and clear, Ethan. But how? She made it absolutely clear she doesn't want a bodyguard."

"Too bad," Ethan said dryly. "She's got one. She just doesn't know it."

She may have lied about why she'd fainted, but there was no way she could have faked a racing heart. Something had scared her, sent her pulse through the roof. He wanted to know what it was.

A few minutes later, Ethan stood in Georgie's dressing room while she was in Horton's office, discussing her next taping.

He looked around. The space was just big enough for a dressing table with lighted mirror and a few pieces of essential furniture, plus a wardrobe rack. The cookbooks she'd authored were stacked neatly on the table next to a bouquet of flowers—a dozen pink roses, with ferns and those little white flowers they always put in with them. He remembered Cathy had called them baby's breath. Crystals of various sizes and shapes were scattered among makeup brushes and cosmetic pots and other assorted feminine doohickeys.

Though the room was a bit cluttered, it had a light and airy feel to it. Crouching, he checked the baseboards and corners. No mice droppings, no gnaw marks on the wood, nothing to indicate the place had been invaded by any unwelcome critters.

He stood and walked to the window. While it was large enough to let in a fair amount of natural light, the view sure sucked. This side of the Golden Gate Towers was neighbored by a slightly taller office structure. Because it was paneled with nonglare glass, it was easy to observe the goings-on in the interior across the way. Most of the windows offered views of desks and cubicles, people milling around or pounding their fingers on keyboards. Anyone standing at a window would be clearly observed.

Had Georgie seen something in one of those windows that had frightened her? If so, what in the hell could it have been? Except for the darkened glass directly across from hers, the place was bustling with what appeared to be normal activity.

Reaching into his pocket, he pulled out a pad and made a few notes, then calculated where that darkened office across the way would be located in the building.

As he shoved the pad back into his pocket, he heard a tapping on the door. A second later, Horton stuck his head through, then his whole body.

"She's gone to lunch," he whispered clandestinely. "You find anything?"

Instead of meeting Horton's gaze, he looked around the room. "A couple of things. Maybe they'll pan out, maybe not."

"Great. Great, great. What happens now, Ethan?"

"What happens now is, I'm going to put Paladin's best man on it."

Horton's brows shot up and he clapped his palms together in quiet applause. "Your best man, you say? And who might that be?"

With one final glance out the window, Ethan turned back to Horton, met the man's anxious gaze, and said, "Me."

Chapter Three

If life's too much for you to handle lately, here's the cure. Find a large faceted crystal sphere, and using a nine-inch strip of red ribbon, hang the crystal in the center of your house. Then step back and wave buh-bye to all your troubles.

Georgiana Mundy's *Feng Shui for Lovers*

Ethan entered the foyer of the Stanford Building and took the elevator to the thirty-first floor. Exiting to the left, he walked down the hall, stopping in front of a door marked MENDOCINO FABRIC IMPORTERS AND DESIGN. Based on his calculations, the window that faced Georgie's dressing room would be right about here.

Turning the knob, he entered the office. A cadaverous thirty-something woman wearing a boxy black-and-red-checked suit sat behind a U-shaped desk. She stopped typing, but didn't remove her fingers from the keyboard. The plastic plaque on her desk read FIONA NAKAMURA.

"Yes, sir?" Fiona said, and smiled, giving him

the impression she had about a hundred too many teeth for her mouth. "How may I help you?"

He offered her his business card.

"Private investigator?" Her black unibrow arched and she smiled past lips painted the color of charred beef. "*You* are Ethan Darling?"

"Yes, ma'am. I'm looking into an incident that occurred this morning in the building next door. It would help me a lot if I could locate the window that directly faces the office where the incident occurred. I promise, it would only take a moment and I'll try not to disturb anyone."

Her forehead furrowed. "An incident? Like, did somebody get whacked?"

"No, but whoever sits at that window might have seen something that could help my investigation."

She looked confused for a moment, then shrugged. "Well, I guess it can't hurt. Just a sec."

Ethan waited while she called someone named Trent and explained the situation.

A moment later, the door behind the receptionist opened to reveal a man holding a bundle of silky fabrics in his arms, his narrow glasses shoved up onto his forehead, a yellow tape measure wrapped several times around his neck. Giving Ethan the once-over, he grinned. "Fiona, sweetie, you were absolutely right. He *is* darling."

"Wrong team, Mr. Trent," Ethan said lightly. "I just want to look out your window."

Trent rolled his eyes. "If I had a nickel for every time I heard *that*!" With his free hand, he shoved a long lock of frizzy brown hair off his shoulder and again gave Ethan the once-over. "Well, it's true what they say. All the good ones are straight." He snorted a laugh. "Come along, baby doll. This way to the windows."

Ethan followed Trent down a hall that opened into a large workroom filled with cutting tables and people in various sizes, shapes, and colors. Bolts of fabric were shoved onto shelves along the walls or were lying in colorful heaps on chairs and tables. Skinny young women with tape measures gracing their necks discussed sleeve and hem lengths with skinny young men holding scissors or trays of long silver pins.

But what snared Ethan's attention was the bank of windows on the far side of the room. Looking out, he realized his position was a little off. Georgie's dressing room was a few more feet to the right, yet an interior wall prevented him from moving in that direction.

"What's on the other side of this?" Ethan said to Trent, indicating the barrier.

"Storeroom. Just junk, nobody ever goes in there."

"Does it have a window?"

"Oh, sure," Trent said as he set the bolts of fabrics he was carrying on one of the tables. "Door's this way, across the hall from the potty."

As we walked down a narrow corridor and rounded a corner to the closed storeroom door, Ethan said, "Pretty hidden back here. Somebody could go in and out and never be seen."

"Guess so," Trent agreed. "Of course, they'd have to get past Fiona first." He bared his teeth and made a clawing motion with his hands.

Opening the door, Trent walked into the room and flipped on the light. Shelves lining the walls were crammed with dusty fabrics, huge rolls of paper, boxes of scissors, broken mannequins, and God knew what else, but Ethan's only interest was the bare window. He walked to it and stared across the chasm between the two buildings, directly into Georgie's dressing room.

Her dressing table and garment rack were clearly visible, though she probably pulled the drape closed when she changed clothes. Otherwise, it was undoubtedly kept open as it had been this morning.

"Not much of a view," Trent said from behind him.

"Not much," Ethan said absently. While the view afforded glimpses of some of the other KALM offices, only this window faced Georgie's dressing room directly. More importantly, Georgie would have a clear view of anyone standing here.

Crouching a little, he checked the window frame. The dark metal was covered with a thick layer of dust, but it looked as though it had been recently disturbed. He reached into his pocket and pulled out a small plastic box.

"Fingerprints?" Trent squealed. "Fabulous! Oh, God, this is *so CSI!* Can I watch?"

"Sure. It's not as exciting as what you see on TV, though." He grinned as he twirled the small brush across the sill. Blue powder poofed in the air as he worked. Two prints emerged clear enough to lift, so he lifted them while over his shoulder he said, "Mind if I talk to some of your people? Maybe one of them saw something this morning that could help."

"Oh, ask everyone!" Trent said cheerily. "Is this a murder case or something?"

"Nothing so dramatic. Just possible harassment. I appreciate your help."

For the next hour, Ethan talked to every member of the staff, while Trent followed close on his heels like an overeager puppy. But when all was said and done, no one had seen anything.

Ethan extended his hand to Trent, and as the two men shook, he said, "You've been a big help, Mr. Trent. I'd appreciate it if you'd give me a call if you see anyone prowling around who doesn't belong."

"And *you* give *me* a call," Trent cooed, cocking a brow. "If you ever decide to change teams."

Releasing the man's hand, Ethan smiled. "I promise you'll be the first to know."

On his way out, he stopped by the reception desk. "What time do you get in, Ms. Nakamura?"

She paused with a bagel halfway to her lips. "Usually about eight-thirty. Then I go down the hall and get water to make coffee."

"Who sits at the reception desk while you're gone?"

She shook her head. "No one. I'm only gone a minute or two."

And anyone watching Fiona's routine would know that.

As he sat behind the wheel of his SLR McLaren, Ethan's gaze stayed locked on the exit doors of Georgie's building. He tried to relax, but a sense of impatience buzzed around him like an irritating insect, and had all day.

In frustration, he rubbed his jaw. It was after five. What was taking the woman so frigging long? Maybe she was changing out of her "protective white light" into some color more appropriate for after hours. *Protective white light, my ass*, he thought.

Thanks to the information he'd obtained from Horton, he knew that Georgie drove a candy-apple-red Miata MX–5 with California vanity plates that read GEORGIE. He had also discovered the automobile had no car alarm. Perfect. Stupid, but perfect.

When the parking lot attendant went to take a leak, Ethan had moved quickly, obtaining entry to the Miata, attaching a listening device under the dash. Yeah, it was illegal and he was putting his license on the line, but at the moment he didn't care. If she chatted somebody up on her cell phone on the way home, he wanted to hear every word.

Relocking and closing the door, he went to the rear of the Miata and slipped a magnetized homing device inside the wheel well.

He returned to his car with a sense of anticipation. Sexual anticipation. At his age, he knew the feeling for exactly what it was, so why deny it? Rubbing his jaw, he admonished himself for behaving like some hormonal teen on prom night.

A few minutes later, several women exited the building through the double glass doors leading out into the back lot where he waited, parked between an ancient VW camper and a late-model BMW. Huddled in a group, the women were a chattering amalgamation of feminine faces from black to brown to white, tailored gray suits, fluttering print dresses, stacked heels, open-toed sandals, briefcases, straw totes, smiles, and cell phones—and at their center, Georgie Mundy, looking as luscious as ever in her summery pink.

In his pocket, the green silk seemed to have a life of its own, warming his palm whenever he touched it—which had been several dozen times in the last few hours. She had been kind to give it to him, and in remembering the compassionate look in her eyes as she'd placed it in his hand, he felt his heart soften.

No, dammit. Not going there.

Ethan tightened his jaw, warning himself to stay in control. She was a job. Hands off. If his hands had a different agenda in mind, he'd just have to deal with it.

Georgie waved good-bye to the other women, who smiled and waved back as they peeled off one by one to go to their cars. She passed in front of him, her head down, her attention focused on the contents of her handbag as she did a deep dive for her keys.

From behind his mirrored aviators, he tried to ignore how the breeze tousled her silky brown hair, how her tits jiggled real nice under the fabric of her pink top, how her hips swayed. She was at ease with her body; his defiant hands itched a little in response.

She got to her car, started the engine. In his earpiece, he heard her radio, the strains of some bland New Age instrumental had him rolling his eyes.

He pulled into traffic a few cars behind hers, following her along the Embarcadero until she hooked a left onto Bay. A few blocks later, the Miata made another turn and headed up to Russian Hill, where hundred-year-old Victorians were stacked side by side like books on a library shelf.

As he listened, her cell phone chimed. Abruptly, the radio cut off midnote.

"Hey, yeah," she said, her tone anxious, her words clipped. "No, now's good. I'm in my car. You okay?" There was silence for a moment, then, "I'm fine, but I, uh, I have a situation here. Actually, I have several. I saw him. Yes, *him, here*, in San Francisco! I thought he was in Europe, too, but he must have come back. No, he hasn't actually contacted me, but if he's here . . . He hasn't shown up there, has he?"

Her voice rose, as though the thought panicked her, and Ethan wondered who in the hell *he* was.

"Oh, thank God," she said on a rush of breath. "I've been super careful, but if he's following me, we've both got to be extra cautious now. Promise me you'll be on guard."

She turned a corner and downshifted; a moment later, Ethan did the same. With two cars between them, she was still unaware of his presence.

"I've got this other problem," she continued. "Ozzie hired a private investigator. He wanted this guy to be my *bodyguard*. *Shit* is right! God, no. I put an end to it. That's all we need is some guy snooping around, watching my every move."

She listened for a few seconds, then said, "There is absolutely no way this PI could know about you, but keep a lookout, just in case. If you spot him, let me know right away. What's he look like? Okay, yeah, well, he's tall, over six feet. Dark hair, um, sort of green hazel eyes with gold flecks . . ."

Ethan peered over his dark glasses into the rearview mirror. Huh. Damn. They did have gold flecks in them.

"You can't miss him. Broad shoulders, rugged good looks, the kind of guy women dream about going to bed with . . ."

Ethan admonished himself to stay on task.

". . . hot and really sexy. Swear to God. No, I am so not kidding. And get this, his name is Ethan *Darling*. Is that a hoot and a half! Thank God I only have to cooperate with him while he investigates at the studio . . . What? No, I'm not. I am *not*. Because he's an arrogant *jerk*, that's why! He's all scowls and smirks and straight edges and sneers. A real stuffed shirt. No sense of hu-mor. *None.* Never smiles, barely talks. I'd bet my last organic bean sprout his house is decorated sparsely in black and white leather. Nothing that lives or breathes or requires nurturing, like pets or plants. Lives alone. Only has company for sex. It's a onetime deal, then probably sends her home in a cab before midnight."

Ethan swallowed uncomfortably.

Georgie said something that got lost when a truck coming down the hill noisily shifted gears.

He scowled. Just what in the hell was wrong with leather anyway? And he had plants . . . sev-eral of them. A couple anyway. There was that brown-leafed thing in the bathroom. Of course, maybe the leaves weren't supposed to be brown.

". . . very smart. Besides, I get the impression he can't be bought."

Ethan's spine straightened. What did she think he'd discover, that she'd want to buy his silence?

". . . Mrs. Beebes doing? Yeah? That's so great! I can hardly wait to see her. Yeah, tonight. I don't have to be back at the studio until noon on Mon-day."

Her brake lights flared as she slowed, then turned into the stubby driveway of a wood-frame, tan and black Victorian, complete with tiny ga-rage to the right of the staircase.

He kept driving, his tinted windows conceal-ing him from view—not that she looked. Turning at the next corner, he slowed, his hand against the receiver in his ear as he listened.

". . . hate that we're separated all the time, and I wish it could be different, but for now, this is the only way. Mrs. Beebes . . . too risky . . ."

His reception was interrupted as a car pulled up behind him and began blasting its horn for Ethan to get a move on.

". . . was *him* I saw . . . worried . . . watching me, I won't have any choice but to . . . meantime . . . keep that PI distracted . . . or kill him myself . . ."

Georgie zipped the top of her overstuffed suitcase closed and grabbed it by the handle. Glancing around her bedroom, she turned out the lights and headed downstairs to her car. If the weather was good and Friday evening traffic was light, she would be in Santa Barbara by midnight.

The boring five-hour drive to Southern California was worth it, though, and she made the trip as often as she could—which was usually at least once a month. If she didn't have to stop off in San Jose every time, the trip would go a little faster, but she needed to make sure she wasn't followed, so San Jose had become an integral part of her deception.

Tossing the suitcase into the backseat of the Miata, she slammed the door, then slid into the front seat behind the wheel.

A cool summer fog had rolled in, which worked to her advantage. Anyone following her would have to stay close enough that she'd notice them, allowing her to take evasive action.

She checked the clock on the dash. It was a little before seven. By the time she reached San Jose in about an hour, it would be too dark for anyone to effectively tail her.

She'd bought a bright red sports car for good reason—it was easy to spot. The vanity plates removed any doubt the Miata belonged to her, so wherever it was parked, anyone on the lookout would naturally assume she was nearby.

So far, the ploy had worked like a charm, but she couldn't help but worry a little about the Darling guy.

He wasn't her bodyguard, but the look in his eyes when he walked out of the restroom with Ozzie had said he didn't accept defeat easily—if at all. He might hang around, follow her, just to spite her. That wouldn't be good.

And then there was Paul. *Damn* him. What did he want? Did he suspect something, or was he just trying to rattle her cage? If so, it had worked.

The day she'd told him to get out, he'd grabbed her by the arm and shoved her against the wall, pinning her there with his body.

"Nobody leaves me," he'd growled. "Especially not you."

"Let go of me, Paul," she'd bitten out. "Or I'll knee you in the groin. Besides, I've already called the police. If anything happens to me, they'll know it was you."

It was clear he didn't believe her—until he heard the scream of a siren coming up the street.

"*Fuck*," he murmured. He closed his eyes for a moment, and when he opened them, he released her arm, giving her his most charming smile.

"Ah, come on, baby," he coaxed, his blue eyes glittering. "I'm not so bad. I made a little mistake, a lapse in judgment. It'll never happen again, I swear. We're good together, you said so yourself. Hey, I love you. We'll get married like you wanted. Have a kid or two. That'd make you happy, right? Come on, Georgie, don't do this."

Maneuvering around him, she grabbed her purse and keys from the half-circle cherry table against the wall in the foyer.

As the police car pulled up in front, she said, "You *are* so bad, Paul. You're adorable and even sweet sometimes, but what you did is unforgivable. You're spoiled, immature, and criminal. The next time you 'make a little mistake,' go fuck your*self*."

Before the two uniformed police officers reached the steps leading up to the first floor of her house, Paul lowered his voice. Through clenched teeth, he growled, "Okay, Georgie. Okay. If this is the way you want it, fine. Just remember, whatever happens, you brought this on yourself. When you least expect it, I'll take something *you* love. My father has powerful connections—"

"I'm getting a restraining order against you, Paul," she said flatly. "Stay away from me, and tell your father to stay away from me, too, or you'll be the ones who are sorry."

With that, she spun on her heel and hurried down the steps to meet the officers. They escorted her to her car, took her statement, and waited while she drove safely away.

That was nearly two years ago, and she hadn't heard from Paul Corcoran since.

Not until she'd seen him standing in the window directly across from hers, staring at her, and smiling.

Chapter Four

Open yourself to change—the kind of man you
think you want may not be the best man for
you. Forget your old ideas about love (since
they're obviously not working for you anyway).
Romance may enter your life just when you
least expect it, and from a totally surprising
place!

Georgiana Mundy's *Feng Shui for Lovers*

From where Ethan stood watching from the
shadows, the San Jose Cottage Inn was a far
cry from the courtyard of cute, shingle-roofed,
rose-adorned bungalows its name implied. Instead, it resembled a three-story white stucco
cracker box with windows.

What on earth was Georgiana Mundy, media
star, doing on a Friday night at a seedy dump like
this?

He pursed his lips. There really was only one
explanation. Sex. Illicit sex, at that, or she'd have
stayed at home in San Francisco instead of driving

for an hour to park her carcass at some out-of-the-way no-tell motel.

He'd followed her south on 101, until she'd pulled off the freeway and driven straight to this place—like she'd done it a thousand times before. When she parked in front of the office, he'd gotten out of his car to get a closer look, watch and see what she did.

Something here just didn't jibe. For all her loony New Age crap, the goody-goody affirmations, the healing colors, and all that, she was classy to the bone. Coming here for clandestine sex just didn't add up.

Maybe it was her boyfriend who was weird. Maybe he got off on tawdry.

Ethan slid his hand into his pocket, wrapped his fingers around the silky bit of fabric once more. She'd offered it to him—a complete stranger—out of the goodness of her heart. Sure, it was utter bullshit, but she'd thought she was helping. He was still having trouble moving his mind past what a simple, selfless act that had been.

The fact the wound in his side hadn't hurt since then was just some kind of bizarre coincidence.

The homing device he'd planted on her car had allowed him to stay far enough behind her so she wouldn't spot him. In the last hour, she hadn't made a phone call, or even hummed along with the radio. She did sneeze once, coughed a couple of times, and cussed out a guy in a truck who'd cut her off.

He grinned at the memory. Pretty colorful language for such a touchy-feely gentle New Age devotee. Her fans would probably be shocked to discover the smiling Miss Mundy, when crossed, had a pissy streak a mile wide.

From his vantage next to the tall hedge that defined the perimeter of the parking lot, he watched as the Miata's brake lights went dark. Georgie opened her door, stepped out, and looked around casually but thoroughly, pointedly, it seemed to him.

So she *was* checking for a tail. He eased back farther into the shadows.

Apparently satisfied she hadn't been followed, she went into the office. A few minutes later, she came out and drove around to the back of the inn. He followed on foot.

She parked the Miata in the only vacant spot available, between a black Cadillac Escalade and a beat-to-hell silver Dodge pickup.

Carrying that gigantic purse of hers and a maroon suitcase, she glanced around once more, then headed up the metal stairs that reached all three floors of the inn. At the second floor, she turned to the right and followed along the landing until she came to Room 227, where she unlocked the door, looked around again, then slipped inside. Instantly, the big square of window glowed yellow behind the closed drapes.

So her boyfriend hadn't arrived yet. Well, it was still early.

Ethan's stomach growled, and he hoped to hell the guy would show up soon so he could go grab a bite to eat.

He rubbed the back of his neck. What did he care if Georgie met some guy at a motel just to have sex? No skin off his nose. Besides, she was his client, not his girlfriend. He was simply an observer; it wasn't his place to judge what she did.

He rubbed the back of his neck again. Even so . . . bottom line, he didn't like it.

Stakeouts were always tough—and boring as hell. Georgie was safely ensconced in her room; he could leave for a few minutes. But what if *she* left? Not really a problem with the tracking device on her car. So what if the boyfriend showed up and Ethan missed seeing what he looked like? And what if there was no boyfriend? What if she'd just driven for an hour to get out of town and get some rest? *Right.*

His stomach growled again, and he tried to calculate how long it would take to hit the Quik Mart next to the motel for coffee and a sandwich and get back before something happened.

As he hesitated, the door to the room next to Georgie's opened and a blonde wearing tight jeans and a sweater stepped out. She closed the door, testing the knob the way people do to make sure it was locked, then turned and walked toward the stairs.

Damn. It was hard to take his eyes off her. Nice ass, he thought as she sauntered slowly down the metal steps.

Though the stairs were well lit from overhead, they cast the woman's face in shadow. He could see her body clearly enough, though. Very, very hot.

He watched as she descended—small purse slung over her shoulder, black suitcase in hand—and climbed into the Escalade. A moment later, the expensive engine hummed to life, and she backed out of the parking space and disappeared around the side of the inn.

A professional. Definitely a professional. Go figure. The San Jose Cottage Inn was apparently a very happening place.

A few more minutes passed, and he decided to risk hitting the market for some eats, then drive his car around to this side of the inn. So far, nobody else had entered the lot, and Georgie hadn't come out of her room. If he hurried, he could grab a sandwich, get the Mercedes, and be back here in ten.

Nine minutes later, he sat parked in the shadows next to the chain-link fence that bordered the inn's property and the gas station next door. In the time he'd been gone, no new cars had shown up, the Miata was still there, and the light in Georgie's room was still on.

As he tucked into the god-awful turkey, tomato, and bacon sandwich he'd purchased and gulped down half the lukewarm coffee, an elderly couple brought out their dog to pee on the small lawn next to the stairs, a woman on the third floor escorted two little kids who obviously needed to blow off some steam by playing tag in a remote part of the parking lot, and a man and a woman all wrapped around each other climbed the stairs and went into Room 332. The light in the window did not come on.

An hour passed. He finished off his now-dead-cold coffee and concluded he was an idiot.

Why hadn't he assigned an agent to do this? Lucas Russell would have been perfect for this job. But no. Just because Georgie Mundy intrigued him, heated his blood a little—okay, maybe a lot—and she piqued his interest, he should have known better, considering his track record. The last time he'd let a woman get to him, he swore he'd never let it happen again.

Glancing up at the closed door of Georgie's room, for no reason at all he thought of Cathy.

It had been six years, and he still thought of her every day, what he'd had with her, what he'd lost. How he'd lost it. After six years, it didn't hurt any more, but it didn't hurt any less, either.

For Georgie's own safety, he had to stop thinking of her as a woman, and focus on her as a client. Period.

Watching the yellow square of light that was her motel room window, he realized something was nagging at him, had been nagging at him, punching at the back of his brain, for over an hour.

That blonde . . .

True, he hadn't seen her face clearly, but the shape of her body, the way she moved . . .

"Fuck," he snarled, wanting to slap his forehead with the flat of his hand. *Goddammit*. He'd been had. Thoroughly *had*.

Bolting from the car, he rushed up to the door of Room 227, taking three steps at a time. He doubled his fist and pounded on her door.

"Georgie? It's Ethan. Open the goddamned door. Georgie?"

Nothing. Not a sound.

Of course not. She was gone.

He smacked the closed door with his palm and cursed again.

Adjoining rooms, that had to be it. She'd gotten adjoining rooms, gone in one, come out the other. The Escalade had been ready and waiting for her. She'd changed clothes, donned a wig, and now she was halfway to God knew where, and he had no way to track her. *Shit.*

"Very clever, Georgie," he murmured to the night sky. "Very, very clever."

Crossing his arms over his chest, he shook his head, which led to a short snicker, which turned into a chuckle that turned into several more. Finally, he caved, and let it happen, laughing so hard his gut ached and he had to put his hand on the door to steady himself.

When he caught his breath, he realized he should be furious, but she'd fooled him so thoroughly and so well, the only emotion he could drum up was admiration.

Deep inside his chest, he felt his heart soften a little more, but this time he did nothing to stop it.

"And . . . *action!*"

At four o'clock on Monday afternoon, Georgie

watched Gil Vincent, *CaliforniYum*'s director, adjust his microphone and headset, then move back behind the cameras and cross his arms over his chest.

She prayed her makeup would hide the dark circles under her eyes. As if the long drive to Santa Barbara and back weren't enough, she'd tried to cram a month's worth of memories into a mere forty-eight hours. Lack of sleep, and the stress of taking extra precautions to avoid being followed, always wore her to a frazzle.

Glancing down at her notes for a sec, she raised her face to Camera 1, thanking God for teleprompters. If she didn't fall asleep face down in the soy burgers or slice off her pinkie along with the onions, she would be done with the taping, home by six, and in bed and asleep by six-oh-five.

The red light on Camera 1 blinked to life . . . showtime.

"Hi, I'm Georgiana Mundy," she said through a beaming smile. "And welcome to another edition of *CaliforniYum*. Today we're going to discover the benefits of all things soy by whipping up a delicious smoothie you guys are just gonna love. I have a great new recipe for soy burgers, too, that'll knock your socks off, plus we'll discuss the benefits of incorporating feng shui into your kitchen design. Fabulous!"

Another big grin. "First off, let's take a moment to meet my guests for today . . ."

With that, she indicated the five viewers Ozzie

had selected from fan letters to come and watch the show being taped, sample the menu, and be on TV. Sitting at the cozy counter facing the cutting board and stovetop, each of the three women and two men waved and smiled at the camera as she introduced them.

It usually took a couple of hours to film the segment that would be shown during prime time the next night. The boring, repetitive stuff and goofs were edited out in order to fit the program into its thirty-minute format.

Despite the bright lights illuminating her and everything she did, Georgie could see past the cameras into the studio. Ethan Darling lurked behind Camera 2, his hands in his pockets, a scowl on his face as he watched her.

Normally, she wasn't nervous in front of cameras anymore. Today, however, her fingers shook, her heartbeat drummed in her ears, and her sexual awareness quotient kicked up a notch, and then some.

Ethan Darling wasn't her bodyguard, but she couldn't shake the feeling he was in her life whether she wanted him there or not. And worse, he was determined to find things out about her, things she absolutely did not want him—or anyone—to discover. He'd issued the challenge on Friday, and she'd accepted it. If it began looking like he was going to be trouble, she'd have to find a way to keep him off balance.

He was interested in her—she'd seen that on Friday when they'd collided in the elevator, and later, too, in Ozzie's office. He'd called her beautiful. It still made her cheeks flush and her ego dance to think of it. It wouldn't take much effort on her part to throw him a few curves, distract him. To protect her secrets, she'd do whatever she needed to do.

Her stomach tightened as it did whenever she was about to do something her instincts warned her was a mistake. Confusion moved in, muddling what she had thought was clear thinking. What were her instincts warning her against? Trusting him, or *not* trusting him?

There it was again, her one abiding dilemma. For on the drive back to San Francisco late last night, she'd considered confiding in him, telling him the truth, maybe even soliciting his help. There was something about his eyes, his manner that evoked a response in her she thought she'd lost over twenty years ago—the desire to trust someone other than herself.

But trusting Ethan Darling could prove to be a huge mistake. She'd let her defenses down with Paul—an error in judgment both she and Raine had lived to regret. No, Ethan was an unknown quantity, and even though he was working for Ozzie, he could easily transfer his loyalties to a client willing to pay more. And Vaughn Corcoran had more, much more. No, she couldn't take the chance. The people she loved counted on her to protect them. She couldn't let them down.

"So let's get to this soy smoothie," she said, setting the forty-ounce blender jar in its base. "Today we're making my favorite, chocolate—yuh-uum! You'll need four cups of carob soy milk . . ." which she poured from a carton into the container. "Four scoops chocolate protein powder, four tablespoons honey, and two cups soft silken tofu." Adding the ingredients to the blender, she picked up an empty bowl and sidestepped over to the refrigerator. *Never turn your back on the camera* was the mantra TV people lived by, and Georgie had learned long ago to keep moving, keep talking, and treat the camera like it was going to bite you in the butt if you turned around.

Opening the freezer, she scooped two handfuls of ice cubes from the tray into the bowl.

"You're going to need several ice cubes to chill and thicken the mixture. Five or six cubes should do the trick nicely."

She returned to the blender and smiled at Camera 2.

Keep that personality up; grin, be friendly, be real. Never let them see beyond your face, though. Never let them see the you who's dog-tired at night, and worried, and even a little afraid. This is showbiz. Smile, dammit.

"Drop a handful of cubes into the blender . . ." which she did. "Put the lid on, and let 'er rip."

She pressed the button and the high-speed blender roared to life, whipping the ingredients into a frothy concoction. After a couple of minutes, she removed the lid, tapped it on the rim of the container to remove the excess, then filled six glass tumblers with the chocolaty mixture.

Handing the tumblers to her guests, she picked up the last one and saluted the camera.

"Chocolaty, frosty, low in fat, high in protein, and dee-licious. For a quick pick-me-up, you've gotta try one of these babies."

She offered a toast to her guests, and everyone raised their glasses and drank.

A second went by, and another, then, almost as a single unit, everyone choked and spit the liquid back into their glasses. Wiping their mouths and staring at Georgie, they looked confused . . . and horrified.

"Cut!" Gil yelled. "Georgie, what in the hell—"

"Bitter!" she managed to rasp past her gag reflexes. "Oh, God—"

Immediately Ethan was by her side.

"Set your glass down, Georgie," he ordered. "Everyone, put your glasses down and don't touch anything. Gil, have somebody call 911." When Gil only stared at him, Ethan shouted, "Now!"

Placing his hands on Georgie's shoulders, Ethan turned her toward him. He searched her face, then looked hard into her eyes, deep and down, as though he were scanning her very bones. "Do you feel nauseous or dizzy? Feel like throwing up or—"

She shook her head. Barely able to speak past the wretched taste in her mouth, she choked. "Rosemary. Oil of rosemary . . . concentrated . . . tastes . . . God . . ."

Coughing, she clutched her throat, trying to

swallow past the foul taste that coated her mouth.

As her studio audience gulped glasses of fresh water, Georgie picked up the tumbler a worried Gil had filled for her, and did the same. It had little effect.

"I don't understand how this could have happened," she rasped. "All the ingredients I used were from sealed containers."

Ethan's gaze left her face and shifted to the refrigerator.

"Except for the ice cubes," he said quietly.

Together, they walked to the fridge. Ethan opened the freezer and removed one large cube from the bin. It looked like an ordinary ice cube. He held it to his nose and sniffed it. Immediately he scowled. "Are you sure it's only oil of rosemary?"

Georgie nodded. "Tasted it once before. It's nontoxic, but tastes horrible. They use it in spray form to keep dogs from gnawing on things. I used it once, and got some on my mouth accidentally. It took hours for the taste to go away, and that was only a tiny bit."

"I'm going to have this analyzed," he said. "You got any plastic bags?"

She pulled open a drawer next to the refrigerator and handed him a small bag. He plopped the ice cube inside and sealed it, then flicked his gaze back to her.

Reining in her fear, Georgie shrugged and lowered her head. "Pretty good prank. Somebody must be having a laugh about now. Irritating, but no real harm done."

She felt Ethan studying her. "A prank this time, Georgie. But think about it. Whoever did this could just as easily have put some kind of drug or poison in the ice cubes. Something to make you very sick, maybe even very dead."

She pressed her lips together and tried to breath past the taste still clinging to her lips, while her fear buzzed like flying ants in her ears. "That's ridiculous. This was just a prank, another silly, childish trick. It'll probably show up on some blooper reel somewhere. I—I can't imagine why anyone would want to make the studio guests sick or harm me."

She felt his knuckle under her chin. As he tilted her face up to his, their eyes locked, and he murmured coldly, "I'll bet if you tried real hard you could come up with a reason. Couldn't you, Georgie?"

Chapter Five

Second only to the front door, your bed is the most important object in your house. All aspects of your bed affect your *chi* (life force). To promote a solid relationship with your man, make sure the bed you share has a strong wooden headboard.

Georgiana Mundy's *Feng Shui for Lovers*

"It was oil of rosemary," Ethan said, watching Horton wring his hands as he'd been doing for the last two hours. "I had my own lab rush it through. Oil of rosemary, just like Georgie said. It's only toxic in highly concentrated doses, so even though the ice cubes probably tasted like shit, they were harmless. The paramedics gave everyone a clean bill of health."

"Oh, well, well, thank God! That's all I can say, thank God!" Horton ran his fingers across the top of his head, forking through the few wisps of hair that remained, like a rake through limp grass. "Jesus, what next?" He paced back and forth in front of his desk. Stopping, he lifted his hands in a gesture of helplessness. "Who's doing this, Ethan. And *why*?"

"Who knew Georgie was going to use ice cubes in her cooking demonstration today?"

"Uh, uh, well, that could be any number of people, Ethan. Anybody who'd read the script."

"I want to talk with everyone who had access to that information and who would have had an opportunity to tamper with the set."

Behind Horton's half-moon glasses, his eyes widened. "But, but, but, that's something like fifty people!"

"Then I'll need to talk to fifty people. Arrange it. I'll need a room where I can have some privacy. I'd also like to take a look at your employee files, especially for anybody who might be unhappy with KALM in general, or Georgie in particular."

Horton nodded, resettling his glasses on his nose. After a quick phone call to his secretary, asking her to begin gathering the files Ethan had requested, he set the receiver back in its cradle. "It'll take some time to assemble all that information, Ethan. Meanwhile, I can give you a few names, though I doubt any of them would do something like this."

"You'd be surprised what people are capable of, Mr. Horton."

The station manager looked thoughtful for a moment. "You're a very cynical man, aren't you, Ethan?"

Yeah, he thought. *But I've come by it honestly.* A lifetime of trying to do the right thing, trying to protect the vulnerable, trying to follow the straight and narrow, be a good kid, a good man, a good cop, only to fail the most important test of his life. Those things had a way of skewing perceptions, stealing away the simple joys that other people appreciated, closing some doors that could never be opened again.

He thought of Georgie. Now, there was a door he wouldn't mind opening.

It had been a long time since he'd considered a real relationship with a woman again, but Georgie Mundy seemed to be knocking on that door, whether she knew it or not. She'd already somehow broken the latch. If he wasn't careful, she'd ease it open and walk on in, and he wasn't sure he could let that happen.

She intrigued him in a way no other woman had, not even Cathy. The look in her eyes today on the set . . . there wasn't only surprise in those expressive eyes, there was fear, and he hadn't liked it or his response to it. He'd wanted to pull her against him, tuck her close, and draw his sword against her unseen enemies. Even though she was tough, something about her brought out all his protective instincts, and he found he wanted to put himself between her and anyone who would hurt her.

To the world, he was one coldhearted son of a bitch, focused, relentless, driven. In his line of work, it served him well. But there was something about Georgie that made him hope she might look beyond the façade.

He scratched his jaw. They'd gotten off on the wrong foot and now she viewed him the same way the rest of the world did. She knew a whole lot more than she was telling, and it bothered him, even pissed him off. She needed to trust someone, and he wanted it to be him.

Ah, hell. Maybe her reticence was for the best. After what had happened with Cathy, he must be crazy to be thinking about ruining another woman's life.

So many questions. Why had she made sure nobody followed her over the weekend? Where had she gone; who had she seen? What was her secret? Was she trying to protect someone, or was she up to no good? And did it have anything to do with the games somebody was playing with her?

His lab was putting a rush on matching those latents he'd lifted from the storage room at Trent's office. Maybe once he knew who'd been standing at that window on Friday, he'd know a little more about what was going on with Georgie.

Or maybe not.

Horton was still rambling on. ". . . seem like the kind of man who—"

"A lot of people in law enforcement are cynical, Mr. Horton," he finally said. "Comes with the territory."

Horton cocked his head. "I'm sorry to hear that, Ethan. I really am. Nevertheless, back to business. You wanted to know if we've had any trouble with personnel recently?"

"You saying you have?"

"Oh, yes, yes, indeedy," Horton replied. "Three incidents I'm aware of. Hildy Nelson . . . she does *Hildy's Haute Chocolate* . . . well, Hildy's ratings were slipping, so we were forced to give her show a new time slot. Not a happy camper, and she let everybody know it."

"Who got her old time slot?"

"Well, Georgie, of course. Wasn't Georgie's fault, but Hildy didn't see it that way. A time slot can make or break a show, you see."

Ethan pulled the notebook from his pocket and scribbled down the information. "I'm going to want to talk to Ms. Nelson. You said there were three incidents?"

Horton slumped back in his chair, tenting his fingers in front of him. "Hmm, yes. Well, the next one was Iona Jameson."

"She a TV cook, too?"

"No. Nuh-uh, no. She was in charge of Georgie's wardrobe, but she just wasn't capturing the silhouette we wanted for Georgie, so we replaced her."

"And she blames Georgie?"

"I didn't think so. Actually, she's done quite well in the end. Advanced herself up to head wardrobe mistress for all of KALM, but she was pretty cranky for a while over the change." He wrinkled his nose. "People don't like change, you know."

Ethan made more notes. Looking up, he said, "And the third incident?"

"Ignacio Quincy." Horton rolled his eyes. "Brilliant showman, excellent chef, but a bit of a prick, if you ask me," he said in a hushed tone. "Top-rated shows, until Georgie came along. He approached me a few months ago and wanted her fired."

Ethan's brow furrowed. "What for?"

Horton shook his head. "Just on general principles, apparently. Accused her of stealing his recipes, but since Iggy prepares ethnic cuisine and Georgie's focus is natural foods, I didn't see how or why she would. Besides, that's just not Georgie. Not a deceitful bone in her body."

Hmm. Now, there was a subject for debate, as far as Ethan was concerned. "And old Iggy was pissed about her higher ratings?"

In an exasperated tone, Horton sighed, "Ah, the artistic temperament. His ratings are still right up there, but . . . well, the ego, you see." He gave a helpless shrug.

Ethan flipped his notebook closed. "I'm especially interested in talking to those three." Checking his watch, he said, "It's nearly six. I'd like to get started about eight tomorrow. Have them here."

"Sure. You bet, will do, Ethan." Horton leaned forward, absently adjusting the three framed photos on his desk until they sat perfectly aligned.

"Your family?" Ethan asked, gesturing to the photo of a man with his arm around a small boy.

Horton beamed. "Yes. My partner and our son, Josh. The light of our lives. I don't know how I ever thought I was happy before . . . well . . ." He sighed and released the photo. His grin faded and his voice became serious. "This, uh, this set-tampering business, it has to end, before somebody really does get hurt. I desperately want this whole thing to be over."

Rising to his feet, Ethan offered his hand. The two men shook. "I understand, Mr. Horton. Until tomorrow, then."

As Ethan left Horton's office, his cell phone vibrated. Checking the readout, he pressed the button. "Lucas? You got a name on those prints for me?"

"Sure do, boss," the agent replied. "And I think you're going to find this very, very interesting."

It had taken nearly a full pint of Häagen-Dazs Vanilla Bean ice cream to finally neutralize the foul taste in Georgie's mouth.

Standing in front of her oval bathroom mirror, she smirked into her own eyes. Full-fat, nonsoy, nonorganic, guilt-inducing, thigh-dimpling *real* ice cream—a terrible infraction, all those calories, but after what she'd been through, she certainly deserved to indulge herself. She eyed what little remained in the container, then ate it as well.

Sex would have been a far better treat, but that simply wasn't an option at the moment. She watched as her smile drooped into a pity-party pout.

Sex. How long had it been? She was nearly thirty, single, smart, accomplished, nice-enough-looking—eh-hem, *some* would say beautiful—

financially independent, had curves in all the right places, and was acquainted with many eligible men—none of whom she wanted in her bedroom at the moment.

The arrogant image of Ethan Darling swaggered across her mind. Talk about frustrating. Now, there was a man who probably knew his way around a woman's body. Without so much as having kissed him, she knew that he'd get the job done and leave her panting for more.

Deep inside her body, her blood heated, sending a trill of excitement up her spine. Tossing her head, she threw his image aside. Why torture herself with lusty thoughts of Ethan? Besides, he was the enemy.

She picked up her natural-bristle hairbrush, absently stroking the soft tufts with her thumb. In frustration, she let it clatter back onto the vanity.

It wasn't just sex she missed, although a few major male-induced orgasms would certainly cure what ailed her. It was the emotional and physical closeness, the man-woman stuff she craved—quiet conversations, hugging, tender kisses . . . the sheer happiness of being in love.

There was a gleam in Ethan's eyes that had her thinking he might be a man who could give her those things. When he looked at her, his eyes held an elusive something that promised a softer side, hinted of a facet to his personality he allowed few people to see. She'd glimpsed it a couple of times now, catching her off guard, confusing her, making her think that if tough-guy Ethan Darling ever fell in love, it would be completely.

Even though she'd be hard-pressed to define her suspicions, the attraction, the connection between them couldn't be dismissed. It was *there*. For good or ill, or whether anything would ever come of it, it was definitely *there*.

But intimacy with any man came with a price, one she couldn't afford to pay at the moment. If she had to go without romance a little longer, she could manage. There were people who loved her, even if they were hundreds of miles away. It was just the way it had to be right now, until she was sure things were safe. She'd gone into this situation with open eyes; loss of intimacy was simply the price she'd have to pay for her deceit. To protect her family, it was worth it. Besides, a lifetime of indifference inside an unresponsive system hadn't exactly equipped her for love.

Orphaned at five, she'd been ricocheted around inside the system like a runaway pinball. Twelve years of abuse, neglect, and just plain apathy had left a thick layer of rust on her soul. Love was under there somewhere, if a man took the time to chip away at the residue. So far, no man had.

The first of her three foster families had been wonderful. She'd spent two years with the Dowds before being moved. The next situation was horrid, but fortunately, her time with The Man and The Woman, as she and Raine had called them, hadn't lasted long. And while the last place had been tolerable, the Bakers had too many kids and too little time for her.

The only real good to have come of it all was Raine, and then later Mrs. Beebes. Despite their lack of a blood bond, the three of them were family in every way that counted, and she'd fight to the death to protect them.

Snapping off the bathroom light, she picked up her cell phone from the nightstand beside her bed. After a quick call to Santa Barbara to make sure everything was okay, she stripped out of her clothes, took a shower, and slipped into her comfiest pajama bottoms and stretchy tank. The white knit top was a little tight, cupping around her breasts like a second skin, but it wasn't like anybody was going to see her in it, so what the hell.

Padding in bare feet down the hall to her office, she sat down and opened the laptop sitting on the small desk by the window. A few seconds later, the Green Day screensaver flickered to life. Just as she went to open her e-mail, the phone next to the computer rang. She checked the read-out; that was weird. Who would be calling her from her own dressing room phone? Was there a problem at work?

"Hello?"

Nothing.

"Hello?" she repeated. "Who is this?"

Silence. A sick tickle feathered up her spine and her breath stopped in her throat. She swallowed, but didn't speak, only listened. A million scenarios blasted through her head, none of which were good, and all of them starred—

"Paul. It's you, isn't it?"

"Wow." He chuckled. "You *are* good—"

"Get out of my dressing room, you fucker!" she whispered, her voice harsh and raspy. "Get out of my dressing room and get out of my life!"

"Aren't you gonna ask me how I got into your inner sanctum?"

"I can guess. I'm hanging up now and calling the police."

He laughed, a loud boisterous guffaw, ending on a lilting sigh. "Ah, Georgie. Silly, silly goose. By the time anybody gets here, I'll be gone, and you know it."

She closed her eyes. "It *was* you in the window the other day. What do you want?"

He can't know. He can't! He's just being an ass. He cannot know anything.

"Well, I'll tell you, Georgie. The way you treated me when we broke up cut me, it really did."

"You're a criminal, Paul. A common criminal. You should be in prison, and would be if—"

"Really," he snorted. "I have it on good authority that you've been playing fast and loose with the shady side of the law yourself."

"What in the hell are you talking about?"

"You know *exactly* what I'm talking about. Give it up now," he warned, "or you'll be the one paying the price."

"What? You're not making any sense. I—"

"Just be aware," he interrupted again, "I'm not interested in dollars, I'll take it out in . . . trade."

Fury nearly made her go blind. After all the pain he'd caused, he had the nerve to come back into her life and cause more?

"Leave me alone, Paul, or despite all your father's money, this time I'll get a restraining order that will stick!"

"Whatever. Just remember what I said. Be seeing you, sweet thing. And I mean that."

"Paul! No, wait . . . What are you . . . Are you still there? Paul?"

Damn! She slammed the phone down and lowered her head to her hands. Paul Corcoran, in her dressing room, threatening her. Why? And why now? Did he know what she was up to? But how could he; *nobody* knew. Nobody except Raine.

The good news was—if there was any good news—he was in San Francisco, and not Santa Barbara.

But why was he hassling her, what did he *want*?

The urge to rush down to KALM and see what he'd done to her dressing room sent her jumping to her feet. He'd most certainly gone through her things. Fortunately, she left absolutely nothing of a personal nature at the office. Not a thing there could point to Santa Barbara.

On the one hand, if he had rifled through her things and left fingerprints, she had evidence he'd broken in and she could prosecute.

On the other hand, he probably hadn't broken

in. He didn't need to. He was Paul Corcoran and had carte blanche to go wherever he wanted—his father made sure of that.

Maybe she should find a way to contact him, meet with him, find out what he wanted.

Her stomach roiled at the thought. No, seeing him in the window was bad enough; seeing him in person might actually make her vomit—or stab him with whatever sharp instrument was handy. She arched a brow. Killing him would be so unsatisfying. Now, cutting off his testicles, *that* would be poetic justice.

Pacing in front of her desk, she realized she'd been hearing a noise, but had been too distracted pay attention.

There it was again, her doorbell. Who on earth was—

Paul? Oh, my God . . .

No. It couldn't be Paul. There was no way he could have gotten from her dressing room at the studio to her house in under half an hour.

She raised her head. It could be one of Paul's goons. No, wait. Paul didn't have goons; Paul *was* a goon.

Her heart pounding in her ears, Georgie stared toward the office doorway. The bell trilled again. She'd chosen the nine notes to emulate the sound of brass wind chimes, thereby bringing new energy into her living space. Nine, and multiples of that number, were powerful feng shui elements, so she tried to use them wherever she could. But tonight, instead of easing her stress, hearing her doorbell sent a cold chill across her flesh. She licked her lips, unsure what to do.

Outside the window next to her desk, the early evening sky was still bright. If she sneaked a peek through the little round etched-glass window in the foyer, she could catch a glimpse of her visitor and then decide whether to let whoever it was in or not.

On tiptoe, she left her office and approached the front of the house, hugging the wall like a cat burglar in her own home. If she eased around the bookcase, she could just see that little window . . .

Her body froze, but not her heart, which slammed into overdrive like a rabbit who'd spotted a raptor.

Him! What in the hell did *he* want? Her emotions were frazzled enough without having to deal with Ethan Darling.

He turned, and his gaze met hers through the etched-glass, his narrowed hazel eyes challenging her as though he knew she'd considered pretending she wasn't home.

Several ideas crashed inside her brain at once. A, she could open the door, feign a headache, and send him away. That would be good. After what had happened on the set, he'd believe her.

Or, B, she could fling the door wide, yank him inside, rip his clothes off, and beg him to relieve her sexual suffering. That would be good; more likely great. He might even do it. On the one hand, *Oh, boy!* On the other hand, *Oh, boy!* followed by guilt and remorse.

But newly forming plan C carried the most appeal. Invite him in, but not for sex. While her hormones would have to live with the disappointment, her gray matter would be appeased: Ethan Darling knew stuff about her, and she wanted to know what he knew. The old *keep your friends close and your enemies closer* thing.

Of course, the infamous D, *None of the above*, was always an option. But that would mean ignoring him, turning on her heel, dousing the lights, and going straight to bed, but since he'd already seen her, she would go with C. Yes, C, final answer.

Besides, if Paul did decide to drop by, the SOB might think twice about hassling her with Ethan there.

Her lips pressed together, she padded toward the door, threw the deadbolt, and turned the glass knob.

His gaze first went to her face, then immediately dropped, traveling quickly down her body and back up again. She watched his pupils dilate and his stance change. Then she remembered what she was wearing—or, more precisely, not wearing.

Fighting the urge to throw an ugly army blanket around herself, she raised her chin and met his stare head-on.

"I already bought cookies," she snapped. "I have a discount coupon book and plenty of life insurance, don't want my house number painted on the curb, my car's been washed and the broken windshield repaired, I haven't seen any lost

Yorkie-poos, I know who I'm voting for, and I'm very happy with my religion, so whatever you're selling, kid, no thanks."

To her astonishment, his mouth quirked and a smile came into his eyes. "You forgot magazine subscriptions."

"Oh, shoot!" she blurted, determined not to let him captivate her by his showing signs of being human. "Listen, kid. Get a student loan like everybody else. No magazines." When she pretended to close the door on him, he put his hand on it, pushing it open. His eyes held the intensity of a green laser, primed to cut right through every defense she had.

"Lady, you drive a hard bargain," he said. "We're running a special this week on *Feng Shui Illustrated*. Every page is just where it should be."

She blinked up at him, a baby sparrow shocked by the looming form of a hungry bobcat. Who in the hell knew Ethan Darling could be charming? Dammit, she wanted information out of him, maybe his protection, not to be enchanted by him . . .

Resolved to make him work a little harder, she said in a haughty tone, "As you can see, I'm hardly dressed for a sales pitch."

His intense gaze flicked down her body once more, lingering for a moment on her breasts. "Won't hear me complain," he murmured, easing the door all the way open. Stepping inside, he closed it behind him.

Georgie didn't budge. *Fine*, she thought. *I can do this. I can let a man ogle me, if it'll get me what I want . . . what I need. It's not like I dressed this way on purpose to distract him. It's his own fault for showing up unannounced.*

On the one hand, her revealing clothes put her at a psychological disadvantage, and made her nervous as hell. On the other hand, he was obviously distracted by the unexpected sight of her in a tank top and jammie bottoms and no underwear.

The fact he was a little off balance might give her the advantage she needed to outmaneuver him.

Spinning on her heel, she walked into the living room, completely aware his eyes were glued to her butt. Equally distracted by the knowledge he was watching her, she barely missed crashing into the curio cabinet under the archway. As she plopped down on the soft sofa, she hoped her boobs jiggled ever so slightly. Stretching out her legs, she crossed her ankles on the coffee table.

"Take a seat, Darling," she drawled, gesturing to the deeply cushioned chair directly opposite her. Folding her hands in her lap, she waited to see what he would do.

He eyed the chair, then her. With a curt nod, he sat and leaned forward, resting his elbows on his knees.

Testosterone seemed to swirl around him like electrons orbiting a nucleus. Georgie'd had men in her house before, but this one seemed to suck the air right out of the place, making her dizzy with awareness. She was afraid any second now she'd start to wheeze, he'd give her mouth-to-mouth, and all would be lost.

His gaze caught hers. "You feel okay?"

It occurred to her to tell him he should feel her and find out for himself, but she thought better of it.

"I'm good," she said curtly.

His gaze dropped to her mouth, lingered there, then lifted to her eyes. "If you say so." Glancing around at the décor, he said, "This all what you call feng shui?"

Georgie cringed. "After hearing you butcher the term countless times, I have to tell you it's not *feng shooey*, it's *fung schway*, and yes, my home adheres to feng shui principles. A grand master helped me with the interior design."

"So, like, do you have to join some special church or something?"

She nearly choked. "Feng shui isn't a religion," she huffed. "It's simply a philosophy that deals with the organization of things around you, to attract goodness into your life and repel anything unwanted." She eyed him suggestively at the *unwanted* part. "Feng shui emphasizes colors, the dynamics of movement, the benefits of affirmations and positive thinking. It's actually quite simple, makes a lot of sense, and anyone can do it."

He looked around some more. "Hmm. Pretty."

She shrugged, which made her breasts jiggle. Like, finally. Her cheeks warmed, but she stood her emotional ground. "To what do I owe your visit, Detective?"

"Ethan."

"Ethan, then."

For a moment, something flared in his eyes, and she felt that invisible connection between them again. In a quiet voice, he asked, "What can you tell me about Iona Jameson, Ignacio Quincy, and Hildy Nelson?"

Oh. So he wanted to talk about business. Okay, she could do that. Easy enough to slip in a few questions of her own while they were having a little chat.

"They all work for KALM," she said. "And they all hate me, if that's what you're driving at."

"Horton explained the circumstances. I'm going to talk to each of them tomorrow. Do you think any of them hates you enough to put oil of rosemary in your ice cubes?"

She lowered her lids and thought about it for a moment. "Not really. I mean, I don't think so. They're all professional enough to understand how these things work. I'm not responsible for decisions the station's management makes. They know that and—"

"Georgie."

His using her name startled her. She raised her head and looked him in the eye. "What?"

"Are you really okay?" His tone was gentle, and there was genuine concern in his eyes. To see him this way was far more disturbing than if he'd been angry or accusing. Anger she knew how to handle; compassion was an entirely different matter. She couldn't love an angry man, but a compassionate one . . .

"No aftereffects from the oil of rosemary?" he said.

"No."

"I don't mean physically," he added gently. "I mean, it must hurt your feelings a little to think somebody dislikes you enough to do something like this."

He understood that? Oh. Oh, dear. She felt her heart respond in a way she'd been trying to guard against since she met him.

"Um, I, uh, I'm okay. Thanks, though, for asking." She plucked the fabric of her sleep pants. "I don't think the staff blames me for the switches the station has made."

"Doesn't make it go down any easier for them."

"No. I'm sure it doesn't. I'm on top right now, but I won't always be," she said candidly. "My turn will come. That's showbiz."

He settled into his chair. "What'd you do over the weekend, something fun? I came by to see you, but you were out."

Her stomach tightened and she wrapped her arms protectively over her middle. "I took a drive up the coast. Helps clear away the cobwebs."

"You clear the cobwebs every weekend?"

Silence.

"Mostly. What about you?"

Silence.

"Mostly."

They eyed each other for a moment.

So he *had* followed her. She *knew* someone had. Not because she saw anything, but just because she'd sensed it, sensed it in him when he'd challenged her. Well, ha! And ha, ha, ha! She'd lost him at San Jose, she thought smugly. That'd show him.

Suddenly she was dying of thirst. Pushing herself to her feet, she started for the kitchen door. "You want something to drink?"

"Sure."

Over her shoulder, she said, "You want to come?"

As he stood, he mumbled something that sounded like, "Ladies first."

The west-facing kitchen was bathed in light from the setting sun. Everything, from the row of cookbooks lining the counter, to the vase of fresh flowers on the table, to the crystals dangling from the curtain rod in front of the window, was brushed with a soft, pink-amber glow.

Pulling open the refrigerator door, she said, "I have iced green tea, carob soy milk, strawberry yogurt smoothies, organic orange juice, naturally effervescent mineral water—"

"Oh, get real," he said softly, from too close behind her. He peered over her shoulder, trying to see into the fridge, but she blocked him. "I know you don't practice what you preach, Georgie. Five bucks says you've got a beer in there. Ten says it's imported."

She jerked her head in his direction, and their

eyes met. His gaze was one of open challenge. "What do you mean by I don't practice what I preach?"

That sexy mouth of his quirked into a sly grin. "The day I met you on the elevator, remember? You had on your Georgiana Mundy, New Age, organic, nurturing, love everyone, dimpled sweetness persona. But we both know that's just for show."

She swallowed and averted her eyes. "It is not."

He scoffed. "Oh, you're nice enough when it suits you, like in front of an audience. But the real Georgie Mundy has a hot temper, probably eats big juicy steaks when nobody's looking, and has a tendency to be just a little bit pissy."

"No beer for you," she snapped. Grabbing the pitcher from top shelf, she slammed the door. "You'll drink green tea and like it." The cold pitcher in one hand, she stalked toward the pantry at the end of the kitchen to retrieve a glass. When she was halfway there, Ethan spoke.

"I like the little armored tanks on your jammie bottoms. What are those, M1A2 Abrams? Most women would have puppies or rainbows or something. Where do you shop anyway, the Marine surplus store?"

With her back to him, she sniped, "None of your busin—"

"Who's Paul Corcoran?"

Georgie's feet froze in place, but her body kept moving, causing the heavy pitcher to slip from her hands. It crashed to the floor, sending shards of glass and two quarts of cold tea splashing across the linoleum like a pale green tsunami. She cried out and made a grab for the tile counter, hoping to keep herself from stepping barefoot into the broken glass, but an iron band suddenly encircled her waist, yanking her off her feet, and straight into Ethan's arms.

Chapter Six

Feng shui is not a religion, simply a philosophy of balance. Your home is divided into eight guas (areas). Each gua represents an aspect of your life. When you place powerful items within each gua, you will gain incredible results. The gua for love and romance is located at the back right corner of your house; fill that corner with hearts and flowers, photos of couples, tokens of love. Do it, and he will come to you!

Georgiana Mundy's *Feng Shui for Lovers*

It felt good to have her in his arms again, as she had been in the elevator, only this time he wasn't in pain. Quite the contrary. He backed up a few steps so they weren't standing in the broken glass and tea anymore, then lowered her until her feet touched the floor.

Her eyes were wide and wary, and he knew he should let her go, but his palms hadn't been filled with the flesh of a woman for a long time, and his fingers flat-out rebelled. Inhaling the orange-blossom scent of her clean hair, he allowed himself to get lost in it.

"You, uh, you didn't get cut, did you?" he stammered, more aware of her than was safe.

She slowly shook her head.

"You sure?"

She nodded.

Somehow, his left hand had ended up on her butt cheek, while his right had skidded to a halt on her back, under her stretchy top. The warmth of her bare skin seeped through his palm, igniting charges of pleasure throughout his body.

Against his chest, he felt the hard pebbles of her nipples. He closed his eyes for a moment, letting his brain craft a picture of what it would be like to ease up the edge of her shirt, expose her breasts to his gaze, then take one sweet tit into his mouth.

Licking his lips, he returned his attention to Georgie. Her brown eyes held a soft glimmer and went all sort of dreamy-like. She wriggled against him—but not to push him away. Bringing herself closer, she crawled her hands up his chest until her arms encircled his neck and he felt her fingers smooth through his hair. She parted her lips, wet them with her tongue, then raised her face in obvious invitation. His gaze dropped to her mouth . . . and he went for it.

He kissed her, taking everything she offered, demanding more. His tongue slid over her teeth, then thrust inside her mouth to tangle with hers. Mmm. Luscious, creamy vanilla . . .

Breaking the kiss for a moment, he found himself panting, trying to catch his suddenly elusive breath.

"You . . . you're good at this," she whispered, nearly out of breath herself. "I . . . you—"

He took her lips again, crushing them, bringing her body so tightly against his, he could feel her heartbeat pounding through his chest like a hammer.

His hands moved around her rib cage, never breaking contact with her skin, edging up her shirt as he went until he palmed her naked breasts. His brain spun as he thumbed the velvet peaks of her nipples, and she moaned into his open mouth.

Rolling her hips against his crotch, she whimpered in the back of her throat, and he thought he'd go crazy with need. He'd been hard since he walked in the door; it would be so easy to shove down her bottoms, lift her, wrap her bare legs around his waist.

But the instincts and iron will he'd relied on as a kid burdened with too much responsibility, and then as a cop bent on dogging the truth, slapped his brain, reviving him, saving him from making a catastrophic mistake. Georgie's words rang inside his head: *keep that PI distracted . . .*

He broke the kiss, yanked her top down over her breasts, and pushed her to an arm's length.

"If I didn't know better," he rasped, desperate to pump some air into his lungs, "I'd say you were trying to sidetrack me."

Georgie ran her fingers through her hair and smiled up at him, blinking innocently like Scarlett O'Hara bending witless fops to her will. "Now, why would I want to do that, Mr. Detective Man?"

"So I'd forget about asking you about Paul Corcoran," he accused, anger and sexual frustration morphing his words into bullets. "How far would you have gone, Georgie? Would you have let me fuck you?"

She gasped and shoved at him. "You're horrible! Let me go!"

"Answer me!"

She was nervous now that he had her on the ropes. Staring defiantly into his eyes, she bit out, "You don't strike me as a man who lives with breaches of ethics easily, and since I am technically under your protection, having sex with me would . . ."

"What are you hiding, Georgie? And what's it got to do with Paul Corcoran?"

"I'm not hiding anything," she snapped. Wiggling, she tried to break free, but he held her tight. "My life's an open book—"

"Yeah, if you've got a crowbar and a magnifying glass. Tell me about Corcoran."

"Nothing to tell."

"You saw him Friday in the window across from your dressing room at the studio, didn't you?" He watched her carefully as she gave him a *how would you know?* lift of a brow. "He left fingerprints behind, Georgie. He *was* there and you *did* see him, and it scared you."

He had to give her credit; she didn't so much as flinch. "Okay. So he was there. Caught me by surprise, that's all."

"You screamed when you saw him."

"It was a mouse—"

"Cut the crap, Georgie," he growled, his fingers tightening on her shoulders. "When you broke up with Corcoran, you filed an injunction against him."

"I tried, but the judge denied the order." She shoved his hands off her shoulders and turned away. "Just filing did the trick, though. I haven't seen him since then."

He jammed his fists into his hips, staring at her rigid back. "You saw him because he wanted you to. It was an act of intimidation. Has he contacted you?"

"Butt out, Detective," she warned. "This is none of your business. If he does start to hassle me, I'll call the proper authorities."

She was lying, and they both knew it. She was scared of her ex-boyfriend, but unless Ethan could get her to trust him, she was so damned stubborn he might never get the truth out of her.

"Look at me, Georgie," he said softly. "C'mon. Turn around. Talk to me, here."

She pivoted on her heel, facing him, her jaw set tight, a mixture of fear and fury in her expressive eyes.

"Why'd you file the injunction against Corcoran?" he coaxed. "Did he hurt you? If he did, I swear to God, I'll take him apart."

He meant it. The thought of Corcoran, or any man, lifting a hand to Georgie sent an unexpected spike of anger through his body, tensing his muscles, piercing his bones. His fingers curled into fists.

She seemed to consider the question for a moment. Then, "He didn't hurt me, not like you mean. Paul is a rich man's son, used to getting whatever he wants, whenever he wants it. He asked me to marry him, and when I said no, he got a little . . . aggressive in his pursuit. End of story."

"Why'd you say no?"

"He fooled around on me. Slept with other women. That's all there is to it."

"That's all there is to it for breaking up with him, not for trying to get a restraining order. There's something else."

Her eyes remained locked with his. "No. There isn't."

Yeah, there is, Ethan thought. But why wouldn't she admit it? What was she really afraid of?

In spite of the barriers she'd erected between them, he would still get to the truth.

At his request, Lucas Russell, one of Ethan's best PIs, had begun compiling a file on Georgie— and on Paul Corcoran as well. Sometime in the next forty-eight hours, Ethan would know all there was to know about the lovely Georgiana

Mundy, including her relationship with Corcoran, whether she cooperated or not.

Grabbing a handful of her hair, he tugged her gently toward him, planting a kiss on her lips she'd never forget. When she was breathless, nearly begging for mercy, he pulled back.

"Stay put," he mumbled against her mouth. "If you'll tell me where the mop and broom are, I'll clean this mess up before I leave."

"I can do—"

"I'll do it," he insisted, then kissed her again. "I want to. For God's sake, Georgie, let somebody do something for you without kicking them in the head for it."

"I'm not like that!"

He grinned into her eyes. "The hell you're not," he said softly. "But that's okay. If you can dish it out, believe me, I can take it. Now, where's that mop?"

An hour later, Ethan violently cut into his porterhouse steak, shoving the chunk of rare beef into his mouth, chewing as though he were grinding galvanized six-penny nails into metal kibble.

Frustrating woman. He raised his wineglass and knocked back a huge gulp, letting the rich burgundy complement the savory meat in his mouth. *Frustrating damn woman.* Swallowing, he tucked into his steak once more.

He'd kissed her. It had been the last thing on his mind, and the first thing he'd wanted to do when he'd seen her. Jamming another bite of steak into his mouth, he tried to focus on his meal, and not on Georgie's hot little body and what he wanted to do to it.

God, her outfit had about driven him wild, and it had taken every bit of restraint he possessed to walk away from her after that last kiss, especially after he'd had his hands on her.

What he needed was to get laid. Find a woman and get down to business. That'd take his mind off Georgie, her curves, her big brown eyes.

But it wouldn't erase the fear he'd seen in those eyes at the mention of Paul Corcoran's name. Why was she so afraid of him? Ethan wanted to tear the guy apart, if for no other reason than he'd put that look into Georgie's eyes.

Leaning back in his chair, he refocused his energies, tuning out the bustle of the five-star restaurant, the clatter of dishes being cleared from a nearby table, the chatter of friendly conversation. He sat alone. In the entire dining room, only he sat alone.

He rubbed his thumb along the stem of his wineglass. What the hell did it matter? Being alone suited him. After all, he'd spent years struggling to meet the demands of other people, talking when he'd've preferred silence, cleaning up one disaster or another of someone else's making. He deserved a little peace and quiet; he'd earned it.

It had been six years since he'd pulled out all the stops and painted the town, taken a beautiful woman to her favorite restaurant, enjoyed her company, laughed at her charm and wit, and later, reveled in her body. Those days were behind him, and any social activities he'd participated in since then were either for business or simply to blow off a little testosterone.

Until Georgie. Why her, and why now?

Maybe it was because she was in trouble, needed a champion, and he'd always been a sucker for women like that—never mind that he was a paper tiger, hardly the kind of man a woman could depend on when the chips were down.

Except that Georgiana Mundy was nobody's victim. She kept her own counsel. Didn't trust him enough to confide in him, preferring to fight whatever battles she faced alone.

That made her one smart lady, and more attractive to him than she could possibly imagine.

He lifted the wineglass to his lips and started to take a sip when he heard a man's voice behind him.

"And here I thought this place had class." A second later, a tall blond man wearing wire-rimmed glasses moved from behind Ethan to slide into the vacant chair across the table.

"Mind if I join you, big brother? Thanks," the man said, without waiting for Ethan's reply. Raising his hand, he caught the waiter's attention and waved him over. "I'll have exactly what he's having. Oh, and put it on his tab. It's my birthday."

The waiter smiled and nodded, then scurried away.

Ethan's mood tripped and fell down a few

flights. Jamming another bite of steak into his mouth, he mumbled, "Your birthday's not for another three months."

Inspector Nate Darling of the SFPD, and Ethan's younger brother by two years, grinned. "How cool of you to remember. Thought I'd better cash in my birthday chips now, though. Who knows if we'll even be speaking in three months? I'd hate to have to wait another twenty years just to tell you what a prick I think you are, even when you step in front of me to take a bul—"

"I thought you were on your honeymoon," Ethan snapped. No need to rehash the past. He'd done what he had to do, and if he'd been shot in the process, well, those were the breaks. It sure as hell didn't make him any kind of hero. "And stop looking at me like that, Nate. You'd've done the same thing for me."

"Yes. I would have. But in my scenario, it would have brought us closer together."

The two men eyed each other for a moment, neither speaking, neither looking away. Their bond had been fragile for years, and even now teetered on a precipice. It could tumble either way, and both men knew it.

But fate had given them a second chance at a relationship, and while Nate seemed poised to leap into the void, Ethan wasn't sure he could survive the risks. What if he did go for it, and it pushed his brother farther away than ever? He leaned back in his chair. "Why are you here?"

Nate shoved his glasses up on his nose. Cocking his head, he said lightly, "Paris was great, thanks for asking. Yes, we had a fabulous time. Incredible food, beautiful art and architecture. The websites really don't do it justice."

"You never even made it out of your hotel room."

"Not very often, no, but when we did, well, you know what they say—Paris is for lovers." He grinned again, and Ethan tamped down a twinge of jealousy.

Nate looked relaxed and happy, like a man who'd just spent the last ten days in bed making love to his bride. It was actually kind of disgusting, but somehow, Ethan just couldn't drum up any ill feelings over it. His brother was no longer a *he* . . . he was a *they*. Obviously in love, he'd found a great woman in Tabitha—well, a woman who was willing to put up with his crap anyway, which was what it usually boiled down to. And someday they'd probably have a kid or two . . .

The fundamentals of a fulfilling life, Ethan thought. The things most men wanted, fought for, sometimes even died for. Things even he had once craved, once upon a time.

". . . got home a couple of days ago," Nate was saying. "Tabby's teaching her dream interpretation class tonight, so I called Andie, but she's offline, so I talked to Mom. And *she* said she thought you were still in the city. Told me this was one of your favorite haunts."

Ethan swallowed a sip of wine. "You came looking for me? What in the hell for?" He eyed his brother for a moment. Good-looking, easy-going Nate. Nate, who had gone off with their dad when their parents had divorced, leaving Ethan to clean up the emotional wreckage. "If you came by just to tell me about married life, I don't give a rat's ass."

Nate didn't bat an eye. "I see we missed taking our happy pills again this morning." He gestured toward Ethan's injured side and his brown eyes grew serious. "You healing up okay?"

The waiter returned, bringing a second wine-glass, a salad, and another basket of hot dill bread. After filling Nate's glass with burgundy, the waiter departed.

"I'm fine," Ethan said, as he ripped off a hunk of bread and slathered it with butter. But his mind went once more to the green silk cloth in his pocket, the silly gift of healing Georgie had given him, and suddenly he wanted to push himself away from the table, jump in his car, and go see her. Maybe she'd let him kiss her again, let him touch her again, let him make her smile. He loved her smile. "When do you have to report for duty?"

Nate's fork spiked through several crisp chunks of romaine. "Tomorrow," he said, then shoved the bite in his mouth. "So, how's it going? You getting any?"

Before Ethan could form a reply, inside his jacket pocket his cell phone vibrated. Checking the read-out, he swallowed a groan. Not now. He should let his voice mail take it. She'd never know.

The phone pulsed again, and the guilt of a lifetime washed over him.

"I've, uh, I've got to take this," he said to his brother, busy digging into the basket of bread. Pressing the button, he put the phone to his ear. "Hi, Mom. What's up?"

Across the table, Nate's eyes locked with Ethan's.

Ignoring his brother's inquisitive stare, he said, "Do you need something, Mom?" Keep it light, keep it casual, he admonished himself. Maybe, if he was lucky, he could bring this conversation in on time and under budget. But when his mother sighed, long and loud, he knew he was in for an earful.

Across the table, Nate grinned wryly and returned to his meal.

"Oh, Ethan, honey," Lydia gushed. Then she sighed again, starting very high and ending very low, almost as though she were falling from a cliff and he heard her in passing halfway down. "You *know* how I hate to bother you."

Uh-huh. Gently, he said, "Tell me what's wrong, Mom." Or not. Not would be better.

"Well, it's my back again. Now, you know how I was seeing that one doctor in the city, and I really thought he was helping me for a while? But then, on Tuesday, no, wait, I think it was Monday. Yes, yes, that's right, it was Monday. I remember because that's the day the boy comes to mow the lawn and he came that day, so that's how I know—"

"What happened to your back, Mom?" Ethan sat back in his chair and patiently waited.

As though he hadn't interrupted her at all, Lydia continued, "—because he *never* comes on Tuesday, so it was *Monday*, and I wanted to make a hamburger noodle casserole, so-o-o-o-o I went out to the garage to find one of the big cans of cream of mushroom soup, you know, in the pantry that you built for me that summer? Well, I was bending down to look on the bottom shelf . . . I don't know why I put the cans there, because, really, bending is so difficult, but the higher shelves have the cereals and grains and flour, and I don't want bugs—"

"You sprained your back again, Mom?" He furrowed his brow. "Are you in pain?"

Nate stopped chewing, and sent Ethan a look of concern.

"Well, honey," Lydia whined, "now, you know I'm always in pain, it's just a matter of degree. But I try not to complain about it too much, because I don't want to be a burden to you kids with my misery, but what with my sciatica acting up . . . Oh, and lately I've had just this horrible ache in my side? Well, I try to ignore it, of course . . ."

Years ago, when his parents had divorced and his father and Nate had moved to Washington state, Ethan and Andrea had opted to stay with their mom. Now, not only did Ethan understand why his father had left the woman, he had occasionally cursed the day he'd decided not to go, too.

If ever a woman felt she needed a man in her life in order to survive, it was Lydia Darling. Without one, she flailed about helplessly, incapable of functioning on even the simplest level. The problem was, if some man did show an interest in her, she just plain bled the life right out of him until he crawled away to die in the Graveyard of Broken Suitors.

But Ethan was her oldest son, the man of the house, her protector; he couldn't crawl away, and they both knew it. Besides, in spite of everything—the grousing, the obvious bids for attention, the constant medical conditions, real or imagined—he loved her.

From the time he'd been sixteen, Ethan had been the man of the family, taking care of Mom and Andie, working two jobs, struggling with the finances, plundering his mother's purse to snare and cut up her credit card whenever she got a new one—and immediately ran it up to its limit. Even though his dad never missed an alimony or child support payment, somehow Lydia failed to understand that it wasn't free money to be spent on whatever caught her fancy.

After over twenty years of this kind of insanity, sometimes the burden was a bit much to bear.

"What do you need for me to do, Mom?"

She sighed again, a sound that Ethan should be used to hearing by now, but that occasionally set his teeth on edge.

"Nothing, I suppose," she grumbled as though she were a little girl who knew she'd misbehaved, but should be excused simply because she was a little girl, and therefore not responsible. "Are you coming by the house soon? Since your sister moved out, it's been so quiet here and, well, I could pass the time by working in the garden, but my knees, you know—"

"Mom," he said as gently as he could. "I hired a gardener for you. You have a cook and a housekeeper. You don't have to lift any finger you don't want to lift, and I'm sorry your back and knees hurt."

"Really?"

Across the table, Nate lowered his eyes and focused on slicing into the steak the waiter had brought.

"Of course, really. Tomorrow, I'll see if I can find a specialist who might be able to get you some relief. How does that sound?"

"Good. That's good. But maybe you could come by and see me? I can make chocolate chip cookies, like when you were little. They're still your favorite, aren't they? With toasted macadamia nuts?"

He smiled. "Yeah, Mom. They're still my favorite. It's going to be a busy week, but I'll try to make it by in the next couple of days, okay?"

"Sure. Okay, honey." She sounded a little dejected, which pinched his heart a bit, but it couldn't be helped.

"Uh, in the meantime, do you need anything?" *Like money?* Even though Ethan was worth millions, he tried to curtail his mother's spending habits just for her own good. It was a hopeless endeavor.

"No, no," she trilled. "I just wanted to see my baby boy. You're such a busy man these days. I, well, I miss seeing you."

He arched a brow and looked over at Nate. "You could always call your other baby boy."

Nate stopped chewing, lifted his head, and stabbed Ethan with a stare.

Lydia giggled. "Nate called earlier asking where you were. Did he get in touch?"

"Yeah."

"Good," she cooed. "I love that my boys are together again. All grown up into such handsome men! And Nate, married! Do you think Tabitha will get pregnant right away? I'll be a grandmother and you'll be an uncle! Oh, but Ethan, being a husband and father *yourself* would be *so* much more ful—"

"Okay, knock it off, Mom." He chuckled, trying to find a way to assuage her without thinking too hard on what she'd said. "We've already gone over this. Nate's the one who's going to provide you with grandkids, hopefully sooner rather than later."

Nate's eyes widened, then narrowed. He pursed his lips, then picked up his wineglass and drained it.

"I have to go now, Mom. I promise I'll try to come by soon."

Ending the call, Ethan set the phone on the table, leaned back in his chair, and closed his eyes.

A husband and father. Not him. Not if there was any justice in the world.

Cathy. Yeah, he'd had his chance, and he'd literally blown it away. Let brother Nate do the husband-and-father thing. Let Andie find some guy, settle down, pop a few babies. He'd be Uncle Ethan and that would suit him just fine. Between his mother's clinging, and losing Cathy, his destiny was clear, so why fight it?

He chugged the last of his wine and set the glass down, licking his lips, recalling the taste of Georgie's mouth under his. Better commit that little episode to memory, because it would never happen again.

From across the table, Nate said, "You were a lot nicer to Mom than you are to me."

"That's because you're a dick."

"Damn, that slipped my mind for a minute," Nate drawled. "Thanks so much for reminding me."

Ethan shrugged. "Happy to oblige."

"Listen, Ethan, I did have a reason for coming by. There *is* something I wanted to talk to you about."

"Shoot."

His brother's mouth tilted on one end. "You must have read my mind. I wanted to say thanks, you know, for—"

"I told you to forget it," Ethan said harshly, returning his attention to his plate. He probably shouldn't blame Nate for the years of struggle catering to their mother's every whim, the financial obligations, the emotional turmoil, but the fact was, he resented Nate for having taken the easier path. After two decades of separation, the two brothers who had once been so close had grown into men divided by a gulf so deep, Ethan wasn't sure it could ever be crossed.

Slowly, Nate's smile faded into a scowl. "Do you always have to play the prick, Ethan? Shit, you want to make an effort here, or do we just say screw it, lost cause, and forget the whole damn thing?"

When Ethan made no reply, Nate doubled his fists and shoved himself to his feet. Yanking out his wallet, he extracted a couple of bills and tossed them on the table. With a sardonic laugh, he said, "Guess I was right about that twenty-year thing, huh? I'll buy my own fucking birthday dinner. Brother."

Ethan watched as Nate strode through the busy restaurant and out the door, never once bothering to look back.

Chapter Seven

To create harmony with the one you love, position a Chinese Double Happiness symbol in the
Marriage Area (the far right corner) of your
bedroom. This beautiful and ancient symbol is
usually painted gold on a red background, and
represents unity and mutual happiness for you
and your man.

Georgiana Mundy's *Feng Shui for Lovers*

"What in the hell did you think you were
doing, Paul? I told you to stay clear of
that bitch and let me take care of everything. I got
you out of it the first time, but there's only so
much I can do. Christ, you haven't got the common sense God gave a goat—"

"Cut it out, Dad!" Paul Corcoran watched as the
veins in his father's neck stood out in angry relief.
"I didn't do anything wrong. I just thought a couple of little pushes might get her going in the
right direction, that's all."

Vaughn never gave him any credit for having
even a few brains. Okay, he may not be swimming

in the deep end of the gene pool, but he wasn't exactly stupid. With a casual shrug, he said, "I stood at the window and smiled. Hey, you know, it took a lot of math to figure out exactly which window was directly across from hers in another whole building. *And* how to find it, and then to slip in without anybody seeing me." He gave a sharp nod, picked up an almond from the bowl held in his hand, tossed it into his mouth, and crunched down.

"Sorry," Vaughn sighed. "I forgot what a mental giant you are."

"Don't insult me, Dad," he said, tossing few more almonds into his mouth. "I'm all you got."

Vaughn sent him a look that said, *And don't I know it.*

At sixty, Vaughn Corcoran looked fit and sharp. His blue eyes missed nothing, and though he was soft-spoken and deliberate, Paul figured it was a safe bet his employees were all afraid of him. Like the way swimmers are with sharks; you didn't know you were doomed until it was too late to get the hell out of the water.

"And you called her," Vaughn accused.

Paul smiled at the memory. "Yeah. From her own phone at the studio. *That* shook her up. Didn't touch anything besides the phone, then I wiped it. No evidence. See? I'm not so stupid."

Behind his massive desk, Paul's father eased back in his office chair, making the soft leather squeak. "It still escapes me why you got involved with Georgiana Mundy in the first place. For Christ's sake, you went to school with some of the most beautiful women in the world. Women who came from families of wealth and status nearly equal to my own. Why didn't you screw around with one of them?"

Paul settled into the plush sofa in his father's San Francisco office and put his feet up on the coffee table. "She was cute, she was a TV star, and I thought she'd be a good fuck."

"Was she?"

"Never found out." The image of Raine What's Her Name flitted behind his eyes. "Her friend was hot, too, but I knew neither of them would go for a three-way, so I—"

"Which brings us to where we stand this very day!" Vaughn picked up a pen, twirled it between his fingers, then slammed it down on his desk. "Your predilections—that means idiotic tendencies—"

"I know what it means!" Paul snapped. "The cops didn't prove anything. No charges were brought."

"Only because I called in every favor I was owed in the entire state and put out a shitload of money, Paul. Stay away from her, do you hear me? Jesus, if the tabloids ever got ahold of this, it'll be Gary Hart all over again."

"Who?"

"Exactly my point!" Swiveling in his chair, Vaughn turned his back on Paul to gaze out over the city. "I'm taking care of everything, so just sit tight. I'll let you know when it's time for you to get involved. Right now things are still in the investigative stage. I'll have more information in a few days."

Paul leaned forward, dusting bits of salt from his raw silk tie. Setting the nut bowl down on the coffee table, he said, "So which one do you think it is—Georgie or her friend?"

Vaughn blew out an exasperated breath, then swiveled back to face Paul. "Which one do I think *what* is?"

Paul shrugged. "You know, like, which one of them is blackmailing you?"

"I didn't work my derriere off at Le Cordon Bleu in Paris, Detective, then hone my skills for a decade in the finest restaurants in France, Italy, *and* New York, just to have some nouveau twit with more cleavage than brains grab the spotlight from me simply because she has perky knockers!"

It was Tuesday morning, and across the conference room table from Ethan, Ignacio Quincy's dark eyes snapped. His puffy face gleamed with a sheen of perspiration, and his thick lips turned down in a sea-bass scowl. In his mid-forties, he was dressed in the traditional white double-breasted culinary jacket, and wore his chef's hat straight up on his head, like a brilliant atomic mushroom cloud just after impact.

While Ethan couldn't argue with the perky knockers part of the chef's assessment, he'd have to disagree; as beautiful as Georgie was, her brain just might be her best feature.

"So you hold Ms. Mundy personally responsible for your dip in the ratings and the schedule changes?"

Quincy grumbled under his breath, then shrugged. "I hold the station's management responsible. Idiots in suits. Not only does one have to be good at what one does—delight *and* entertain one's audience—one also has to be—dare I say it, can I utter the term aloud? *Sexy!*" He raised an indignant brow. "Why, if I were a hundred and seventeen pounds thinner, twenty-three years younger, and good-*looking*, this never would have happened!" He gestured wildly with his hand. "Take away her big brown eyes, tight little tush, the aforementioned rack, her long, silky hair, alluring smile, and all she'd have left is her pitiful tofu and bean sprout soufflé!"

Tofu and bean sprout soufflé? Ethan fought to suppress his gag reflex.

"I have to tell you, Mr. Quincy," he said. "I'm getting some real mixed messages from you about your feelings toward Ms. Mundy."

The man set his jaw and averted his eyes. "Nevertheless, if *she* hadn't come along, I'd still be number one."

Ethan let the pen in his fingers drop to the open file in front of him—Ignacio Quincy's file. The TV chef was everything he claimed to be, from his humble beginnings as the son of a male nurse in a suburb of Davenport, Iowa, to his culinary studies in Europe, to his top-rated cooking shows.

"Did you put the oil of rosemary in Ms. Mundy's ice cubes?"

Quincy scowled again, then snorted. "Such an act is *far* beneath me, my man. If one wanted to discover whom it is behind all this mayhem, one needn't look very far."

"One wouldn't?"

The chef's ample mouth twisted. "One would be well advised to have a chat with Hildy Nelson."

"Hildy's Haute Chocolate?"

"Hildy's Haute *Temper,* if you ask me. She was boiling mad the day Ozzie shuffled her time slot."

"Mad enough to make trouble for Ms. Mundy?"

"Madder," Quincy snarled, lifting his bushy brows to the rim of his toque blanche. "Methinks, mad enough to kill."

About fifteen minutes later, Ethan put that question to the lady herself. Tiny, bespectacled, and prim, Hildy Nelson apparently tried to offset her petite stature by overteasing her silver white hair. Instead of the elegant coif she'd undoubtedly gone for, she looked more like a Q-tip that had been used to light a barbeque.

Aside from that, she was an attractive older woman whose smile could have melted the hardest chocolate heart.

"You suspect me?" she tittered, rapidly blinking her blue eyes. "Me, make trouble for that adorable creature? I'm sorry, Detective. You're not only barking up the wrong tree, you're in the wrong forest altogether." She squared her shoulders and brushed an invisible piece of lint from the lapel of her red jacket. "Do you know how old I am, Detective?" She smiled at him once more, lifting her chin to elongate her somewhat creped neck.

"Your file says you're sixty-two."

"A damn lie!" she snapped, then recovered herself and smiled demurely. "What I meant to say was, I'm barely fifty. My agent was supposed to, ehm, take care of that, you see. It's an unfortunate typo." She licked her lips and lowered her eyes.

Ethan watched as her shoulders slumped just a little. Gently, he said, "I thought it must be a mistake. Anyone looking at you would realize the error immediately, Ms. Nelson."

She sucked in her bottom lip and raised her eyes to meet his gaze.

"Thank you, Detective," she whispered. "My point is, I am a mature woman who's worked in this business a long time. I've seen them come and I've seen them go. I have no reason to resent Georgie, and I'm certainly not hassling her." She met Ethan's gaze. "Georgie is young and hip and now, but trends always fade, and when this one does, I'll still be here."

"What makes you say that, ma'am?"

She blinked at him as though he'd just asked her weight. "Feng shui is *transient*, Detective," she stated with emphasis. "*Chocolate* is *forever*."

Since he could hardly disagree with that, he said, "Ms. Mundy's success may not bother you, but can you think of anyone who might have taken issue with it? Maybe even had the means and opportunity to cause a little trouble?"

Her gaze shifted up and to the left, the way people's eyes do when they were trying to recall something. "Iggy wasn't too pleased. He wanted to get to know her." She wiggled her thinly plucked brows meaningfully.

"Get to *know* her?"

"In the biblical sense," she said, leaning forward as if to impart a state secret. "Fancies himself God's gift. Thinks his fame can replace youth and good looks." She eased back in her chair and lowered her head again. "It can't. Silly man should know that."

Ethan picked up his pen and tapped it on the stack of files in front of him. "He asked her out, and she rejected him?"

Hildy nodded. "Yes, but in all fairness, she rejects everybody. Iggy took it personal, though. Pinhead."

"Anyone else take her rejections personally?"

"Maybe. Hard to say." Checking the watch on her delicate wrist, she said, "I'm sorry. I have to prepare for a taping."

When she stood, Ethan rose and shook her hand. "Thank you, ma'am. You've been very gracious."

"And you," she replied softly, "so very gentlemanly."

As she raised her face to smile up into his eyes, Ethan could see the beauty in her bones and realized she must certainly have broken her own fair share of hearts along the way.

Iona Jameson probably hadn't broken as many

hearts as she had jaws, Ethan thought as the woman entered the conference room, kicking the door shut behind her with one booted foot.

According to her file, she was twenty-seven and had worked for the station since she'd graduated from USF with a BA in graphic arts. Tall and broad-shouldered, she was dressed in black leather pants and what appeared to be a black rain slicker. Her too-black hair shot out from her scalp in pointy spikes, while her lobes, lips, brows, nose, tongue, and God knew what else had been pierced with small gold hoops. Eyeing him like a Goth pugilist taking her corner, she dropped her body into the chair, spread her knees, and crossed her arms over her chest.

Mary Poppins she was not, and a far a cry from what he'd pictured a wardrobe mistress might look like.

"I'm, like, not a lesbian, if that's what you're thinking," she stated, her voice oddly high-pitched and feminine for her looks, sort of like a squirrel on helium.

"Your lifestyle is none of my concern, Ms. Jameson," he said, "unless it involves criminal activity. Can you think of why anybody would want to cause trouble for Ms. Mundy?"

She sneered, showing straight white teeth. Apparently trashing her looks stopped at dental care. With a casual shrug, she settled down into her seat and uncrossed her arms.

"Georgie was, like, cool to me when I did her duds for her. She's good-lookin', ya know? Has good bones, elegant lines. Has a good bod, too, and I dressed her that way, kind of classy-like. But the Suits wanted more T&A, and I wouldn't go there, so they, like, replaced me. Wasn't Georgie's fault; in fact, I heard she went to the mat for me."

"She fought to keep you?"

"Yeah, for all the good it did. But she's, like, turned into this real stuck-up bitch now, so maybe somebody thinks it would be fun to rattle her cage a little."

Ethan twirled the pen in his fingers. "She wasn't always stuck up?"

"Naw, like, only for the last couple of years. We used to do stuff, you know? Girl stuff." She laughed, and he was caught off guard by the pleasant, musical sound of it. "Yeah, I know. We made a pair, all right, her all pretty, and me all Gothed up. But Georgie, she, like, sees past that and shit. She's cool. Or was. We'd go out for drinks or a laugh or, like, to meet some guys."

Her deeply purple lips flattened. "Course, most all the guys wanted Georgie, but that's okay. Sometimes they wanted me." She shifted in her chair. "We've got different styles, so the guys she liked, I didn't want, and vice versa. But now that she's, like, this big star, you ask her to do something, and it's always *too busy*, or, *gotta work*, or *maybe next time*, except she never does the next-time thing. I finally stopped askin'. It's been like that ever since she first met Paul, but more since she dumped the bastard."

Ethan felt his heart miss a beat. Straightening in his chair, he said, "You met Paul Corcoran?"

She shifted again, looked at him, looked away. "Tall Paul? Yeah. He was hot. Even I thought so. A little eyeliner and a leather jock, and I'd've been the goner, not Georgie. She was crazy about him, though. At first anyway. But, man, like, what an asshole." She scratched her nose, then sniffed. "I don't know all what happened, like, but one day they're all cozy, and the next day she's got the law on him. I'm surprised they didn't fire her."

Ethan's brow furrowed. "I didn't hear about any scandal. Why would the station fire her?"

Iona blinked her eyes at him and scratched her nose again. "Well, because of Paul, of course. The Suits."

"What about them?"

She looked a little puzzled by his question, then shrugged. "Guess you don't know the whole enchilada, then, huh? Some private dick you are."

"Why don't you fill me in?"

She grinned, shifted in her chair, recrossed her legs. "Well, Paul Corcoran's dad is, like, this Vaughn Corcoran guy. You musta heard of him."

Who hadn't? Vaughn Corcoran was one of the West Coast's wealthiest businessmen, had fingers in every pie worth tasting, oversaw a huge conglomerate out of the priciest offices in San Francisco, and if word on the street was right, had his eye on making a run for governor. He was a ruthless businessman who had a reputation for always getting what he wanted. Always.

Ethan nodded slowly as the puzzle pieces started clicking into place. There weren't enough of them yet to make a picture, but he was getting there.

"Yeah, I've heard of him," he said. "So Vaughn Corcoran is Georgie's ex-boyfriend's father. How would dumping Paul get her fired?"

Iona sucked in her lower lip and gave Ethan the once-over. "You know, you're hot. I mean, under that button-down look you've got going. A little eyeliner, maybe a studded collar—"

"I left them at home. How would Georgie's relationship with Corcoran get her fired?"

She shrugged, rolled her eyes, and sighed. "Okay, Mr. Dick. Your loss. It's like this . . . 'cause way, way up the food chain, I mean, like, way, *way* up the food chain, Vaughn Corcoran is sort of our boss."

"*What?*"

"Yeah, he, like, owns KALM. Didn't anybody tell you that?"

Chapter Eight

If you eat food prepared by an upset or unhappy person, it will taste bad, and you may
even get sick. More importantly, the *chi* of
your stove corresponds to the quality of your
relationship, and the degree of harmony you
experience. Yes, your stove! For best results,
position it where you can see the door, and
who's approaching. And for the best *chi*, make
sure your stove is clean!

Georgiana Mundy's *Feng Shui for Lovers*

Without so much as a courtesy knock, her
dressing room door swung open, revealing what appeared to be a very irritated Ethan
Darling. She swiveled in her seat, presenting him
with a dry look. "Crawl out on the wrong side of
the cave this morning, Conan?"

His jaw seemed glued shut as he grabbed her
arm, yanked her to her feet, and marched her
down the hall toward Ozzie's office.

"Oh, I know why you're so pissy this morning."
She lengthened her step to keep up with him.

"Pissy is the right word, isn't it, Detective? Because somebody recently referred to *me* that way, and while it didn't fit me at all, I think it describes you perfectly."

When he still didn't respond, she said, "If this is about somebody writing *Ethan Darling wears girls' panties* on the bathroom mirror, I can neither confirm nor deny—"

Her tirade was cut short when Ethan shoved open the door to Ozzie's office, slamming it shut behind them.

At his desk, Ozzie jumped to his feet, a look of dismay on his face.

Ethan shot a look at Ozzie, then at Georgie, and back to Ozzie again. "Is there some reason why neither of you felt it necessary to mention that Vaughn Corcoran owns this television station?" With a jerk of his chin, he indicated Georgie. "You. Speak."

She crossed her arms under her breasts. "Woof."

"Elaborate," he snapped. "And it better be good."

"I can't imagine why you'd be so worked up over this," she lied. "It's hardly important."

For a heartbeat, he simply watched her, then shifted his attention to Ozzie. "Tell me *you* didn't think it was important, either."

Poor Oz shook his head enthusiastically, dislodging his glasses from his nose. His cheeks flushed. "Well, uh, well, well, no. No, I didn't, Ethan. Do you, uh, that is to say, do *you* think it's important?"

In a charcoal Hugo Boss suit, white silk shirt,

and pearl-gray tie, Ethan looked powerful . . . and dangerous. If she were some kind of criminal he was interrogating, she'd be nervous as hell.

All right. She was nervous as hell anyway.

Their eyes met, and she felt her lower limbs go numb. In spite of how they were glaring at her now, he had the most beautiful eyes.

He shoved back the edges of his jacket and thrust his hands into his pants pockets, flashing that hard gaze back and forth between her and Ozzie.

Did this man never smile? Did nothing ever touch him, amuse him, make him laugh? Since she'd met him, he'd been serious, solemn, even when he'd kissed her, run his hands over her body. He hadn't seemed to derive any pleasure from it. He must have an iron-encrusted conscience.

Or he was very good at hiding his true feelings behind a mask. That was something she understood completely. If that were true, then they had something in common . . .

"To answer your question, Mr. Horton," he said with a tension in his voice that warned of an impending storm, "I think it might be damned important. Georgie had a relationship with Paul Corcoran that nearly ended in legal action. If the senior Corcoran is the kind of man to take issue with that kind of thing, he could have planted, bribed, or intimidated someone at the station to make trouble. It's no secret he has lofty political goals for himself, maybe even for his kid. Georgie's attempt at a restraining order could compromise those goals in the eyes of the voters, so maybe he wants to discredit her."

"If what you say is true," Georgie granted, choosing her words carefully, "why didn't he simply have me fired?"

"Makes him look magnanimous, forgiving. His public image stays intact. But if the media dogs got hold of the fact KALM's star tried to get an injunction against her former boyfriend, the son of the station's owner, they'd never rest until they found out why you filed it. It's amazing they missed it before, which makes me wonder just how many people Corcoran has in his pocket."

A lot, Georgie thought. The Corcorans had a lot of people in their very deep pockets, which was just one reason why she never trusted anyone. Not *anyone*.

"Firing you would only make Corcoran look vindictive," Ethan said. "Since the injunction was denied, he could twist that into a mark against you. Turns it into a he-said-she-said thing, with no proof of anything. And if the rest of your credibility were taken away, *you* come off looking like the vindictive one, and Corcoran Junior comes out smelling like a rose, his father's reputation unmarred."

Ozzie nodded, scratched his chin. "Yes. Yes, yes, I could see that might happen. Yes, indeedy. Hmm." He adjusted his glasses and looked up at Ethan. "Do you have any leads? Any idea who might be aiding Mr. Corcoran?"

Blowing out a long breath, Ethan said, "No.

Fifty people knew what Georgie was going to prepare that day, and fifty people all had access to the freezer. Fifty-one," he said quietly, "counting you."

"Ha!" Ozzie blurted in obvious surprise. "That's a good one, Ethan!" He laughed again, then his brows snapped together and he mumbled, "Oh, I see you're serious. But, but, but *I'm* the one who hired you."

When Ethan said nothing, Ozzie removed his glasses from his nose, let them dangle from two fingers for a moment, then slipped them back on again. "I have to ask, do you have any proof Mr. Corcoran is behind this? I can't believe a man of his stature—"

"I didn't say it *was* him," Ethan corrected. "Only that it *could* be him. I've never met the man, but I remember hearing of his proclivities from when I was a detective. Some things happened, his name was bandied about, but nothing was ever proven. He's got a rough reputation and high aspirations. Behind that polished public image, he's a very dangerous man."

Ethan turned toward Georgie, standing so close she wanted to take a giant step back. But she stood her ground.

"Is there anything you want to tell me about your relationship with Paul Corcoran? Anything *beyond* the restraining order that might make his father want to rattle your cage?" His glittering eyes stared deeply into hers, intimately, and she saw the message plainly. *Trust me.*

Suddenly she *wanted* to. Oh, she wanted to confess *everything*. She was so tired of the games, the hiding, the worry, the constant vigilance. The urge to confide in Ethan, spill her guts, share the ordeal with him beckoned like a shelter from the storm. If she told him the truth, she might be able to relax a little. It would be so nice to have someone strong to lean on for a while.

But there was too much at stake. If it had been just her, if it had been only about *her* . . . but there were others involved, people she loved with all her heart and all her soul, and she was their only shield, their only protection.

Vaughn Corcoran did have a lot of people in his pockets; and maybe Ethan Darling was one of them. He'd zeroed in on Vaughn awfully fast. Either Ethan was every bit as brilliant as he seemed to be, or he had been put on her trail . . . ask the right questions, get the right answers.

"Nope," she choked, lowering her head. "Can't think of a thing. Pretty cut-and-dried, so if that's all, I have work to do."

As she scurried past him, her body brushed his shoulder, and she wished for one second, just one brief second, she could stop and lay her head against that broad shoulder. His arms would come around her and he'd pull her close. He'd rub her back with his wide, warm palm. She could sink into him and let it all go.

She was so tired of being strong. Feeling like a victim one minute, a criminal the next, never knowing who to trust . . . God, it would be so nice to give it over to someone else for a while. If she did, maybe she could get her life back. She could close her eyes at night and dream sweet dreams once more.

Swallowing a sigh, she straightened her spine, walked on by the stalwart shoulder Ethan had silently offered, and right on out the door.

Betrayal. That was the name of the game, baby.

Slumped over his desk at Paladin's offices, Lucas Russell let his fingers slide across the covers of the two files sitting in front of him.

He'd done a good job, and felt a sense of professional pride about it. This was just the kind of thoroughness and dedication that had made him Ethan's top agent, earned him his boss's trust—after a fashion. Yeah, in spite of his history, he was goddamned good at what he did. The data he'd gathered included everything Ethan had asked for, with a few surprises tossed in just to keep things interesting.

But then, in his experience, there were always surprises. After all, that's why people hired private investigators.

He leaned back in his chair, shut his eyes, and ran his fingers through his hair, scratching the back of his skull out of force of habit, since it didn't itch.

It seemed, at this point anyway, he was the only one who knew where all the bodies were buried, so to speak, and now he had to decide what to do with that information.

He'd been tasked to find out everything there was to know about Georgiana Mundy, her relationship with Paul Corcoran, and how Raine Preston and a Mrs. Beebes figured into the equation. And he had, in spades. Vaughn Corcoran would be *very* interested in what Lucas had turned up and would probably be willing to pay through the nose for it.

Flipping open the file under his right hand, Lucas shuffled through the papers until he found them—the photos of Raine Preston. What a knockout. Golden hair, sexy mouth, hot body. Dressed in jeans and a white shirt, she stood facing the camera, unaware she was being photographed, simply going about her business at the grocery store. The snitch Lucas had paid to track and photograph her had zoomed in on her face, probably as captivated as Lucas was by her eyes.

Summer-sky-blue. He'd always been a sucker for blue-eyed blondes, but this one beat out all the others.

He stared into those eyes, seeing again what he'd seen the first time he'd looked at her pictures. Yeah, there it was. She had a sort of lost quality about her that brought out all his protective instincts—instincts he thought he'd traded for his soul a long time ago.

Now that he knew so much about her, he understood why she seemed so damaged, and why he was faced with a decision he'd never in a million years thought he'd have to face.

He cursed under his breath.

The two files in front of him contained nearly identical data. One held information Corcoran would pay him a king's ransom to have; the other, while equally informative, was somewhat . . . incomplete.

Being a PI involved learning all kinds of stuff about all kinds of people, and then delivering that information to the party who'd hired you. It wasn't up to Lucas to judge what he discovered, only to dig deep and come up with what the client wanted to know—or suspected anyway.

Over the years, a man in Lucas's line of work had to develop a certain *let the chips fall where they may* attitude. Pass along the information, then just walk away. Sometimes, what he discovered made him hate the subjects of his investigations; other times, he hated his clients. Regardless, he'd always done the job he was hired to do.

The title of that old story popped into his brain . . . "The Lady or the Tiger?" Two options, his choice. Would he open the door on the lady, or would he end up being eaten alive? Which file did he give to Ethan, and which to Corcoran? Which man would he betray?

Cursing again, he rose to his feet. His hand hovered over the files. Finally, he grabbed one and shoved it into a special zippered compartment in his briefcase. The other he simply tossed inside, then closed and locked it.

Betrayal. Yeah, that was the name of the game, all right. Maybe he should feel bad for what he was about to do, but he didn't. Perhaps too many years as a cop on the take had hardened him, shut him off from that little nagging voice in his head that had always tried to steer him straight, but that he'd occasionally ignored. Even so, he'd moved past the bad old days, or thought he had until Corcoran's offer had stopped his good intentions cold.

He checked his watch; the meet was in less than an hour. Time enough to take a leak, then hit the machine to grab a candy bar or a bag of chips, get to his car.

Briefcase in hand, he headed for the door, still uncertain which file he would hand over. Corcoran's payoff would set him up for life, allow him to retire, move back to the Midwest. His ex-wife had remarried, but it didn't make that son of a bitch father to his boys. Lucas was their dad, and always would be.

He thought about how the money would change everything. No more midnight surveillance, no more shitty assignments, people spying on each other. He would take his kids fishing and camping, and only work when he damn well felt like it.

Yeah, money was a great thing. More money was even better.

Pausing at the doorway, his hand on the light switch, he turned to face his empty desk, letting his eyes linger on the framed photo of his two boys. Grinning ear to ear, they looked out at him from their innocence. He missed them so much, he thought his heart would crack and splinter.

And as he stood staring at his only two reasons for living, in that moment, he clenched his teeth and knew what he had to do.

Even though the alarm clock made a pretty musical sound, Georgie was loath to hear it at six on a Thursday morning. Without opening her eyes, she sent her hand flailing at the nightstand until her fingers met with the offending gadget. Pressing the snooze button, she sank back down into her pillow and sighed in relief.

Now, where was she? Oh, yes. She'd been dreaming, and it had been a damn fine one. Flinging her arm over her closed eyes to keep the early morning sunlight from penetrating her lids, she tried to pick up where the dream had left off. Ethan had unbuttoned her blouse and was trailing kisses down and down and down, until finally his tongue had reached her—

"Judging from that smile on your face, I guess I'm missing something good."

At the sound of the man's voice, Georgie's eyes flew open as a jolt of panic seized her. Her brain emptied, and her blood felt as though it had been zapped with a cattle prod.

He stood directly over her, his face only inches away. She gasped for air, trying to sit up as she blinked him into focus . . .

"Paul! How . . . how did . . . what are . . ." Shock and terror stole her voice, leaving her with nothing but a strained choke.

Immediately he slapped his palm over her

mouth and shoved her back down in the bed. She tasted salt on her lips, smelled the coffee on his breath. With a muffled squeal, she doubled her fists and slammed them into his shoulders, wiggling and squirming against his weight, trying to throw him off. Though she aimed for his face, his arms were too long, turning her hits into frustrating misses.

"Settle down, sugar tits," he warned. "You're getting me all excited."

She froze, glared into his eyes, her lungs pumping air in and out. Under his palm, she parted her lips farther, then bared her teeth and clamped down, biting the fleshy part of his hand until she was close to drawing blood.

"*Fuck!*" he yelped, pulling his hand away. Examining it, he swore again.

Taking advantage of the opportunity, she screamed with all her might, punching him in the neck with her fists until he grabbed her wrists, holding her arms on either side of her head as her legs kicked under the tangled blanket.

"Shut up, you stupid bitch," he snarled. "I'm not here to hurt you." He smiled then, but it only contorted his handsome face into something pathetic and ugly. His blue eyes sparkled with menace. "Not because I couldn't if I wanted to."

She stopped struggling, eyeing him with disgust. "Damn straight, you're not going to hurt me," she panted. "I'll kill you if you do, you bastard."

His grin widened. "Ah. The old Georgie. That's my girl."

"Get out!"

Releasing her, he walked to the bedroom door. As she made a grab for the phone on the nightstand, he said lightly, "Relax. I'm leaving. Besides, I have witnesses that will place me clear across town, so you'd be wasting your time." He stood in the threshold, arms crossed, his eyes narrowed on her. "I just wanted you to know that we know what you and your friend are up to, and if you go public, my father will see to it you and dear little Raine are put out of business permanently. Euphemistically speaking. Do I make myself clear?"

Georgie sat up. In the struggle, her top had been torn, exposing her bare breasts to Paul's view. Staring at him across the room as his leisurely gaze drifted to her chest, she made no effort to cover herself. Let him look, the prick. Besides, if he came back to the bed and made a move on her, she'd castrate the son of a bitch.

"I don't know what you're talking about," she said slowly, shaking her head. "And what gives you the right to break into my house and threaten me?"

Did he really know what she and Raine were doing, or was this some kind of bluff to get information out of her?

"Whether you have phony witnesses or not, Paul, I'm calling the police right now."

He shrugged. Dressed in black denims and a navy T-shirt, stubble on his jaw, he looked like the petty criminal he was. "Suit yourself. Just know this. My father's worried, and when he gets worried, people . . . disappear. But, well, see, you and I were something to each other once, briefly." He shrugged again, then averted his gaze. A moment later, he sought Georgie's eyes once more. "Okay, we're done here. I've been an upright Boy Scout and done my good deed for today. Consider yourself warned."

Georgie twisted her body, reaching for the phone. Quickly stabbing in 911, she turned to face Paul once more, but he was gone.

Chapter Nine

Feng shui's goal is to maximize the beneficial movement of *chi* through your home. Shapes, sounds, colors, light, texture, symbolic imagery, and the arrangement of your possessions, create a particular *chi*, which allows you to be at peace, move forward in your life, and connect with the man of your dreams.

Georgiana Mundy's *Feng Shui for Lovers*

Just after dawn on Saturday, Ethan slowly closed the cover on the file Lucas had compiled. Slouching in his office chair, he scrubbed his chin with his knuckles, giving his brain some time to process, analyze, recover from what he'd read. He'd met her just over a week ago, but now that the last twenty-nine years had been filled in, he knew a week would never be enough time to get her to trust him.

Reaching forward, he picked up a small photograph, the only personal item of his in the entire suite of offices. In his palm, the metal and glass frame felt cool, remote.

By rights, a man his age, in his position, should have more photographs decorating his space. But he'd lost the desire to cultivate that kind of relationship, the kind that would put a pretty wife and a couple of kids in frames on his desk for him to check out as the day progressed. Pictures of the people who kept it real, kept a man grounded, helped him remember that everything he was, everything he did, in the end, was for them.

He stared down at the old photo in his hand.

Two little boys sat close together on a couch, smiling for the camera, as they held a crying baby girl awkwardly in their arms.

Nobody who worked for him knew for certain who those kids were, had been, would never be again. If anybody asked, Ethan simply redirected the conversation, and since he was the boss, the issue was dropped.

Gently, he put the picture back in its place.

He was only thirty-seven, but some days, he felt older than goddamned dirt. But hell, he had no right to complain. Paladin was a success. He had everything in life he'd ever wanted, and then some.

So what? his conscience jabbed. *So the hell what?*

Absently, he opened Georgie's file again. Now he understood, saw how her mind worked, what drove her. She was tougher than he'd imagined, and had made her way in the world alone. She'd crafted a family out of love and loyalty, clung to them, and guarded them more fiercely than a wolf protecting its young.

Everything she'd done in her life had been designed to move herself ahead, and yet she hadn't screwed anybody over to get there. She might have a stubborn streak as wide as the Pacific, and a short fuse—both of which she'd deny—but she also had a strength and a sense of honor and integrity he found admirable, and wildly attractive.

In more ways than he wished to count, she was perfect for him.

Yeah, right, his conscience poked. *That's not going to happen, pal, and you know why.*

He knew. He'd made a mistake, and now he'd pay for it for the rest of his life. Not in coin; that would be too easy. But in the things he would be denied. Six years ago, his brilliant future had been knocked completely on its ass.

In a way, he'd always chased catastrophe—it came with the job—but it usually belonged to somebody else. This time, though, chaos had pivoted on its heel and smashed him in the nose. A sucker punch followed by an uppercut that had shattered his career, and his dreams.

Cathy. They'd had it all ahead of them, him and Cathy. All of it—house, kids, the works. In an instant, it had been snatched from him, leaving a hole in his life he thought he'd never recover from.

Until the day Georgie Mundy collided with him in an elevator, and he felt something stir inside him he hadn't felt in six long years.

Though he was young and healthy, he hadn't met a single woman in all that time he wanted so damn much that just seeing her put breath in his lungs, desire in his blood. He'd kissed her, tasted her, felt her flesh in his hands, and it had both excited and terrified him.

He shook his head, trying to dissolve the images of them together. He needed to stop thinking about her as though she were the one who might ease the shadows from his soul.

"You need to move past this, Inspector," the official shrink had advised him. "Put it behind you. Sometimes things happen in life that are nobody's fault, Ethan. Cathy—I mean, Inspector Vandermere—was a cop, too. She knew the risks, same as you . . ."

Words. Bullshit words. Rationalization for his failure as a police officer, and as a man.

"Thanks, Doc," he'd mumbled on his way out the door. "I'll keep that in mind."

Though the investigation and the psych eval had cleared him of all wrongdoing, the fact he'd been vindicated left him feeling worse than before, more guilty, more responsible. The investigation had forced him to drag the incident from his memory, stare at its ugliness a good long while, analyze it, and pick it apart. Every action, every second, every decision. By the time he was done, he knew that, whether they called it an "unfortunate accident" or not, *he was responsible*.

As a result, he deserved to be punished, just like any perp. The fact that nobody was willing to dole out thirty lashes or send him down for hard time meant only one thing—if he was going to be properly castigated, he had to do it himself.

For a couple of months after Cathy's death, he'd tried drinking himself into oblivion, but alcohol had only made him sick. Drugs were out just on basic principle. Women had worked for a while. A different woman every night, or as often as he could manage it, just to keep the loneliness and the guilt at bay for a few hours. Nameless, faceless women, willing, certainly, but if they'd been interested in him as more than a bed partner, he'd never noticed. Besides, all sex had done was make him miss Cathy more; not only had he killed her, with every woman he laid, he betrayed her memory.

So he'd left the force, borrowed a shitload of money, and immersed himself in getting Paladin off the ground. Fifty, sixty, eighty hours a week or more. He worked until his brain was so filled with it, there was no room for Cathy, for what he had done to her.

Exhausted as he was, though, each night when he fell into bed, each time he lowered his lids, he remembered Cathy's eyes as clearly as if she were standing in front of him. When the bullet struck, she'd raised her head, and her eyes locked on his. He watched her expression change from mild surprise, to horror, to pain, and then . . . nothing at all. She was nowhere; she was gone.

Before he could get past the human debris standing between them, her body tumbled from the wharf into the bay. They told him later what he'd already known in his gut—she was dead before she hit the water. It hadn't stopped him from plunging in after her.

His throat tight with panic, he'd fought the rolling waves, tangles of kelp, blackness, in his desperation to get hold of her, pull her to him, save her. It was what he *did*, for Christ's sake, *save* people.

As lights danced across the water, he shouted her name. Then he saw her, floating near him no more than three feet away, face down, her hair swirling around her head like ribbons of golden seaweed.

Salt water and salt tears filled his mouth as he slapped at the hard sea, grabbing her and tugging her limp body to his chest. He called her name, trying to call her back, demanding she return to him.

But he was too late.

Things happen in life that are nobody's fault, Ethan . . .

Rising from behind his desk, he jammed Georgie's file under one arm and stalked toward his office door.

"Maybe sometimes, Doc," he muttered as he locked it behind him. "But not this time."

As he exited the building, he looked around at the city, still quiet this early on a Saturday. It was barely eight A.M. and most people were probably still zonked, lazing about in bed, reading the paper, maybe even making love. A cool fog had drifted in overnight, hiding the hot August sun behind a screen of soft gray mist.

The breeze wafting in from the bay was thick and salty, and he inhaled, trying to clear his head. Sliding behind the wheel of his car, he realized his dour thoughts had gotten to him. He needed more than a breath of fresh air; he needed Georgie.

Her street was silent, her curtains drawn. He should probably call her first, give her a little warning.

Nah, he thought. Where was the fun in that? For all her pissyness, Georgie was fun, and God knew he needed some right now.

Besides, if he was lucky, he'd catch her in those hot jammies again. In spite of how wrong getting involved with her would be—wrong on so many levels—his heart thrummed a little faster, and his nerves rode along the sharp edge of reason at the mere thought of seeing her again.

He knew she was home. With the weekend coming, he'd decided to put a guy on surveillance last night, just in case. But her car hadn't left the garage, and she hadn't had any visitors. Climbing the steps to her front door, he nodded, giving his man the all-clear to take off.

In his left hand, he held a pressboard container sporting two steaming Starbucks coffees. With his free hand, he pressed the doorbell. There went those pretty chimes again.

When she didn't answer, he peered in through the etched-glass window to see Georgie standing in the living room, stock-still, her arms straight at her sides, staring at the front door as though he were Attila the Hun come to carry her away. She blinked a few times, rubbed her eyes, then seemed to recognize him. He knew the moment she registered who he was, when what appeared to be apprehension on her face morphed to definite disgust.

He suppressed a laugh, then pressed the bell again and smiled at her through the glass.

Her hair was all mussed up and hung loose around her shoulders. The sleep pants she wore were rumpled and hit her just below her hip, revealing her belly button. It was a tight little innie, and for a second it drove him wild.

Her sleep pants were white, and printed with what looked like green frogs wearing gold crowns. It didn't take a rocket scientist to extrapolate the message. His sister, Andie, had once told him that a girl had to kiss a lot of frogs before she found a prince, if she ever did. He wondered how many frogs Georgie had kissed, and whether she considered *him* a frog.

While the pants were cute, it was the tank top that riveted his attention. It was thin and pale pink. One strap had slid down her arm, taking the neckline of the top with it, nearly exposing her left breast.

He swallowed, sucked in a deep breath, then rapped his knuckles on the door.

"Come on, Georgie," he mumbled, as she meandered with slow deliberation toward the door. "Open up, or I'll huff and I'll puff and I'll—"

The door swung open. She put a hand on her bare hip and gave him the once-over.

"Well, if it isn't the one and only big, bad wolf.

You really need to come by once in a while when I'm fully dressed."

"What would be the point in that?"

Then she spotted the coffees, and her breath caught in her throat. Her eyes narrowed on him. "Tell me it's not that decaf crap."

"Do I look like a decaf crap kind of guy?"

She sniffed the air. "Oh, God. Um, orange mocha full-caff, uh, two percent, and whipped cream." Her eyes drifted closed in what appeared to be orgasmic ecstasy, and she sighed. Through the sheer fabric of her top, he could see the small thrust of her dark nipples. Jesus, he'd never met a woman in his life he'd wanted so much to get his hands on. Guilt immediately assailed him, and he forced it aside.

She opened her eyes, smiled, and stepped back. As she reached for one of the cups, she said, "Do you have the foggiest idea what time it is, Detective?"

He nudged the door closed behind him with his hip, then popped his own coffee from the holder.

"Hell, yes. Any later, and I'd've missed seeing those frogs hopping all over your ass."

She scowled, took a sip of coffee, then padded into the living room. Dropping into the couch in front of the bay window, she said, "Thanks for the breakfast. What do you want?"

Easing himself onto the sofa across from her, he said, "I'm here to guard the aforementioned frog-encrusted ass of yours."

"Touch one pollywog and I'll scream." She popped the top off the coffee container, then puckered those luscious lips and blew across the steaming liquid. Over the rim of the cup, her eyes met his. "I *told* Ozzie I don't like bodyguards."

"Yeah, well, I don't like coconut-mango-flavored chewable vitamins, but they keep me healthy." He took a sip of his own coffee. "I think you need a bodyguard, and I'm bigger and stronger than you, so I win."

In her hand, the coffee cup seemed to tremble and a strange look crossed her face. "Has anything happened that you suddenly think I need your personal protection?"

"Not that I know of," he said slowly, trying to get a sense of what had happened to suddenly put her on guard. "You tell me. *Has* something happened?"

She took a sip of coffee, swallowed, licked her lips. "No," she said. "Just curious."

A lie. She'd taken too long to answer, as though she were debating what to tell him, or not tell him. The wary look in her eyes and her closed body position told him plenty.

"So," he said, "what's the plan for the day?"

Averting her eyes, she seemed to study the wall for a moment, then returned her attention to him. With a sexy little shrug, she said, "I'm leaving town for the weekend."

Ethan's heart gave a jump. She'd left town last weekend—but he'd lost her trail. Surely she wouldn't go wherever she'd gone last time, knowing he would follow. "Horton didn't say anything about your taking a vacation."

She slid the strap of her top up her arm to her shoulder. "It's not a vacation. I'm scheduled to visit a winery in Napa. A family operation. I went to college with the daughter. It'll be boring, I'm sure. You won't be missing a—"

"I love Napa. I drove the sedan today, a very smooth ride."

Georgie straightened. Wrapping both her hands around the paper coffee cup, she said, "Well, tough noogies. You're not invited. Besides, I'm staying overnight, so unless you packed a suitcase—"

"Don't need one," he said lightly. When she sent him a warning look, he shrugged. "Hey, I'm a guy. The clothes I've got on won't start smelling for at least two more days. I wasn't due to change underwear until next Wednesday, anyhow."

God, she looked pissed. She was one of those women who was gorgeous when they were mad. Her cheeks flushed and her eyes snapped. For the first time in a long while, he wanted to laugh, but if he so much as chuckled, she'd probably punch him in the gut.

She stood, her jaw tight with restrained fury. Assessing him for a moment, she tossed her head, then laughed casually.

"You know what, Detective? It's a free world. You can do whatever you damn well please."

Placing her hand against her collarbone, she said, "As for me, I'm going to shower and change, then hit the road in my car, by myself. You can follow me or not, I simply don't care. But we are not, under any circumstances, going to drive to Napa together, spend *any* time there together, do anything of any *kind* there . . . together. Do I make myself clear?"

Chapter Ten

When you take a vacation or travel, don't invite snafus by leaving disorder behind. If you leave your house in a mess, you can expect the same energy to greet you during your trip. This can manifest as problems with bad rooms, muddled transportation, and difficult people.

Georgiana Mundy's *Feng Shui for Lovers*

"You're driving too fast," Georgie groused, as her unwelcome bodyguard downshifted the luxurious four-passenger Mercedes, veering north onto I-80.

She watched Ethan's jaw muscle jerk. So he hated backseat drivers, did he?

"I never driver faster than is safe, ma'am."

Tapping her finger on the padded leather cup holder by her left hand, she cooed, "Oh, come on, now. Fess up, Detective. You're a frustrated Le Mans driver, aren't you? Or maybe it's Monte Carlo? *Vroom-vrooming* around the city streets, edging out the other drivers to speed across the finish line first, have them hand you that big gold cup, not to mention getting your photo taken with a giggling nubile young thing wearing a scrappy bit of nothing with her boobies falling out."

He sighed, loud and long. "Fast cars, trophies, boobies. Yeah, throw in some red meat, a keg of beer, and a remote control, and you pretty much have my dream life nailed, sweetheart." He clicked his tongue. "If I didn't know better, I'd say you were jealous."

"Jealous? Look, it's a nice day," she huffed. "I'd like to enjoy the scenery instead of blasting through the valley at warp speed, Scotty."

"Aye, Captain," he said in a very iffy brogue, then mumbled something under his breath.

Late morning sunshine splashed across the nearby hills, washing the towering stands of eucalyptus lining the ribbon of highway with summer magic. Overhead, the sky was a brilliant blue.

Ethan had popped in a Nirvana CD and the music flowed beneath Georgie's consciousness like a riptide of raw emotion. The rhythm of her heart kept time to the visceral beat of Kurt Cobain begging to apologize.

How on earth had she let Ethan talk her into this? Well, she hadn't. He'd bullied her with scare tactics, crime statistics, a laundry list of the things somebody out to get her could do to her if she wasn't protected. All the while, he'd stood too close, enveloping her with the scent of spicy soap and healthy man, and she'd found her will to resist him dissolve.

Besides, with Paul on the loose and acting so strangely, maybe a little protection wouldn't hurt.

She knew how he'd gotten into her dressing room, of course. His father owned KALM, where all doors were open to the Corcorans. But she still had no idea how he'd gained entry to her house. Though she didn't think Paul knew where she kept her spare key hidden, she checked and found it still in its hiding place. Even so, he might have used it, then put it back. Just in case, she'd called a locksmith and had the front door lock changed.

All the uncertainty had weakened her defenses, and she'd capitulated to Ethan's demand to drive her to Napa for the weekend. Now that they were on the road, the reality of her idiocy struck home; the last thing she needed was to spend two days, and a night, alone with a man she found so utterly attractive—and who had made no secret of the fact he wanted her.

As Nirvana speculated about a girl, Georgie's thoughts turned inward.

She was sure of herself, knew what she wanted, didn't want; there were things she needed to hide, keep hidden, defend. Yet there she was, flying along a country highway with a man capable of discovering every secret she'd ever harbored. In no uncertain terms, she was courting disaster.

But God, he was so appealing. Underneath that stoic veneer, behind those solemn hazel eyes, he had a sense of humor. He was caring, and could be surprisingly charming.

And when he'd kissed her, and she'd felt his heart beating against her body, she'd felt a sense of connection with him she'd been trying ever since to deny, but simply couldn't. Everything she thought she knew about him since the day they met had begun to shift.

She liked him, wanted to be with him, and yearned to put her trust in him.

It had been so long since she'd been in love . . .

Her heart jolted like she'd just had a triple shot of pure Colombian, straight up, no foamed milk, no nothing.

Love? No, she wasn't falling in love with Ethan. Stupendous, over-the-top uber-attraction. Lust, even. Want, need . . . but not *love*. You had to know somebody a whole long while before you could let your defenses down enough to allow love to replace doubt and fear. She *might* sleep with him . . . maybe. She *was* human, after all, and she hadn't had sex in, God, how long had it been? But give him her heart? Her trust? No. If it came to that, she would draw the line at her body and keep her heart and her trust locked away, as they had been most of her life.

But he was so . . . and together they were so . . . and being with him made her feel so . . .

Dammit. A tangle, that's what this was. An emotional, sexual, moral tangle, and she didn't know how to extricate herself.

She turned her attention to the passing scenery. The day was lovely, the sky a miracle, the air fresh and warm and sweet. She and Ethan were young and single and in each other's company. Anyone seeing them would think they were a couple, and maybe they were—for today. But not for always.

Because when you let yourself love somebody, when you finally let someone in, you had to tell him things, trust him with certain secrets, certain truths.

Georgie suppressed a frustrated groan. She needed to decide what she wanted, and before too much longer. Did she dare trust him with her body, her secrets, her truths? Something deep inside her core promised her she could. Still, she'd trusted before, and look what had happened. If she could just switch off her brain, life would be so much easier!

"Better now?" he asked, peering at her over the top of his aviators.

"What?"

"My driving. I slowed down, even though I'd always heard that getting there fast is half the fun."

"Then you've been sadly misinformed."

He laughed, and her breath snagged in her throat. Since she'd met Ethan, he'd barely allowed a smile to curve that sensuous mouth. Now he was laughing, and it was deep and melodic, masculine. The sound of it reached down inside her, stroking her soul like the strains of a tender melody.

Crossing her arms over her stomach, she set her jaw and turned her attention to the rolling hills all around them. Thousands of grapevines stood in shoulder-high parallel rows, their rough brown vines twisting, reaching toward each other like skinny line dancers dressed in costumes of summer green.

She slid a covert glance at Ethan, his attention no longer on her but on the road. No man on earth had the right to look so hot in jeans, an open-collar white shirt, and dark glasses.

She was so engrossed in watching him, she nearly jumped when he said, "What's the name of the place we're going again?"

"The Casa del Giordano Winery," she answered, adding a bit of sarcasm to her voice for his failure to remember the destination he so ardently insisted he accompany her to. "Family-owned and -operated for six generations. I went to college with Sophia Giordano." She paused for effect. "*I* am staying as a guest at the main house."

Ethan nodded, leaned back in his seat, one hand on the wheel. "Yeah, Giordano. Good stuff. I especially like their '97 Cabernet. I'll be staying with you."

She jerked in her seat and sucked in a gaspy breath. "You are *not*. You can*not* stay with me. I'm an invited guest, and there on business. You are an intruder."

"Tell them I'm your bodyguard."

"I will not!" she choked. "How embarrassing. This is a nice Italian family winery, not a Mafia stronghold."

"Then tell them I'm your boyfriend and couldn't bear to be parted from you for even forty-eight hours."

"No."

"Clinging brother?"

"No."

"Devoted hairstylist?"

"God forbid."

"Factotum?"

"You're enjoying this far too much," she challenged. "I only let you come along because you promised to guard me without getting underfoot."

His easy smile faded. "After what happened on the set the other day, I want to be a more conspicuous presence around you. It might discourage our bad guy from doing some real damage."

Georgie's stomach rolled over a few times at the memory of that foul mixture, and how the taste had sickened her. She thought of Paul, his phone call, the twisted fury of his face as he'd leaned over her while she lay in her bed.

"You got awfully quiet," Ethan observed. "Everything okay?"

"Sure," she said, and left it at that. "Take the next right."

As Ethan veered off onto Highway 37 toward Napa, Georgie said, "Why you, Detective?"

"Why me what?"

"Why didn't you assign an agent to escort me? Why is the big cheese of Paladin Private Investigations my own private bodyguard? I have a simple TV cooking show and have written a couple of books, but I'm not exactly high-profile enough to warrant your personal attention."

She felt as though an electrical current ran between her and the man next to her. When he turned the wheel, his arm occasionally brushed against hers, and she liked it. She'd never been more aware of anyone in her life, and it made her uncomfortable and excited at the same time.

She cleared her throat. "I didn't realize it was that difficult a question."

"Okay, look," he said. "The truth is, I'm in a tough position here."

"Meaning?"

"Meaning I'm a professional, and as such, never mix business with pleasure. To do so could impact Paladin's reputation, and that's something I would never do."

Georgie took in a deep breath. "Understood. But how does that—"

"I like you, Georgie," he said slowly, his tone low, his words measured. "I shouldn't, but I do. I'm attracted to you. You must have figured that out by now."

"It occurred to me."

"Before or after I kissed the hell out of you?"

"No comment."

"I haven't been involved, let myself become involved with a woman for . . . a long time."

Georgie lowered her head, nodding slowly. "How, uh, how long is a long time, if you don't mind my asking?"

He squirmed a little in his seat. "Six years."

She lifted her head and looked over at him. "Oh. Well. Six years. That's not so long. Unless you're a dog. In which case that's forty-two years, and that *is* a long time."

Turning to her, he smiled. "Thanks for not asking for details."

She pursed her lips and tilted her head. "Doesn't mean I'm not curious."

So he had secrets and trust issues, too. On the one hand, she understood it; on the other, it made her feel as though she were on the outside looking in. And for some reason, she suddenly wanted in. She wanted him to confide in her, share himself with her, which was ridiculous, since she had basically no feelings for him at all, and any secrets or issues he had were certainly none of her business.

"The bottom line," he continued, his tone indicating they were getting back to her original question, "you need to be protected, and I thought I could handle the job, stay detached. But I'm frankly finding it very difficult."

"I see."

"I'm committed to staying by your side this weekend, and that's exactly what I'll do, but first thing Monday morning, I'm going to assign Lucas Russell to take over."

She nodded. "Lucas Russell."

"He's Paladin's best. You'll be in fine hands, er, you'll be safer with him than you would be with me."

"Safer? I don't understand what that means. You just told me I'd be safer with you, so . . . What are you *doing*?"

As she'd been speaking, Ethan had cranked the wheel, sending the Mercedes off the road, onto the grassy shoulder. When the car came to a halt, he pulled the e-brake and released his safety restraints.

"Yeah, *safer*," he hissed, sliding his hand around the nape of her neck. "Because Lucas Russell would never do this."

She looked up at him. Her pulse hammered in her ears. Her eyes widened and her mind raced.

Ethan's lips were inches from her own. He paused for a moment, searching her face. Then he lowered his mouth, and kissed her.

Chapter Eleven

Colors play an important role in feng shui. Each shade and hue has significance—positive and negative. Take brown—quiet, neutral, and woodsy. Whenever you feel frightened or insecure, brown helps ground and comfort you. Wear it when you want your man to put his faith and trust in you. Since brown isn't a power color, however, avoid it when he's being obstinate and hardheaded, or he'll roll right over you—so to speak.

Georgiana Mundy's *Feng Shui for Lovers*

Ethan yanked his dark glasses off and eased back a little so he could see Georgie's eyes. Her lids were half closed, her irises glazed with the same simmering need he felt. Blood pounded in his ears in a primal beat as he reached down and unsnapped her seat restraints, then slid his arm around her waist and pulled her toward him. She exhaled in a sharp burst against his mouth as he lowered his head and captured her lips once more.

Her mouth was soft, sweet, her tongue languid as it tangled with his own. She made a mewling sound at the back of her throat, and he thought he'd lose it right there, drag her out of the car and into the bushes at the side of the road, shove up her skirt, and relieve the lust he felt every time he looked at her.

His hand managed to find its way under her shirt to cup her breast. Against her open mouth, he breathed, "This was why I shouldn't have assigned myself to your case."

She licked her lips, then she licked his. "Because Lucas Russell," she panted, "would never do this."

"Not unless he wanted me to rip off his balls."

"God, pure poetry," she whispered. "Such a romantic."

He chuckled, nuzzled her neck, bit it softly, the craving for the taste of her flesh overcoming the will to push himself away. She arched back, and he pressed heated kisses to her throat, then returned his attention to her mouth.

The blare of a horn from a passing car brought him back to his senses. Pulling away slowly, he tugged her shirt down, then eased himself into his seat.

They sat in silence for a moment, while Ethan tried to decide whether he should apologize or not. He shot her a glance. She seemed to be as shell-shocked by the encounter as he was.

Her hair tumbled around her shoulders, her silky knit top in disarray. Instead of looking at him, she stared out the window on her side of the car, so all he could see of her face was the curve of her flushed cheek.

"I'm not sorry that happened," he stated flatly as he worked to slow his heart rate to normal. "But it won't happen again."

She let her head fall against the headrest, then slowly turned in his direction. When her sleepy eyes met his, she murmured, "Too bad."

"Look, Georgie . . . I don't know what do to about this."

"Don't you?" A come-hither smile tilted her swollen lips.

Something sharp jabbed him in the heart. He didn't want to feel this way about a woman again; didn't want to feel this way about *her*, because there wasn't a damn thing he could do about it, and he *wanted* to do something about it. He wanted to do something about it until he'd sated himself on her, gotten her out of his system, ridden himself of this terrible need he felt every time he so much as thought of her.

Furious at his own lack of control, he reached for his seat belt and snapped it back in place. "Buckle up," he ordered, shoving his dark glasses on. "We'll be there soon."

As Georgie straightened her clothing, finger-combed her hair, and refastened her seat belt, Ethan pulled back into traffic. In another twenty minutes, they'd arrive at the winery. There'd be other people around all weekend—he wouldn't be alone with her, wouldn't be able to kiss her, touch her. And thank God for that, because the next time he had her in his arms, he wouldn't be able to stop.

As Georgie fought to settle her nerves, she tried to keep her attention on the purpose of her visit, and not on how she'd rather be anywhere else in the world, as long as she was with Ethan . . . naked, his hands on her, his mouth capturing her moans of pleasure . . .

Off to the right, a carved wooden sign reading CASA DEL GIORDANO hung from the center of a tall stone arch, which served as the winery's main gate. The drive up the narrow paved road that wound through acres of vineyards should have been delightful, but Georgie was only vaguely aware of the lushly rolling fields outside her window, people in straw hats bent to their tasks, and the sweet and musky scent of sun-ripening fruit.

At the very top of the hill, the main house resembled a sprawling, two-story Italian villa. Surrounded by elegant cypress trees, its cream-colored stucco walls, earth-red roof tiles, arched windows, and classic statuary were complemented by gray fieldstone steps and walkways.

In front of the house, the driveway curved around a huge formal garden set off by an intricate pattern of neatly trimmed boxwood hedges. The fountain centerpiece offered a beautifully carved nude holding an urn on her shoulder. The pale marble sparkled in the sunlight as water splashed down her body onto the lilies floating in the large circular pool at her feet.

Everywhere, there were flowers. Crimson, bronze, and pale pink roses bloomed in a garden to the left of the villa, while bright magenta bougainvillea rambled up the façade to tumble across the columned portico that shaded the front door.

As the Mercedes pulled to a stop, Georgie released her seat belt and practically jettisoned herself from the car. Maybe once she put a bit of distance between her and Ethan, her head would begin to clear and her nerves settle.

She heard a friendly, *"Ciao!"* as the massive oak door swung open and a smiling Sophia Giordano stepped onto the tiled porch.

Sophia was exactly as Georgie remembered, from her mass of gorgeous sable hair, to her brown eyes, to the flawless complexion Da Vinci could easily have rendered in oils.

And yes, the attitude was still there in the way she held her head, the way she walked—well, slunk seductively—and most especially in the way she slid her eyes over Ethan in that *hello, hot guy; I can get you, if I want you* kind of way she'd always had.

Sophia came from a long line of dollars that bought her everything from clothes to cars to men, while Georgie waited tables to put herself through college. They'd been acquaintances, but never friends.

However, doing a segment on Casa del Giordano would serve KALM's desire to put a spotlight on a local winery, while giving free advertising to the Giordanos. A win-win for both parties, so when Ozzie had proposed the piece, Georgie'd had no choice but to accept.

"Welcome to the Casa del Giordano Winery," Sophie said coolly as she meandered down the steps to throw her arms around Georgie in an air hug. "It's so good to see you again."

As the two women almost embraced, Sophia whispered into her ear, "Hey, you didn't mention you were bringing your movie-star boyfriend. What's his name?"

"Ethan Darling. But he's not my boyfriend," Georgie rushed to add.

"His name is *Darling*? Oh, my God!" Sophia squealed.

And how many women had he gotten into bed using that *ridiculous* name of his?

"Ethan's my, uh—"

"Your boy toy?" Sophia said suggestively.

"Uh, no. Actually, he's my . . . feng shui master!" she blurted, then swallowed. "It was a last-minute kind of thing. I remember what a huge follower of the discipline you are, and thought you'd like to meet—"

"Perfect!" Sophia rushed, eyeing Ethan once more. "How fabulous of you to bring him!"

"I apologize for not calling to let you know. Like I said, it was very last-minute—"

"Believe me, it's okay," Sophia murmured, eyeing Ethan. She gave him a thorough examination as he busied himself retrieving Georgie's overnight bag and laptop from the trunk. Tilting her head, she mused, "He's awfully young to be a feng shui master. And he doesn't look Chinese at all."

"Oh, well, he's a very old, uh, soul. Reincarnated many, many times." She gulped some air. "He is Chinese, actually, a little. Way back. Way, way back. A great-great-great-grandfather or something."

"Hmm." Sophia tapped a painted nail to her full lips. "Yes, I think I see it a little, around the eyes, maybe. And he does have that dark hair." Her brow lowered as though she'd just had a disturbing thought. "So are feng shui masters like monks? Does he, you know, like, abstain?"

"Yes," Georgie hurried, then slowed to consider the implications of what she'd just said. "Uh, why, yeah, actually. They're *exactly* like monks. Absolutely no sex."

"Never?" Sophia's greedy eyes looked disappointed.

Georgie leaned forward in a conspiratorial way. "Never. They can't, you see. They're, uh, well, it's because they're, uh . . . eunuchs."

Sophia's eyes widened. "No!"

Georgie shrugged and gave her hostess a *sad but true* look.

She wanted to laugh out loud. She'd fix his wagon for barging in on her plans this weekend, kissing her until she ached with lust, then leaving her hanging. Sophia wouldn't come on to him now, plus the Giordanos would never suspect Ethan was a detective or her bodyguard, or that she was in any kind of trouble. Damn, she was clever! She felt so relieved, her knees nearly buckled.

"You see, feng shui masters must keep their minds clear," she elaborated, warming to her subject. "Abstinence is a huge, huge, *huge* part of their being able to focus entirely on the basic principles of feng shui, and not become distracted by tawdry physical desires." She wrinkled her nose in feigned disgust.

Sophia shook her head and narrowed one eye. "You sure couldn't tell by looking. Kind of pitiful, when you think about it. I mean, he's so . . . so . . ."

"Hot?"

"Yeah, that's the word, all right."

Georgie nodded in fake empathy. "I hear you, sistah. A real loss to womankind."

"Yeah," Sophia said absently. "I didn't think I'd ever find myself drooling over a feng shui master." She squinted her eyes and stared directly at Ethan's crotch. "Those jeans don't hide much. I'd swear, if I didn't know better . . ."

"Bunched denim," Georgie assured her with a knowing nod. "Sitting in the car will do that. Trust me. Nothing there."

Both women watched Ethan close the trunk and stalk toward them, graceful and predatory, like a strong, healthy animal. For a moment, she nearly smiled. He really was the most beautiful creature she'd ever seen.

Next to her, Sophia gasped deep in her throat. Shaking her head, she murmured, "Are you positive that's just bunched denim? I mean, it sure looks to me like he's got an enormous—"

"Try not to stare," Georgie admonished softly, so the object of their discussion couldn't hear. "Makes him feel self-conscious."

"Ah. Sure. Of course. Sorry."

He stopped in front of them. Removing his dark glasses, he flicked a look at Georgie. His hazel eyes snapped with intelligence . . . and suspicion. Then he smiled at her, a sort of secret smile, and she couldn't help but smile back.

For all his arrogance and pigheadedness, he could be a real nice man. He had a gruff, dictatorial manner, but there was always that elusive something in his eyes when he looked at her that spoke of deeply held convictions, compassion, honesty. Qualities that drew her in, making her want to get closer to him, maybe even learn to trust him.

"Um, Ethan, this is our hostess."

He extended his hand. "Pleasure to meet you, Ms. Giordano."

"Please call me Sophia." Georgie watched as the two shook hands. Sophia grinned up at Ethan like Santa had finally brought her that spotted pony she'd been waiting for all her life. Then her smile faltered a bit, as though she suddenly reminded herself of Ethan's "condition."

"Do I call you Master?" she asked.

"Excuse me? I—"

"Oh!" Georgie intervened. "Yes, um, well, Ethan, I mean, *Master* Ethan . . . I've been telling

Sophia how you're my feng shui guru, and how you guided me through every decorating and lifestyle decision I've ever made, and how you wanted to come with me this weekend, in spite of my many, many, many, *ma-n-n-ny* protests that it would take you away from your very important work, but that you, knowing what a devoted follower of the discipline Sophia is, *insisted* on coming along, in spite of those many aforementioned protests." She gave a little high-pitched musical laugh and sent him her biggest grin. "It might be nice, though, if you could loosen the rules a little, just for the weekend, so we can all address you as *Ethan* instead of . . . *Master*?"

Time stood still. He gazed down into her eyes for what seemed an eternity. Except for the muscle working in his jaw, his face gave nothing away.

She fluttered her lashes, smiling hopefully.

He blinked, and a glint of something akin to malicious mischief appeared in his sharp hazel eyes.

She was in trouble.

His gaze never leaving hers, he sketched a brief, mocking bow.

"Sorry, but the rules are clear," he stated. "You will call me *Master*." He pinned her with a meaningful glare. "*Grasshopper*."

She bristled. So he was going to play rough, was he? Well, she'd see about that.

"This is fantastic!" Sophia said, apparently oblivious to the battered gauntlet lying in the dust between her two houseguests. As she took

Georgie's arm, she cooed, "Everyone's so looking forward to meeting you. And bringing Master Ethan is the frosting on the cake!"

"Ev-everyone?" Georgie breathed, panic suddenly overtaking her. "You mean your family?"

"Not just my family."

As Ethan picked up the overnight bag and laptop with his left hand, Sophia hooked his right and began walking the three of them toward the house.

"*Everyone* is a couple of dozen of your biggest fans, Georgie. Hey, you're a celebrity!" Was it Georgie's imagination, or was Sophia's suddenly very toothy smile painted on?

"As soon as some of my friends and neighbors found out the *famous* Georgiana Mundy was researching a show on Napa Valley wines . . ."

Yeah. Painted on. Definitely.

". . . and that you were going to be my houseguest this weekend, *wild horses* couldn't have kept them away. They're all having lunch on the terrace in back. I hope you don't mind the intrusion. You don't have to pay a whole lot of attention to them. They just wanted to meet you."

Kiss, kiss, hug, hug, and all that.

"That'll be fine," Georgie said. "I'll be happy to meet them. I enjoy meeting my fans. I really do."

And normally she did, but now, with the feng shui "master" thing, and the eunuch thing . . . oh, no . . . what had she done? She'd had no idea anyone else was going to be around. Well, maybe Sophia wouldn't say anything to them.

"Hmm. One problem, though," Sophia remarked, as they reached the bottom of the stairs. "All the guest rooms are filled. But we'll figure it out. We certainly want a man of Master Ethan's stature to have his own room, so I'll give him yours, Georgie, and we'll find something else for you." The trio started up the steps. "Nonna has twin beds in her room, and she doesn't snore too loudly anymore since the doctor put her on those new meds. And she usually takes her teeth out at night, so you won't have to worry about her grinding them. And if the yelling in her sleep gets to you, well, there's always earplugs." She scrunched her nose and nodded. "Nightmares."

Sophia was giving away her room to Ethan? She was going to have to bunk with Sophia's snoring, tooth-gnashing, nocturnally garrulous grandmother? Not bloody likely!

With a placid smile, Georgie said, "Ethan's not all that special. He doesn't really need—"

"So sorry young Grasshopper has forgotten her manners," Ethan interrupted in an imperious tone. "*Master Ethan*, please to remember." He arched a dark brow. "Simply 'Master' will do, of course."

"Of course," Georgie said through clenched teeth. "Many apologies, *Master*. Sophia, why don't you go on ahead? Master Ethan and I need to discuss the proper feng shui positioning of . . ." *My knee in his groin*, she wanted to say, but didn't. "My, uh, laptop. I need to set it up somewhere where it will allow my thinking to be clear."

"No problem," Sophia said, then walked a few steps ahead. "I'll meet you two on the terrace." With a smile, she pushed open the door and disappeared inside the villa.

As soon as she was gone, Ethan grabbed Georgie's arm and growled, "Why in the hell did you tell her that? I don't know a fucking thing about feng shui—"

"It doesn't matter, *Master*," she snapped. "She's been practicing feng shui for years. Just compliment everything in sight, and leave it at that."

"What if she asks me about the technicalities of feng shui theory, or wants an opinion on the color of her underpants?"

"When exactly are you planning on seeing her underpants?"

"That's beside the point! What am I supposed to *tell* her?"

"I don't know! Say something inscrutable. It shouldn't be a stretch. Hell, you do it to me all the time!" She scowled. "And I want my room back, *Master Frickin' Darling*. No way I'm giving up a private room in this luscious villa to *you*, so I can sleep in an itty-bitty twin bed in Grandma's room. You horned in on my weekend, so you can just sleep in your stupid car, for all I care!"

He presented her with an exaggerated pout and drawled sarcastically, "Now, is that any way to treat the man who has guided you through every decorating and lifestyle decision you've ever made?"

"Don't make me hurt you."

"Like you could," he muttered under his breath. Her suitcase and laptop in his left hand, he slipped his right arm through hers. "Come on, Grasshopper. It's showtime. Remember to keep a simpering look on your face, ask me often if there's anything you can get for me, and occasionally bow respectfully."

"In your dreams," she groused.

They stepped through the threshold and into the grand foyer. Light and airy, it was filled with afternoon sunlight from the arched windows that reached nearly to the ceiling. The high walls had been covered with trompe l'oeil images of the rolling green, blue, and gold hills of Tuscany, while small olive, cypress, and poplar trees in enormous terra-cotta planters sat on the tile floor, complementing the gardenlike illusion.

As they walked through the living room, Georgie noted the tasteful and muted earth tones in both the furnishings and artwork. Excellent feng shui. What an incredibly lovely place for Sophia to live. The bitch.

"Remember what I said," Georgie whispered, a smile plastered on her face. "Just keep your comments vague and your opinions obscure, and nobody will be the wiser. Most people don't know a thing about feng shui, so they'll probably ignore you all day."

The sounds of laughter and conversation trickled off to silence as Georgie and Ethan stood in the open threshold that led to the terrace. Everyone looked at her for a moment, then, as if on some unseen cue, two dozen pairs of eyes slowly left her face to drift toward Ethan, where two dozen curious gazes came to rest . . . on his crotch.

"Everybody," Sophia said as she approached them from a nearby table where she'd been chatting in close quarters with an older couple, "this is my special guest, Georgiana Mundy."

She smiled her best TV smile, and was rewarded when all two dozen guests grinned at her and applauded.

"And her personal feng shui guru, Master Ethan," Sophia continued. She beamed with obvious delight, flicked a quick glance at Ethan's beltline, then arched a brow at Georgie.

Out of the corner of her eye, Georgie saw the wine steward smirk, the woman serving canapés titter, and the violinist by the dessert table raise his instrument and resume playing, a sardonic grin on his face.

None of this was apparently lost on Ethan, who reached out and snared her arm, tugging her so close, she could see every gold fleck in his eyes.

"Grasshopper," he said lightly, belying the iron grip he had on her, "is there some little detail about being a feng shui master you forgot to mention?"

Chapter Twelve

Long live the queen—the queen-sized bed,
that is! Sleeping on a mattress the size of
Rhode Island won't spark intimacy, so lose the
king, and get yourself a comfy queen-sized
bed, then snuggle up and let nature take its
delicious course.

Georgiana Mundy's *Feng Shui for Lovers*

Georgie blinked up into Ethan's accusing gaze,
unsure how she should answer. If he found
out what she'd told Sophia—who obviously
hadn't waited more than a gnat's heartbeat to
spread the word—he'd kill her. Really, he would.

Swallowing, she gathered her courage. With a
bright smile, she turned her face away from the
murmuring crowd. Under her breath, she said,
"You have to understand, I was really, *really* mad at
you for commandeering my life. So, uh, I may have
given Sophia the wrong impression of . . . certain
things."

His grip tightened. He wasn't hurting her, but
there was no way she'd be able to escape his grasp

without pulling out a gun and shooting him. And even then . . .

"What did you tell her?" he bit out.

Georgie swallowed again. "It's nothing terrible," she insisted. "I told Sophia that you were Chinese. Partly."

"Well, judging from the direction of their stares, I'd have to ask which part."

She snorted a laugh, but didn't elaborate.

He cocked his head and eyed her for a moment. "That's it? They're all staring at my fly because they think I'm partly Chinese? What do they think I've got in there, a firecracker?"

"You tell me," she quipped, thrilled he'd bought the half-truth. When he looked as though he might just answer, she rushed, "Actually, it's not your crotch they're looking at, it's your eyes they're *avoiding* looking at. I told Sophia that it was disrespectful to look a feng shui master in the eye. I imagine they're all simply trying to show you their, uh, reverence."

He tugged at her arm and raised her face, forcing her to look him in the eye.

"You don't seem to have any trouble being irreverent to your feng shui master."

"Well, I'm a close, uh, personal friend. It's different. Besides, we both know you're not a real feng shui master."

"Listen, Grasshopper," he drawled. "I'm not sure I'm buying your story, but unless you want the truth to come out, you'd better start staring at my crotch like you mean business."

Georgie felt her knees go weak and her throat close. "Not a problem."

Sophia, who'd been pouring wine for a couple at a table across the terrace, rushed back to them. "No fun hogging all of Master Ethan's time," she interrupted, grinning at Ethan. Taking his arm, she yanked him away from Georgie and guided him to the middle of the terrace.

Immediately the assembled guests and staff showed Ethan their veneration with curious stares and pursed lips. *Two* of the men winked.

Georgie put her fingers to her mouth, biting her lip to keep from busting out laughing.

"Master Ethan," Sophia said, tossing her long hair over her shoulder. "Why don't you sit right down here at my table, and let me serve you some of the best Cabernet on the planet? Our '94 was an exquisite year."

She led Ethan to a chair, leaving Georgie to follow in their wake. It seemed her "celebrity" status had taken a backseat to one gorgeous hunk of fake feng shui master.

Once the three of them were seated, the rest of the guests returned to their meals, but their eyes never strayed far from Ethan.

As Sophia filled their glasses with the dark ruby liquid, she gestured with her free hand to the terrace, stuffed to overflowing with baskets of red, pink, and yellow flowers, potted acacia palms and ferns, and glazed planters offering variegated crotons, philodendrons, and mother-in-law's tongue.

"Tell me, Master Ethan," Sophia cooed. "Does the feng shui of the terrace meet with your approval?"

For a moment he looked a little nervous, then he picked up his wineglass, took a sip, and settled imperially back into his white wrought-iron chair. With a quick glance at Georgie, he said, "Green is for healing."

"So it is!" burst Sophia. "I knew I'd done the right thing by spacing the tables just this way, and decorating with plants. I'm thrilled you sanction what I've done, Master. It *is* healing out here, isn't it? After a long, hard day in the vineyards . . ."

Georgie took a bite of her salad and relaxed while Sophia emoted for the next twenty minutes on how she had used color and lighting, vegetation and various textures to create the proper *chi* throughout the villa. All the while, Ethan said nothing, but nodded at the appropriate times and occasionally threw in a knowing, "Ah, so," then returned to his meal.

What a ham. Olivier had nothing on Ethan Darling.

After lunch, Sophia took them on a tour of the vineyards, explaining the growing process, careful to point out that great winemaking begins with great farming.

The harvest had begun earlier that week, and gigantic gondolas sat staggered along the rows for the pickers to dump their heavy boxes, before returning to the trellises to gather more of the sweet, ripe fruit.

Ethan walked silently beside Georgie, his hands in his back pockets, his dark glasses shielding his gaze. She suspected he was still angry, and suspicious, but nobody would dare say anything, so he'd never discover her deception.

Georgie asked questions as they strolled between the rows, taking copious notes on everything involved in viticulture, from training the vines along the wires, to how the grape varieties were planted in "blocks," to what lees, soft tannins, and finings were.

Sophia promised to show them the vinification process during a tour of the cellars tomorrow morning. Then it would be back home to San Francisco, and whatever reality awaited Georgie there.

She inhaled the hot summer air, forcing her mind to the task at hand, and not the fact that somebody—maybe Paul, maybe his father—was actively doing things to shake her up, possibly hurt her. This weekend so far had been a respite from fear, and she had to admit that Ethan's presence had a lot to do with it.

The day spun away into evening and soon all the guests reassembled in the large dining room for a wonderful meal of lobster bisque and steaks grilled to perfection, smothered with garlic herb butter. Chaos for your cholesterol, Georgie mused, but damn, it was good.

All evening long, people approached Ethan, asking for advice on one thing or another. Having embraced his role, he generally smiled and made some obvious remark, which people seemed to accept as wisdom, even though she knew it was a total crock.

After the last woman thanked him and wandered away, Georgie said, "You're pathetic. Everybody's going to think I'm a moron for having an idiot for a feng shui master."

"You're pathetic . . . *Master*," he corrected. "When will young Grasshopper learn she sleeps in bed of own making?"

"You're not frigging Lao-tzu," Georgie snapped. "You're not even David Carradine, so stow the pithy remarks."

"Hey, I'm just playing the role you cast for me, Grasshopper." Looking around the room, he said softly, "I've gotta tell you, this is the most reverent crowd I've ever seen in my life. The pope should get this kind of ardor. Nobody has looked me in the eye for hours."

"Uh, well"—she gulped—"they're obviously very devout."

As Georgie scowled up at him, she saw a flash of movement to her left, and their hostess appeared.

"Master?" she breathed, virtually ignoring Georgie. Placing her palms together in a gesture of prayer, Sophia bowed slightly. "A favor, if I may?" She was clad in a form-fitting yellow dress that allowed a generous view of her deep cleavage. How disgustingly obvious.

Ethan turned to Sophia and smiled blandly. "Yes, my child?"

Why in the hell was the woman standing so

close to him? Sophia couldn't imagine that he would be interested in her, him being a *eunuch* and all, unless her hostess suspected Georgie's deceit and was testing the waters. Sophia had always been a little on the slutty side, in Georgie's opinion, but the woman wasn't stupid. She knew a *man* when she saw one, and had always gone after the best-looking guys in school . . . and gotten them.

Georgie sipped her wine. Why in the hell should she care what Ethan did or didn't do with Sophia? It wasn't like he was Georgie's personal property; it wasn't like they had a relationship.

As Sophia fawned over Ethan, engaging him in some stupid-ass conversation about the appropriate positioning of tableware in order to aid in digestion, Georgie fumed a little more. She slid a glance toward him just in time to catch him casting an appreciative look at Sophia's bountifully displayed bosom.

Damn! Maybe it was the wine, or maybe it was the fact she *did* have a relationship with Ethan, whether either of them wanted to admit to it or not, but she suddenly felt very possessive of her counterfeit feng shui master. Sophia had no right to sink her hooks into Georgie's man, especially not right in front of her, eunuch or not.

She was about to speak up when Sophia slipped her arm through Ethan's. "Pardon me for being forward, Master," she said softly, her brown eyes earnest yet somehow calculating. "But your discipline simply astounds me, and I wondered if

I might, just for one moment, impose on your serenity and ask an intimate question?"

Bells clanged inside Georgie's head like fire alarms. *No, Sophia. Don't do it. Don't go there. For God's sake, don't go there.*

Georgie shot a nervous look at Ethan, whose brow was furrowed in confusion.

"My child," he said evenly, "to what are you referring?"

Sophia's catlike grin said it all. "Well," she simpered, "I'm wondering why a man such as yourself, so . . . well, *manly*, and all . . . would make such a drastic and irreversible decision."

When Ethan looked dumbfounded, Sophia said to Georgie, "Excuse us, would you?" Tugging at his arm, she eased Ethan back into a secluded corner of the room where Georgie couldn't hear what they were saying.

Sophia wasn't *that* forward, was she? But if Georgie protested her dragging Ethan off, he'd probably get suspicious. *Oh what a tangled web we weave . . .*

Judging the number of ounces remaining in her wineglass, she knocked them back in one gulp. When he killed her, she didn't want to feel it.

She stood frozen in place, watching their heads bent together as Sophia whispered something in Ethan's ear, then giggled.

His head snapped around, and he shot Georgie a look that could only be described as murderous. Everything she needed to know about what

Sophia was saying could be read in Ethan's glittering, narrowed, homicidal eyes.

He pursed his lips, turned back toward Sophia, and bent his head to hers once more. A second later, Sophia's head snapped up and her jaw dropped. She looked directly at Georgie, astonishment clear to see in her wide, rapidly blinking eyes.

The two continued with their nods and whispers for a few moments more while Georgie's stomach began doing the cha-cha, and not in a good way. By the time Sophia all but stumbled off, she looked as though she needed a straight shot of something, and Ethan, the rat, looked like he'd just consumed the most satisfying meal of his life.

Georgie turned her back on his mocking stare. Dammit. If she at least had her own room, or *any* room, for that matter, she could go there now, lock herself in, and wish this whole ridiculous weekend had never happened!

Looking for a potted palm large enough to go hide behind until morning, she felt a hand slip around her waist. "Not so fast, Grasshopper," he drawled. His arm tightened in a move obviously designed to intimidate. Too bad it didn't work.

"Let go of me, Master," she hissed between clenched teeth. "It's getting late and I need to find a room—"

"Not a problem. Let's go."

A few minutes later, Georgie found herself in

Ethan's darkened bedroom—well, *her* darkened bedroom, she reminded herself. Moonlight filtered in through lace sheers fluttering at the arched window, mottling the bedcover with quicksilver flecks.

Behind her, the door closed. She heard the lock snap against the brass plate.

She didn't turn to him; she didn't dare.

Silence reigned for a heartbeat, then another. She felt him move up close behind her.

"A eunuch, Georgie? A fucking *eunuch*?"

"That's an unfortunate turn of phrase," she drawled, "since it's a physical impossibility, or would take a force of will I doubt even you could muster."

She felt his hands on her shoulder. They were trembling. Oh, God. He was so furious, he really was going to strangle her.

Then she heard it . . . a low rumble, then a snort, then it burst forth. Laughter. Loud, and raucous, and hearty.

His hands dropped from her shoulders as he made his way past her to the bed, where he collapsed, clutching his stomach. He seemed to be trying to speak, but every time the words would form, he'd begin to laugh again and they'd get lost.

He sat up, wiped his eyes, looked at her, then started over, laughing so hard, she thought the walls would shudder.

"Oh, God," he gasped. "Oh, Jesus. That's why they were all staring. Oh, my God." Then he was off again, the deep laughter making her want to laugh as well, but all she could do was stare at his prone body, the long, lean length of him on that bed, and the bulge in his pants that most definitely was not bunched denim.

She crossed her arms over her stomach. "Are you done?" she sniped, waiting for him to quiet himself and sit up. Finally, he did. "You have some 'splaining to do yourself, Master," she accused. "What did you tell her about me?"

In the shadows of the room, she saw his mouth curve on one end. Leaning back against the headboard, he crossed his arms over his chest. "Uh, sorry, Grasshopper, but I was mad, you know, about the eunuch thing. All I can say is, maybe they looked at my crotch all day today, but tomorrow they'll be looking at yours. George."

He grinned like a Cheshire cat. His gleaming eyes met hers in challenge.

Her breath caught in her throat and she gaped at him. "No!"

"Yes." His smile widened.

Well, that *did* it. She'd had enough. She didn't care if she had to sleep with the grapes in one of those damn gondolas, she was not spending the night in the same room with a man who'd just told blabbermouthed Sophia Giordano that she was a transsexual!

But as she raised her hand to flip the deadbolt, Ethan was suddenly behind her, his steady fingers curling over hers, preventing her from turning the lock. She felt the heat of his body envelop her, caught the sent of his skin.

"Don't go," he whispered. "Come to bed. Make love with me, Georgie."

She whirled on him. "What! Sleep with you? After what you've done?"

"What have I done?" he said lightly. "Besides, you started it."

"Well, I was angry at you for—"

"For what? For wanting to protect you? For doing my job? You haven't made that job easy, either. You haven't exactly been up front with me, have you?"

Her mind went to Paul, the phone call, the visit, the threat, the secret she carried about what she and Raine and Mrs. Beebes were doing. No, she hadn't been up front with Ethan, but she had nothing to feel guilty over. She was protecting the ones she loved.

Glaring up into his eyes, she said, "I didn't ask you to be my bodyguard. I didn't ask for you to come along this weekend. The only way I could fight back was to make you a eunuch, figuratively speaking. But what you did was reprehensible. I'm on TV. Now all these people are going to think—"

"Georgie." Ethan's lids lowered, took on a sleepy look. "It was simply tit for tat. And speaking of which . . ." His gaze drifted down to her breasts, then returned to her eyes. "I want to make love to you. And I think you want the same thing."

She swallowed. "So now you're psychic as well as being a feng shui master?"

He slowly shook his head. With one hand, he

brushed her hair aside, placing his mouth on the sensitive spot just beneath her ear. His kiss was teasing, his lips soft, the light flick of his tongue erotic.

Her pulse quickened and she knew she should push him away.

"We're . . . I'm still mad at you."

"Mm-hmm," he murmured as his hands eased around her waist and he tugged her closer.

"We haven't resolved this yet."

"Nuh-uh." His lips trailed along her collarbone while his hands slowly crept up her sides.

"I don't have sex with men I don't like."

Okay, sure, like that ever stopped a determined male.

Pulling her closer, he kissed her, and she let him. Her head spun with desire as his mouth and tongue seduced her, making her skin too warm, too sensitive. Her body screamed for the release she hadn't enjoyed for so very long. With Ethan, it would be good, it would be incredible. His hands moved under her blouse, his thumbs slid along the top of her bra, then tugged the silky fabric down so he could rub her nipples. The buds peaked, and she felt a thrill like an electric shock shoot straight down between her legs. In that moment, her resistance evaporated like a San Francisco mist.

"I want to see you naked," he whispered. "You can still be mad at me. I won't hold it against you. C'mon Georgie, make love with me. Let me make you feel good."

Her eyes drifted closed and she let her head fall back. The sensation of his fingers playing with her nipples drove her wild, making her want, need. She felt edgy, hot. It had been such a long time. It seemed she'd shut herself off from intimacy forever ago, unable to trust any man with her body.

As big a mistake as she knew it was, she wanted him desperately, wanted to get close to him, feel his strong arms around her, drown in his kisses. Maybe it was time she really did shut down her brain and just let it happen.

Sliding her arms around his neck, she lifted herself up on her toes and kissed him. His arms wrapped around her, pulling her so tightly against him, she could feel the rhythm of his heartbeat, as rapid and frantic as her own. She felt something else, too.

She pulled back from the kiss a fraction to nibble on his damp lower lip. Rolling her hips against his jutting length, she murmured, "It seems whoever performed your operation missed a couple of things."

He panted, "Yeah. That's what happens when the low bid gets the job."

Then his lips took hers in a kiss that turned quickly desperate, ravenous. Their tongues tangled. He tasted of sweet, salty wine, and she moaned.

She tugged his shirt free of his waistband and slid her hands underneath the fabric. Muscle and flesh, warm, silky hard, met her eager palms. His body was perfect, and she wanted to see it, touch it, taste it. She wanted it over hers, under hers. She wanted the feel of him between her legs, rubbing her there, that place where sensation was everything and mindless pleasure would send her tumbling into oblivion.

He moved his hands, and her top came off over head. A second later, her bra dropped to the floor. His hands and his mouth were everywhere and she squirmed in his arms. A moment later, her skirt and panties joined her other clothing. She was naked . . . except for her heels.

Ethan stepped away, his breathing hard and raspy. Though the room was dim, she knew he could see her, so she eased back against the door, her arms behind her, and let him look. His hungry eyes raked her body as he unbuttoned his shirt and cast it aside.

Now it was Georgie's turn to stare.

As she'd imagined, he was perfect. The hard planes of his chest, the lean waist, taut abs, begged for her hands, her mouth. She went down on one knee, fumbling for his belt buckle, opening it. Tugging at the zipper, she shoved his jeans away, closing her mouth over the hard ridge beneath his soft briefs.

"Georgie," he groaned. His hands stroked her hair. "Georgie . . ."

His lungs were bellowing when she dipped the elastic down to let his shaft spring forward. Sliding her hand along its length, she moved, taking the satiny tip into her mouth.

He made a low, guttural sound she took as pleasure, which only increased her own.

Suddenly he pulled back, reached for her, and brought her to her feet. "Have to stop," he choked. "Or it'll be over way too soon."

"I want to lie on the bed," she demanded. "I want to feel your weight on me."

In one smooth move, he picked her up and laid her on the coverlet. A moment later, when he came down on top of her, he was naked.

One hand cupped her breast, and then she felt his mouth on her nipple, suckling, licking, tasting, and teasing until her body felt like a tightly coiled spring. Colors burst inside her head as he took her to the edge of insanity, and she squirmed, whimpered, begged.

With one knee, he parted her thighs and moved between them. He fumbled with a condom. Quickly, he sheathed himself.

"Something you want, Grasshopper?" he teased as he settled between her thighs. "You need only ask . . . in the appropriate manner."

She would have laughed, but she was too desperate to have him inside her, too frayed around the edges to think of anything to say.

"Do it," she breathed. "Now. Please." Arching her back, she brought her hips forward, easing his head into position. She wiggled again, but he only pushed in a fraction, and she thought she'd scream in frustration.

"Ethan," she begged, her eyes closed, her head thrown back. She was so close to coming, just the touch of his penis had nearly sent her over.

He chuckled in a breathy, labored sort of way.

"Yes, Grasshopper?" he whispered. "A little more?" He eased his hips forward, and she sighed in delight.

"Yes . . . oh, yes . . . please . . . *Master* . . ."

"Georgie," he whispered, and once more crushed his mouth against hers. Grasping her hands, he lifted them over her head, intertwining his fingers with hers as he plunged into her.

Sensation took away her world, leaving only Ethan above her, Ethan inside her. It was the only world she had ever known, would ever know. The taste of him, the feel, the way he moved.

She felt her body stiffen, felt the delicious peak begin, lifting her higher and higher. One thrust, another . . .

"Ethan, oh, my God, Ethan . . ."

He kissed her again, hard, demanding, rough. He went wild on top of her, slamming into her, holding her down, driving himself on, taking her to a place she'd never been before.

She felt it coming. *Oh yes oh yes oh yes* . . .

Her back arched, and his body stilled. She wanted to grab his hips and force him to keep going, but he held her hands imprisoned.

Slowly, he slid back in . . . and she cried out, bursting into flames, her skin scorched, her lungs pumping, trying to pull in enough air to stay alive.

He thrust again, and again, then gave a hard cry and a shout, slamming into her body as though he were a force of nature that could not be stopped. She climaxed once more, the orgasm taking her by surprise as she tried to catch her breath.

Ethan eased down on top of her, gently releasing her hands. Immediately she slid her arms around his strong back as she felt her eyes begin to burn. She swallowed, bit down, but it was too late, and the tears slipped from her eyes in a minigusher.

How could she have let this happen? How could she have let her defenses down, let him in, let him get to her? What was she going to do now?

Her arms tightened around his back as she savored the feeling of him so close, reveled in the heat and weight of him. Pinching her lids tight, she tried to keep the tears at bay, but a tiny sob escaped in spite of her efforts.

Ethan stilled for a moment, then lifted himself a little away. She knew he was peering down at her face, studying her, trying to figure out what was wrong. Any second, he'd say something stupid like, *Do you always cry after sex?* Or *Did I hurt you?* Or the totally clueless, *What's the matter?*

But he didn't.

Instead, she felt his lips brush her flushed cheek, gently kissing away the tears, first one side, then the other. He touched his mouth to hers in a kiss that was at once damp, salty, infinitely tender, and heartbreakingly sweet.

A moment later, he rolled onto his side, capturing her in his arms, bringing her close, spooning around her like a flesh and bone barrier against all the hurts of the world.

She snuggled into him, her back against the hard wall of his chest. Her body shook with each silent sob she wished she could stop, but the tears continued to form and fall, and finally, she just let them.

As she quietly cried, Ethan stroked her hair, then bent his head to hers. "I know, Grasshopper," he whispered. "I know."

Chapter Thirteen

Use your bed for sleeping and sex, and not
necessarily in that order.

Georgiana Mundy's *Feng Shui for Lovers*

Curled around Georgie's warm silky body,
Ethan dozed off just after daybreak, only to be
awakened an hour or so later by the sound of the
shower in the adjacent bathroom. He stretched,
realized he was hard again, or still hard, either
one. Didn't matter. Smiling to himself, he figured
he could fix that.

He tossed the sheet aside and stood.

Georgie. Damn. Talk about the best sex he'd ever
had in his life. She was so responsive, so wild, he
became even more aroused just thinking about
how making love to her all night had felt. What it
had done to him. Not only physically, but deep
inside himself, where he'd fought a six-year battle
to keep tenderness out.

But Georgie had stolen in, and though it
should have alarmed him, he found he couldn't

be sorry. In fact, he was feeling damned chipper about it.

She'd left the door leading to the bathroom slightly ajar. All the invitation he needed.

Standing behind the mist-smudged glass, she reminded him of a fairy nymph beneath a woodland waterfall, her wet hair a silken veil over her shoulders. The long line of her spine led to the two perfect globes of her butt. His hands itched, remembering.

Quickly, he peed, then grabbed a condom from the bathroom drawer where he'd found a fresh package last night, thank God. Sucking in a deep breath, he popped open the shower door. She turned, smiled, maybe blushed. It was hard to tell with all the heat and steam.

As the door snapped closed behind him, he let his gaze slowly wander down her body and back up again. He stepped forward, and their eyes met. Without conscious thought, his hands found their way to her naked breasts, slick with soap, her berry-colored nipples erect against his fingers.

"Hey," he murmured.

"Hey."

Lowering his mouth, he whispered, "You're so damn beautiful."

The kiss was wet and hot, deep and erotic. As water pounded against his back, he reached between them, opened the packet, and rolled on the condom. He lifted her, curling her thighs around his hips, and thrust inside her in one easy motion. She sighed, tightening her arms around his neck. He felt her fingers glide through his hair.

Turning so her back was against the white tile, he continued to move. She murmured words of encouragement, her voice soft and husky. Incredibly aroused, he bent his head to capture her mouth.

She jerked against him, thrusting her hips. A moment later, her body stilled. As she clung to him, her open mouth pressed to his, he felt her body stiffen as her breathing changed into sharp staccato bursts. So did his own. Suddenly she gripped his hips with her thighs, softly keening his name over and over, as she reached her climax.

He wanted to eat her up, take her every way he could think of, take her, and take her, and never let it end.

Holding her hips hard to his groin, he plundered her body. His head fell back to focus on the feel of her all around him, enveloping him, body and soul. He came in a rush of heat and wracking spasms that went on and on and on.

They were both panting, working to pull in air, as he set his forehead against hers. Under the spray of the steaming water on his shoulders, he opened his eyes and smiled at her, and then he laughed.

She pulled back a little, a sassy grin on her face, a satisfied gleam in her half-closed eyes. "Maybe you should put me down," she huffed, obviously still trying to catch her breath, "before you slip on the soap and we both break our necks."

He considered it briefly. "Not yet. You feel too good." They were still mated; he was still inside her, and he didn't want to break the connection. It had been such a long time since he'd felt so close to someone, to set her down and step away was something he wasn't prepared to do just yet.

Her legs wrapped around his hips, they soaped each other and rinsed off, all the while kissing, touching, whispering their likes, their wants, their needs. By the time the shower was over, they were both smiling, squeaky clean, the water had gone cold, and Ethan was starving.

They padded from the bathroom, towels wrapped around themselves, sleepy grins on their faces.

"Is that you?" Ethan said, pointing to Georgie's bag, where a cell phone chirped inside it, like a robin with a pillow over its beak. "A birdcall ring tone?" He arched a brow. He'd heard it before, a week ago, but she'd been in her car, alone.

Georgie shot him a quick glance, a nervous look, if he was any judge. "Natural sounds are healthy and cheerful," she said as she scurried over to where the purse sat on an overstuffed chair by the window.

Digging inside the bag, she pulled out the phone and checked the number. As she flipped it open, she said to Ethan, "Sorry. This won't take a minute."

She licked her lips and tightened the towel around her damp body. Turning away from him, she said softly, "Yeah, hi."

Ethan watched the line of her back as he slid his towel from around his hips, dried his hair, then searched around for his clothes. She listened to the caller intently, nodded, mumbled something, but for the most part remained silent.

He quickly dressed and finger-combed his hair, going about his business as though he weren't listening intently to her every word, not that there were that many of them.

She muttered something into the phone, then flipped it closed. For a long time, she simply stood there with her back to him.

Tucking in his slightly crumpled white shirt, he moved up behind her, slid her hair off her bare shoulder, and placed a kiss there. "You okay?" he probed. "Awfully quiet all of a sudden." He put his hands on her arms. She was trembling.

He quickly turned her to face him, and was shocked at how pale she was. All the blood had drained from her cheeks, her eyes were glazed, her full lips the color of paste.

Alarmed at the abrupt change that had come over her, he bit out, "What in the hell's wrong?"

She blinked up at him a couple of times, like she'd never seen him before. The trembling grew worse. She looked to be on the verge of collapse.

Finally, she seemed to recover herself. "Nothing's wrong," she rasped, her eyes too wide, too innocent. "I, um, I have to go."

"Go where?"

"Uh, back to town. I need my own car. Or maybe I can rent one. Yeah, I can do that. There's, um—"

"Cut the crap, Georgie," he snapped. Sliding his hands up to her shoulders, he squeezed. She averted her gaze. "You've been lying to me from the beginning, and now I want the truth. Who was on the phone, and what kind of trouble are you in?"

She eased out of his grasp, and he let her go. Dropping his hands to his sides, he watched as she pushed past him and went to her suitcase, digging around for a moment, then pulling out some underwear and fresh clothes.

"There's no trouble," she said lightly. "I just have to go, that's all."

"Bullshit." He snagged her elbow, forcing her to stand in front of him, face him, face down whatever barriers to the truth stood between them. He didn't want any barriers anymore. He wanted *her*, and for that to happen, she had to let him in of her own free will. "*Tell me.*"

She cleared her throat and gave him a bland smile. "It doesn't concern you, Ethan. Please drive me into town so I can rent a car."

Sudden anger flared, burned a hole in his gut.

"You can walk, for all I care. I'm not driving you anywhere until you pull those defenses down and trust me."

"*Trust you?* How can I trust you while you work for the station? You're being paid to follow me, keep tabs on me, investigate me, for all I know. You're my *bodyguard*, not my . . . not my . . ."

"I stopped being your bodyguard the minute we landed in bed, Georgie." He ran his fingers through his hair. Jesus Christ, what a stubborn woman. "You trusted me to make love to you, to let yourself be as vulnerable to a man as a woman can get, but you can't tell me what kind of trouble you're in?"

Her eyes snapped up to meet his. Doubling her fists, she slammed them into his chest. Ow. Damn. The woman had some muscle under those curves.

"We had sex, Ethan!" she cried. "That's *all*. Don't think for a minute it meant anything beyond that. You wanted it. I wanted it. It happened. Now it's over. We can go back to being—"

"That's the lamest, most stereotypical line of bullshit I've ever heard!" he shouted. "Surely you can do better than that!" When she only glared up at him, he said, "You really think this didn't mean anything? What, then—you think I fuck all my clients? Huh? *Do you*, Georgie?"

"I don't know what you do with your clients, and I don't care! I need to leave. Now! And if you won't take me, I'll call a cab!"

Her words rang inside the room, inside his head. Fury boiled his blood as he fought a close battle with his temper. Did she think she was just some bimbo he'd scored with? Had he said something, done anything to lead her to believe she was just a hot body for the night?

He'd read the file Lucas had compiled; he knew about her, the facts, anyway. What he wanted was for her to trust him enough to provide the details.

Like the man said, the beauty—and the pain—was in the details.

As she scurried into the bathroom, hugging her clothes to her chest and slamming the door, Ethan stood in the center of the room, his hands clenched into tight balls at his side. Okay, now what? Should he drive her back, even though it was obvious she didn't trust him enough to open up to him?

He rapped his knuckles against the closed bathroom door, but only as a heads-up. He was going in, whether she wanted him to or not.

She stood in profile to him as she faced the mirror, brushing her hair. Not so much as sparing him a glance, she said, "You driving me or not, *Master Ethan*?"

"I'll drive you." Crossing his arms over his chest, he leaned his hip against the doorjamb and let the facts roll around in his head for a moment. He didn't dare confess what he knew about her, but maybe he could provide her with an opening, and then lure her through it. "I may be just a guy, a little slow on the uptake, but I think I figured it out."

For a moment, her brown eyes narrowed, and a flash of something crossed her face. Quickly masking her emotions, she said, "Figured what out?"

"It's not that you don't trust me. I think you do. I think you want to, anyway."

She smoothed a little blusher on her pale cheeks. "You're wrong. Besides, you're a great one to talk about trust."

"What in the hell does that mean?"

Sending him a meaningful glare, she said, "I think you know exactly what it means. You're not exactly Mr. Open Book."

"What's happening to you has nothing to do with me." His hands thrust against his hips, he said, "Regardless, I think you're dying to trust me. But you're afraid, if not for yourself, then for someone else."

Her hand stilled in midair and she gazed into her own eyes in the oval mirror. Slowly, she let her hand fall, setting the blusher on the black marble sink. "Wrong again, Sherlock. Besides, it's none of your—"

"It could be my business, Grasshopper," he said softly. "Should be. And you know it."

She whirled on him, her eyes glittering with fury. "I don't know any such thing! I slept with you; that doesn't change our relationship one little bit!"

"The hell it doesn't! Georgie, what's going on? Huh? For Christ's sake, before you or someone else gets hurt, cut me a little slack and talk to me!" Leaving the threshold, he moved toward her, stopping so close, he could feel the heat radiating from her tense body.

"Trust me," he whispered, fighting off the memory of the last time he'd said those words, shoving away the reality of what that request had cost him. It would be different this time, he told himself. This time, he would not fail. "Georgie, look at me."

Her shoulders slumped a fraction, and she turned her head toward him. As she lifted her eyes to meet his, he could see the hurt and confusion there, the wanting, the hesitation, and wished to God he knew the words to say to make her understand.

"Whatever burden you're carrying, Georgie, you've been carrying by yourself. I have a broad back, strong hands. Let me share the load. Whatever's wrong, I can help. I promise."

For a long time, she said nothing, just stared into his eyes. It was as though she were searching for some ancient truth, some long-sought-after answer to a barely murmured prayer. Perhaps she was checking for signs of deceit, duplicity, treachery. Even though she had every right to look, she'd find none.

Outside, a breeze had come up, and he could hear the rustle of eucalyptus leaves through the open window behind her. Somewhere a crow scolded, a train whistle screamed, a man laughed, but Georgie remained silent.

She lowered her eyes.

Well, then, Ethan thought. That was that.

He pursed his lips and gave a sharp jerk of his head, then turned toward the door, anger fusing with disappointment inside his belly. Screw it. He'd drive her back to the city, call Horton, and give him the name of Paladin's best competitor. After that, he'd never have to see Georgie Mundy or hear her name again.

Curling his fingers around the knob, he flung

the door open, ready to stalk out, when he heard her voice behind him.

"Wait," she whispered, her voice barely audible.

But he'd heard it, and it stopped him in his tracks. He swung back toward her. Her eyes were rimmed with red, her face a study of uncertainty and pain.

"It's okay, Grasshopper," he urged gently. "Tell me."

Licking her lips, she crossed her arms over her body in an ages-old gesture of self-protection. "I don't want to tell you."

"I understand."

She shook her head, her mouth a straight line, her jaw tightly clenched. "I've never told anyone. Why should I tell you? What proof can you give me that you won't betray me?"

He stood before her, facing her squarely. Letting his arms relax at his sides, he sought her gaze, locked on it. "You have only my word."

The arch of her brow spoke of her skepticism. "Words can be bought and sold."

"Not mine."

He waited. She had to decide for herself. He could say nothing now to urge her on. Anything he said, she'd view as coercion or pressure. So he kept his eyes locked on hers, and he waited.

Minutes passed while they stood facing each other, neither speaking, neither moving. Just when he thought he'd lost the game, she let her arms fall to her sides.

"I don't care how big you are," she said flatly.

"Or how strong you are, or how many guns you own, or how I feel about you. If you betray me, if you hurt anyone I love, I'll track you down like a dog and rip your dick off."

He swallowed. "Deal."

She nodded once. Her shoulders relaxed. Finally, she took a breath. "I . . . I have this friend," she said quietly. "In Santa Barbara . . ."

Her heartbeat hammering in her ears, Raine Preston fumbled to unlock the front door. Hanging on tightly to the warm bundle draped over her shoulder, she shoved through the threshold, kicked the door closed with her foot, and slid the deadbolt into place with her free hand.

Was it really him? Had he seen her? Georgie had warned her he might show up in Santa Barbara . . .

Quickly laying the sleeping baby down in the playpen by the archway that led to the dining room, Raine ran back into the living room, yanking the front drapes closed.

After a quick look to see that Caroline was okay, she scurried into the kitchen to make sure the back door lock was secure.

Methodically, she went from room to room, testing windows, pulling curtains closed. She felt queasy, and her head ached. With rubbery legs, she made her way back to check on the baby. Only when she saw the long lashes fanning Caroline's rosy cheeks, the drooly mouth, pouting in sleep, did she let herself relax.

Slumping into the chair next to the playpen, she rubbed her temples and tried to make herself believe she hadn't really seen Paul Corcoran staring at her through the crowded farmers' market. Still, it had frightened her enough to call Georgie.

She shook her head. It *was* him, had to have been. After all, Georgie had seen him, too, but that was in San Francisco, three hundred and fifty miles away. Had he followed Georgie to Santa Barbara last weekend? Had he come *looking* for Raine?

Doubling her fists, she put them to her eyes and rubbed. Should she call the police, just in case? And if she did, what would she tell them?

Her white Taurus still stood in the driveway; she needed to pull it into the garage behind the house and bring in the groceries before they spoiled. But to do that, she'd have to risk going outside, risk being vulnerable.

If Paul had followed her home . . .

A person's blood really did run cold in fear, she decided, rubbing her arms despite the wilting August heat.

Georgie had promised to come, she was on her way, but it would take her hours to get to Santa Barbara from . . . where had she been? Napa?

Rising from the chair, she went to the front window and eased the curtain aside just enough to peek out at the quiet street. It was a beautiful, sunny Sunday, but few people were out walking. Occasionally, a car would drive by, but this part of town was relatively exclusive, quiet, not a lot of foot or automobile traffic. Most of the people Raine saw regularly were her neighbors, though she didn't know any of them well. Because neither she nor Georgie knew how far Vaughn Corcoran's hands reached, by design she really didn't know anyone in town well.

Caroline made a whimpering sound in her sleep and curled in on herself, taking her little thumb into her rosebud mouth.

Raine's heart nearly burst. Her baby. *Hers*. From the silky blond curls to the blue button eyes, this baby beauty queen was hers and hers alone. The only blood family Raine had ever known. As much as she loved and adored Georgie, they weren't related. Only through years of shared circumstances had an unbreakable bond formed between them. In every way that mattered, Georgie and Raine were sisters.

She nearly jumped out of her skin when the living room phone chimed to life. Letting the curtain slide back into place, she checked the caller ID, then grabbed up the receiver.

"Georgie?"

"Did he follow you to the house?"

"I don't think so." She inhaled a deep breath, trying desperately to calm her nerves. "I lost myself in the crowd at the market and hurried home. Do you think he knows? He must suspect something. Why else would he be in Santa Barbara?"

Her worried gaze drifted over to the baby, sleeping like an angel on her tummy. One leg of her denim pants had ridden up, revealing a plump little calf and one bare foot where her sock had come off, exposing five tiny pink toes.

"Raine," Georgie was saying, "listen to me. It'll take us another four hours to get there, but there's a man, one of Ethan's agents."

"Ethan? Who's—"

"He's the private investigator I told you about."

Raine crinkled her nose in surprise. "That hunky Darling guy you mentioned? Did you tell him about Mrs. Beebes?" she said, using their code name for the baby.

"Yes."

"Georgie!"

"It's okay, Raine," Georgie hurried. "Ethan has an agent already in Santa Barbara. His name is Lucas Russell. He's on his way to the house and should be there any minute."

She turned her head away from the receiver just in time to hear a car pull into the driveway and park behind hers.

For the second time that day, her heart began to race.

"Somebody's here. Maybe it's him. Hold on."

Setting the receiver down, she went to the window and peeked through the drapes. A tall man emerged from the car, thirty-something, athletic build, light hair, dark glasses. *Not Paul.*

She returned to the phone. "Describe this Lucas Russell."

Raine listened while Georgie relayed from Ethan what Lucas looked like. It sounded like the right man.

"How do I know I can trust him?" she said. "I mean, I don't know who the Corcorans might have paid off. And why is this guy in Santa Barbara, anyway?"

"There's no way the Corcorans could even know Lucas Russell, so I wouldn't worry about that," Georgie said. "Ethan told me he's in Santa Barbara on another assignment, but he's being reassigned to watch over you."

Rainie's brows snapped together. "Why do you trust this Ethan Darling all of a sudden?"

"I don't know that I do. Not completely."

"Well, then why in the hell—"

"I had no choice, Raine. I swear. I needed help, needed to find a way to protect you and Caroline, just in case Paul showed up. I'll, uh, I'll explain more when I see you."

The doorbell rang, and the baby stirred in her sleep.

"Georgie, promise me this guy's okay."

"Let him in. He'll protect you and Caroline until we get there. I have Ethan's word on it."

She glanced at the door as the bell rang again. "All right. I'll let him in, but if I suspect for one second he's working for Corcoran, he'll never know what hit him."

"If he's working for Corcoran," Georgie said slowly, "there will be two bodies floating in the channel—his, and Ethan Darling's."

Raine said a quick good-bye, then set the receiver back in its cradle. Moving toward the door, she lowered her head. "Who's there?"

A deep, masculine voice answered. "My name's Lucas Russell, Ms. Preston. Ethan Darling sent me. I have ID, if you need to see it."

Dread filled her as she debated whether to let him in. Finally, she eased the deadbolt back. Opening the door a crack, she was met by the sharpest blue eyes she'd ever seen. His arm moved, and her eyes fell on the ID he held up. Scanning it, she decided he was who he said he was.

"All right," she said. "You can come in." Her stomach churning, she stepped aside to allow him entry.

His presence was overpowering. He stood nearly a head taller than she, and seemed even bigger now that he was in the room. Quickly, she put some distance between them by moving back toward the playpen.

That was when she saw what was in his hand. Not the hand that held his ID, but the other one. The hand with the gun in it.

Chapter Fourteen

Make sure "his" side of the bed has easy access (no exercise equipment or overflowing laundry baskets, please!). Empty half of your dresser drawers, leave some space in your closet, and keep an extra toothbrush on hand. If you fill up every square inch of your house with you, there won't be any room for *him*. When you demonstrate your willingness to share your space with someone special, you encourage Mr. Right to make himself at home!

Georgiana Mundy's *Feng Shui for Lovers*

After a hasty good-bye to their confused hostess, Ethan had given Georgie a quick kiss of assurance that everything would be all right, tossed all of her stuff into the trunk, and pointed the car toward the nearest freeway.

An hour had passed, and now they were speeding along U.S. 101—next stop, Santa Barbara. The Sunday morning traffic was light, and they were making good time. Moving smoothly around a lumbering furniture van, he checked his speedometer—slightly over the legal limit, slightly under bat-out-of-hell.

In the seat next to him, Georgie sat with her eyes closed, her fingertips gently massaging the bridge of her nose. Abruptly, she opened her eyes and turned to him.

"You're sure this Lucas guy can be trusted? You're *positive*?"

"Next to yours truly," he assured her, "he's Paladin's best. Former police officer."

"And he won't let anything happen to Raine or the baby."

"He'd die first."

Why make her more nervous than she already was? Going into Lucas's background would only confuse the issue, and the chances were everything in Santa Barbara was just fine, Lucas was doing his job, and all their worry and haste was for nothing.

Out of the corner of his eye, he saw Georgie's brow furrow. "He'd *die* first?" she said. "That's quite a sacrifice to make for an assignment, for woman he doesn't even know."

He kept his eyes on the road. "It's a matter of ethics, Georgie. Commitment. You take the pay, you do the job."

She sent him a skeptical look, then snorted. "He'd actually *die* before he'd let anything happen to a total stranger. I find that hard to believe, and not a little alarming."

"Believe it," he said. "Besides, Lucas knows that if he didn't put himself in the line of fire for a client's safety, I'd kill him myself."

"Between ripping Lucas Russell's balls off for being tempted to kiss me, as you so delicately put it yesterday, and killing him for not protecting a client, it's a wonder the poor man doesn't pee his pants at the mere sight of you."

"How do you know he doesn't?" He shot her a quick grin.

She was silent for a moment, then said, "Can I ask you a question?"

"Sure." He already knew what she was going to ask. They all did, eventually.

"When you were a police officer . . ." Her voice trailed off, almost as though she were afraid to ask, afraid to know the truth. "When you were a police officer, did you ever have to, I mean, did you ever—"

"Yes," he said, sparing her having to say the words. "Once. I was still in uniform."

He could feel her watching him, waiting for more, unsure what to say.

"It was just before I was promoted to detective. My partner and I responded to a domestic. Guy was high on something, beating the shit out of his girlfriend. She was screaming, terrified he was going to kill her. Cath was good at talking people down, so she approached. Out of nowhere, he pulls a weapon, aims it at her head."

"Cath? Your partner was a woman?"

He nodded once. "The guy had her cold. He was going to do it. I had no choice." Then again, softly, "I had no choice."

And he hadn't. A split second's hesitation, and Cathy would have been dead. The board had agreed, his use of deadly force had been deemed justified, and the case had been closed.

But that night had changed everything. Not only had he taken a life, he and Cathy had bonded in a way unique to people who faced down death together. Their relationship had begun that night, and when he'd been promoted to detective, and she'd gone on for special training in hostage negotiations, they'd stayed close. They'd fallen in love. They'd made plans.

Maybe they'd cheated fate that first night. Maybe the next three years of Cathy's life had been borrowed time, and the bullet that finally took her had simply taken three years to find its mark.

"What's it like?" Georgie asked. "Having a woman for a partner?"

"It works."

"What happened to her? Did she become a detective, too?"

He cleared his throat. "No."

She sat back in her seat, crossing her arms over her stomach. As soon as she chewed away on all this new information, she'd come back at him again. It was simply the way she was, but for a few minutes, anyway, he had a little time to think.

Forcing Cathy's memory away, he turned his

mind once more to Lucas. Sure, he trusted Lucas, but . . .

It was that *but* gnawing away at him now. Something wasn't right about this whole setup, and hadn't been from the beginning. In the years Lucas had worked for Paladin, there hadn't been a hint of unethical behavior or unprofessional methods. Ethan knew, because he'd monitored the guy twenty-four/seven, three-sixty-five for nearly three years. What Lucas had done to get himself kicked off the police force seemed to be behind him. But it was like a woman who'd been unfaithful one time. Once, but never again? The doubt would always be there. Broken trust was hell to repair, and when it came to personal security, it could be fatal.

When Lucas had first come to Paladin, Ethan had taken one look at his résumé and shut the file. No way was he going to hire a "bad" cop, reformed or not. But when Lucas explained his motives, and how he'd turned his life around, Ethan had reconsidered, and brought him on board. In time, he'd begun to trust Lucas more and more, until finally he'd become 99.9 percent positive the guy was a changed man.

It was that .1 percent, however, that was like a gnat in his ear. Had he made a mistake in trusting Lucas? Had the guy just been biding his time until he had a scenario he could exploit? If Vaughn Corcoran was involved in Georgie's case, then huge sums of bribery money could be at stake.

Was Lucas really above all that now, or had Ethan put his faith in the wrong man?

"I swear to God, on my mother's grave, on a Bible or any holy book you choose," Lucas had said on the day Ethan had turned down his job application. He'd stood straight, looked Ethan square in the eye. "I swear I've changed. Gotten help. I need a break, Ethan. I take complete responsibility for the shit I was involved in, for my dismissal from the force. My fault. Nobody else's. Jesus, everybody deserves a second chance. I guess I'm begging you for one. If I fuck up, you can deck me and I won't put up any kind of fight."

"If you fuck up," Ethan warned, "I'll do worse than deck you. If you fuck up and you run, you'd better keep running, because when I find you—"

"I won't screw up. I'm on the level, I swear to God. I'm not asking for forgiveness or blind trust, just a *chance*, Ethan. Just a measly second chance to make things right. You won't be sorry." A flash of hope snapped in his sharp blue eyes, cop's eyes. "So you'll take me on?"

He could say no. Even though he and Lucas had been on the force together way back when, even though the guy had been a solid police officer when the chips were down, even though . . .

"You're not expecting any special favors because Cathy was your half-sister?"

"I'm not," Lucas bit out. "No special favors. I don't deserve any. I'm just looking for a chance. If you don't want to give me one, I'm history."

He'd turned for the door, but Ethan's next

words stopped him. "I'll take you on, Russell. But don't expect anything glamorous. You'll pull the midnight-till-dawn surveillance, lost-parakeet patrol, and every shit job Paladin has to offer, and like it."

Facing Ethan, Lucas said, "I can do that."

And in nearly six years, Lucas hadn't fucked up, not even once. He'd excelled at everything he did. No BS, he did his job, kept his mouth shut, satisfied the clients, and lived within his means. He'd given Ethan no reason to question Lucas's dedication or his ethics.

But that damned outside .1 percent had begun ripping a hole in his spleen, and he hated that he couldn't do anything about it.

With one hand on the wheel, he slid his cell phone from his pocket, flipped it open, and pressed the autodial.

No answer. At the end of Lucas's voice-mail prompt, Ethan growled, "Call me."

A thousand reasons ran through his head, reasons his almost-brother-in-law couldn't answer the phone. Lucas should have called in when he'd reached Raine Preston's house. Why hadn't he?

That same .1 percent began turning the contents of his stomach to carbolic acid.

Tossing a quick look at Georgie, he said, "Give your friend a call, would you? Ask her how things are going."

"What's wrong?" she asked, her voice a little on the thin side. "Is something wrong? Who did you just try to call?"

"I just want to make sure everything's all right."

Her small nod wasn't accompanied by a smile. She pressed a button on her cell. A moment later, she flipped the phone closed. "Voice mail."

They sat in silence for a mile or so, tension humming between them like a spindly melody. Everything was okay, he assured himself. Lucas was probably getting settled in, making sure the house was secure.

He shot a glance over at Georgie, who was staring out the passenger-side window. Her hands were in her lap, fingers all twisted around themselves in a white-knuckle knot.

"Ten bucks for your thoughts," he ventured, trying to ease the anxiety they both felt.

Without looking at him, she said, "I heard it was a penny."

"Inflation. Besides, I'm willing to pay the going rate to hear what's on your mind."

"Why don't *you* tell *me* what's on *your* mind?"

"Men don't talk."

"No, it's men don't *listen*."

"Hmm? What?" He gazed vacantly over at her as she turned to face him. "Did you say something?"

"Very funny," she said softly. "Do you really think Raine and the baby are okay?"

"Yes," he said, hoping to hell it was the truth.

Lowering her eyes, she fiddled with her fingers. "Look. Ethan. I, uh, I don't know how to be today, with you, you know, after last night. Our relationship changed from a kind of business arrangement to a really personal, physical, you know, thing, then right into this bizarre scenario where we're flying down the highway, not knowing if my family is in danger . . . but my mind hasn't finished processing the personal physical thing yet, and I feel a little off-kilter. I sort of need to talk about it."

He grunted.

She frowned over at him. "That's it? A *grunt*? No comment?" Her mouth flattened into a tight line, her eyes warning him she was ready to do battle. "Tell me how *you* feel about last night."

Jesus, women and their need to talk things to death. This was neither the time nor the place to delve into his feelings about last night. Distracting Georgie from worrying about her friend was one thing; confessing his emotional attachment to her would have to wait until the situation at hand had been resolved. If he started getting romantic right now, it would splinter his concentration. Raine Preston could be in real trouble, and until he knew for certain she was safe, he needed to stay focused.

"Georgie, you should know by now that men don't talk about their feelings."

She made a clicking sound with her tongue. "That's a pretty pat answer," she charged. "I opened myself up and was honest with you, and now you're shutting down? I hope what I said was worth ten bucks. You can pay on your way *out*."

"I need to stay on task, Georgie. Last night

meant a lot to me, but we need to set that aside until we have more time to get into it."

"We're in a car, alone, with nothing to do but talk about *it* for the next couple of hours, but you need to stay on task? What task?"

He gripped the wheel, trying to keep his mounting temper under control. "Okay, look. Last night was incredible. I want to do it again, soon, very, very soon. But you need to understand—"

"Wanting to have sex with me and having feelings for me are two different things, Ethan." She sank back into her seat and crossed her arms in angry defiance.

He checked the rearview mirror, then changed lanes. "I would think you'd be more worried about your friend than what my feelings are about last night."

She raised her hands in the air, then slapped her knees with open palms. "I *am* worried about Raine! I'm terribly, terribly . . . Oh, *damn*—"

She broke off her sentence, and her hands suddenly flew to her face, covering it in a gesture of helplessness. Between her fingers, she stumbled, "You h-have no idea how worried about her I am. I'm so far away. I've always hated how far away I am, but it was necessary to protect Raine and the baby. And now Paul may have found her anyhow. I'm terrified he'll hurt her, or kidnap the baby, or . . . I don't *know* what!"

When she lifted her face, her eyes were red with unshed tears. "Raine's all I have. I've always protected her, or tried to. But when it came to . . . when

Paul . . . I failed her, Ethan. I *failed*. It's my fault she's in this mess."

He shot her a hard glance. "It is *not* your fault, Georgie. You didn't fail. You couldn't know what kind of man Corcoran was, what he was capable of. He's a bastard who victimized both of you to one degree or another."

"Oh, sure," she shot back. "What do you know about failure? What do you know about somebody putting their trust in you, believing in you, and then you let them down, betray that trust, fail, and they get hurt? You've probably never done anything that—"

"Stop it!" he shouted, his fingers tightening around the wheel in a death grip. "You don't know a thing about me, Georgie. Not a thing. Everybody screws up. Everybody!"

She stared over at him, her eyes wide, her lips pressed tightly together. He should say something, put her mind at ease that he wasn't shouting at her, but at himself. He wanted to tell her just how badly a man could screw up, how badly *he* had. Instead, he locked his jaw and kept his eyes on the road. If he opened his mouth, it would all come pouring out. Six years ago, he'd sworn to himself he'd never reveal to anyone what happened. Not *any*one.

The department had shut the file and sealed it. It was only his superiors' respect for his so-called stellar record that had kept the truth from coming out. In the end, it didn't matter. Just like Lucas, he had resigned the force in disgrace. It was why he'd decided to give Lucas a break. Cathy would have wanted him to.

He wouldn't give himself a break, though. Never himself.

What had he been thinking, making love to Georgie? Ultimately, he could never have her. It was insane. His attraction for her had painted pastel hues over a past so dark, the ugliness was bound to seep through. If he was a gentleman, he'd simply break it off with her. Today. Now. Right *now*.

"I'm sorry, Ethan," she said quietly. "I didn't mean to imply—"

"Forget it," he bit out. "Look, I've got to make a couple of phone calls. Why don't you try and get some sleep? We'll be there in another hour or so. I'll wake you when we hit town."

Before she could say anything, he pulled his cell from his pocket and punched the autodial. Putting the phone to his ear, he shut Georgie out, leaving her to deal with his raw emotions and silence any way she could.

It wasn't right, but he might as well begin shutting her out now. Because when all was said and done, it was for her own damn good.

Chapter Fifteen

Want a man who's a little dangerous? Look for a guy who's tall and rugged, with strong eyebrows and a prominent brow bone. He has a well-defined jaw, slightly indented temples, and a square hairline. This signals a man of action, an entrepreneur, a pioneer, an athlete. But watch out! Along with being intelligent and disciplined, he can be irritable, frustrated, impulsive, impatient, judgmental, pushy, rebellious, and angry!

Georgiana Mundy's *Feng Shui for Lovers*

Raine huddled inside the closet behind a big scratchy coat, the one she'd seen The Woman wear on windy days. The coarse fibers itched the backs of her little arms, but she'd scooted as far into the corner as she could get. If The Man or The Woman opened the door, they wouldn't see her, and maybe would go look for her someplace else.

Wrapping her arms around her thin body, she tried to control the shaking. Her teeth chattered, too, except for the ones in front that were missing. She always shook when she hid in the closet. It was so dark, and it smelled bad, too, like The People. Next to her, the new girl was crying softly.

"It's okay," she whispered into the girl's ear. "They'll be super drunk soon and go to sleep, then we can go out."

The new girl sniffed. In the deep shadows of the small space, Raine saw her wipe her eyes. "A-at my old place, they were nice."

Raine shook her head. Keeping her voice quiet, she said, "They're not nice here. What's your name?"

"Georgie Mundy. I'm eight."

"I'm Raine Preston. I'm seven. You need to whisper or they'll hear. They'll forget about us and go to sleep. It always happens that way."

Or not. The last time Raine had hidden in the closet, the yelling had gone on and on, but she'd stayed put, too terrified to show herself. She'd hidden there so long, she'd wet her pants. When The People found out, they put her back in the closet for a whole day.

"When we get out," Georgie whispered, "we should call the social worker. I don't think they're supposed to do this kind of stuff to us."

"I tried to do that once, but I don't know her phone number." And by the time the social worker had visited on her regular rounds, the bruises were gone.

On the other side of the door, The People were having another really bad fight. Accusations, slurred words, a slap, another. Something hit the wall near the closet door and shattered.

Raine felt Georgie lean closer. "He said fucking," she whispered. "He's not supposed to say stuff like that."

"Do you know what it means?"

"Yeah. Do you?"

"Y-yeah."

Raine's stomach began to ache, and the saliva in her mouth turned sour. Bile rose in her throat while cold sweat made its way down her spine. She crossed her arms over her stomach and hugged herself, squeezing her knees tightly together.

"When they fight," she warned Georgie, "you always need to hide until it's over. But not in the bedroom. Okay? Stay real far away from the bedroom."

Georgie was silent for a moment. Then, "Raine, you need to tell the social—"

"No, don't tell anybody!" she begged. "The Man said that they'd put me in a worse place if I told. I don't want to go to a worse place!"

In the dark, she felt Georgie's warm hand reach for her own. Her fingers curled around Raine's and squeezed. "I'm older than you, and stronger. From now on, I'll watch out for you, Raine. Nobody will ever hurt you again. I promise."

Raine nodded. "And I promise I'll watch out for you, too, Georgie. Forever and ever and ever . . ."

". . . ever gonna wake up, Raine? Hey, babe. Up and at 'em."

Raine slowly moved through the dream, the memory. Was she awake or asleep? What time was it?

She kept her eyes closed and tried to remember.

A man had come to her house . . . he'd walked in the door, then something had happened. She'd been looking at him, then hell had broken loose.

Other men had crowded in the door behind him. Other men, including—

Her eyes flew open as panic seized her heart like a tight fist. Bright light stabbed her pupils, forcing her to shut her eyes again.

"Ah, there you are. Hey, babe. Didn't realize that little tap on the jaw would put you out for so long. Come on, wake up for me. Let's see that beautiful smile."

No. No. Not him. No!

Her heart began to slam in steady rapid beats against her ribs. Slowly, she lifted her lids and blinked a few times until her eyes became accustomed to the light behind him. Her eyes burned, but her gaze never wavered.

He sat sprawled in a chair facing her, one arm under Caroline's bottom as he held the baby to him, her blond head resting on his shoulder, her chubby little arms limp in sleep.

Fury boiled up inside her, searing her throat. She wanted to fling her body at him, claw his eyes out, kick him in his goddamned balls, but she didn't, not while he held her baby.

"Paul." She pushed herself into a sitting position. Her head felt heavy, her brain muzzy. She wanted to rub her jaw, but instead she reached toward Caroline. In a dead-calm tone, she said, "Give me back my baby."

The handsome bastard grinned in that charming way he had. His blond hair was slightly tousled, his jaw fashionably unshaven. Anyone looking at him would have thought he was a model ready for a shoot.

If she had a gun, she'd be happy to oblige.

Paul tilted his head. "Don't you mean *our* baby, sweet thing? Why didn't you tell me I was a daddy?"

As Ethan pulled into the driveway behind Raine's car, Georgie flung her door open and began running up the flagstone pathway to the house. He stepped out of his side and caught her as she tried to move past him.

"Wait," he ordered, his grip on her arm firm as he tugged her close in to his body. "Is that Taurus hers?"

She spared a quick glance at the sedan, the back door on the passenger side standing slightly open. "Yes," she said breathlessly.

His laser-sharp stare flashed up the driveway, then out to the street. "I don't see Lucas's car." Reaching inside the Mercedes, he pulled a handgun from the door panel.

"Maybe they went to the store," she mumbled, unable to take her eyes off the weapon.

"Maybe." His gaze darted around again, up the driveway once more, to the rooftops, across the street. "Stay here, Georgie."

He moved quickly to the Taurus; in a moment, he was back by her side. "Backseat's filled with grocery bags. No keys in the ignition."

"What about the car seat?"

"The what?"

"The car seat, you know, for the baby." She felt her heart tumble around inside her rib cage. "She's not here," she whispered, her nerves riding thin and high on a razor-sharp precipice. "She knew we were coming, so why did they leave? Where would your agent have taken her?"

Before Ethan could make a grab for Georgie again, she rushed past him, taking the flagstone steps two at a time. Just as she reached the front door, his arm wrapped around her waist, yanking her back hard against his chest.

"Me first," he growled into her ear. "You get behind me, and stay there. Understood?"

She nodded, and he released her. The gun in his right hand, he curled the fingers of his left hand around the knob. He turned it, and the door opened.

It should be locked, Georgie thought. *Why isn't it locked? Raine always, always, always keeps the door locked. And the groceries . . . why are they still in the car . . . ?*

Her stomach pitched and she felt as though she might be sick. But when Ethan pushed the door open and stepped through the threshold, she put her open hand on his back and followed right behind.

The house was a disaster, turned upside down, as though someone had either been searching for something or had torn the place apart in a rage.

Georgie's hands flew to her face and she covered her open mouth, stifling a gasp.

She stood frozen in the threshold as Ethan moved through the house, the kitchen, the hallway. He opened the three bedroom doors one by one, then moved into the bathroom.

As though in a trance, Georgie drifted toward the nursery. She and Raine had painted the walls blue, with rainbows arcing across the sky, through puffy clouds, and around the sun. A unicorn frolicked on a hilltop, yellow ducks waddled in a row just above the baseboards. Butterflies fluttered by, and silvery stars peeked out from behind a crescent moon in the darkened upper corner. Over the crib, little sailboats dangled and spun from a mobile, like a fleet of pink and blue Flying Dutchmen. The scent of baby powder and lanolin filled the room, making her heart ache.

She curled her fingers over the railing and looked down into the empty crib. A moment later, she heard Ethan's footsteps halt a few feet behind her. Not knowing what to say, where to begin, she turned to face him.

He stood in the threshold staring at her, his eyes glittering with a ferocity she didn't know a man could possess, and she couldn't help thinking if this were the Old West, Lucas Russell was a dead man.

Lucas Russell was a dead man. Whether he'd sold out to Corcoran or simply failed to protect Raine Preston and her baby, it didn't really matter. Ethan had trusted the son of a bitch.

He had to get control of his anger, rid himself

of the gnawing worry that ate away at his guts. Right now he needed to think, needed a clear head, and all the reason he could muster.

If Lucas had betrayed him, had he had accomplices? Were there other of Paladin's agents who'd sold out? And if so, who could Ethan trust? He couldn't go after Lucas alone. He needed backup, but from where?

It took every ounce of courage he had to meet Georgie's accusing stare. Only hours ago, she'd talked to him about the cost of failure, of promises made, promises broken. And now he stood facing her, knowing he was responsible for the pain and fear she was suffering.

"I'll fix it, Georgie," he said. "Whatever's gone wrong, I can fix it."

She shook her head as angry tears formed in her eyes. "I trusted you," she rasped, her voice nearly too clogged with emotion to be coherent. "*You said* he was okay. *You said* he'd take care of them, keep them safe!"

He raised his hand, palm up, an unspoken gesture that begged her to listen. "I'm sorry. I'll—"

"You'll *what*? You don't even know where they've gone! I trusted you, believed in you . . . I . . . I can't believe I was so naïve and stupid to think—"

The bleep of Ethan's cell phone cut her off. Yanking it from his pocket, he checked the readout, then pressed the button. Through clenched teeth, he bit out, "Where the fuck are you, Lucas?"

"Hey, boss," Lucas said, his tone light, almost

jovial. "Sorry about cutting out like that, but I was under orders from my new employer, and it would have gotten really messy if I was still there when you showed up."

"Do you have any idea what I'm going to do to you if any harm comes to the woman or the kid?" The threat was nothing more than a low growl.

Georgie's eyes blazed as she rushed toward him, making a grab for the phone. Wrapping his arm around her waist, he held her at bay, trying not to hurt her.

"Let me handle this, Georgie," he whispered harshly. To Lucas, he said, "When I get my hands on you, I'm going to wring your frigging neck."

In his ear, Lucas laughed. "Listen, I can't talk long. I just wanted to let you know that Paul says you can give it up now. He says to tell you no cops, and no Feds, or the woman and the kid disappear permanently. Oh, and I'm resigning from Paladin, effective, like, yesterday."

There were voices in the background, then a man's deep laughter. But nothing Ethan heard gave any indication of Lucas's location.

"Who's behind this—that little prick Paul, or his father?"

Georgie stilled, her eyes wide and locked on Ethan's.

"Yes, yes, I'd love to chat, too," Lucas said, "but I've delivered the message, so we're done here."

"I'm going to track you down, asshole," Ethan snarled. "And when I get my hands on you—"

"Well, I tell ya, Ethan," Lucas interrupted, "if I

were you, *I'd* find some cozy spot and just hole up for a while. Get a little rest. Let the old nerves settle down. Trust me, Ethan. Trust me, by morning you should feel a whole lot better."

Ethan's eyes narrowed. "What in the hell are you talking about? Lucas? *Lucas? Shit.*"

The line was silent.

Georgie squirmed and Ethan released her. "Is Raine okay? They haven't hurt her? What about Caroline?"

Ethan clenched the phone in his hand for a moment, thinking, working it through. "Paul must have shown up here with some help. Unless I miss my guess, they're escorting Raine and the baby to San Francisco, to Vaughn Corcoran."

He looked down at Georgie. Her face was pale, her eyes huge. In their depths, he saw fear and hope, and fury.

"You have to get them back!" she snapped, her voice high and shaky. "You said you trusted your agent, and I trusted *you.* And now Raine and Caroline are gone. Get them back, Ethan!"

"He won't hurt them, Georgie."

"How do you know that?" she cried. "Why did he take them? What does he want with them? This doesn't make any sense!"

Running her fingers through her hair, she looked down at the floor for a moment, then back up at him. She licked her lips, put her hands on his chest, curling her fingers into the fabric of his shirt.

"Get them back, Ethan. You promised, you

swore. I *trusted* you!" Her eyes shone with unshed tears as she gazed up at him. "They're my family. They're all I have. You have no idea what Vaughn and Paul are capable of!"

His eyes never leaving Georgie's, he thumbed the autodial on his cell phone and pressed it to his ear. A moment later, the call rang through. "Yeah," he said, forcing out the words he knew he had to say. "It's me. Just listen. I'm in Santa Barbara. Paladin's been compromised and I don't have time to sort it out right now. I, uh . . . I need your help. You're the only one I know I can trust—"

"I'm in. Tell me what you need."

Lowering his eyes, and his voice, he said, "Thanks, Nate. Here's what I want you to do."

Chapter Sixteen

Exposed beams in your home are bad news. The worst are those above your bed. They depress both your romance and your health by creating unseen pressures on you—physically, mentally, and emotionally. To cure this problem, hang two special feng shui flutes at forty-five-degree angles, placing one at each end of the beam. Flutes have powerfully uplifting effects and aid in relieving pressures imposed by the bad bed beam.

Georgiana Mundy's *Feng Shui for Lovers*

Raine paced the dingy motel room, trying to keep her frayed nerves from unraveling completely. Paul's two goons had taken out the phone and locked her in, warning her that if she made any noise, they'd come and take Caroline away, too.

If she'd been alone, she'd bust out a window and make a run for it, but she had the baby to consider. Fleeing a bunch of thugs with a ten-month-old in your arms wouldn't get you very far.

She went to the double bed where Caroline lay sleeping, blankets tucked around her so she wouldn't roll onto the floor. Her silky blond hair, so much like her father's—damn the man—curled softly against her flushed cheek. She was a beautiful baby, a fact that no doubt fed Paul's already inflated ego.

Caroline never napped for very long, and soon she would wake and begin looking for a meal. The room contained a mini-fridge, but it was empty. What did they expect her to feed the poor child? And how could she ask them, when she'd been warned not to make a sound?

Moving to the curtained window next to the door, she edged the heavy polyester fabric aside and looked across the nearly empty parking lot to the western horizon. It would be dark in an hour or so. Were they planning on keeping her here all night? She'd given up trying to get answers out of Paul. In the few minutes they'd spent together, she'd begged him for information.

"You'll know when you need to know," he'd said. "Meanwhile, keep your mouth shut, and you just might get through this in one piece." He'd held Caroline on his lap, and when he tried to bounce her on his knee, her little face had crumpled and she'd begun to cry. He quickly thrust her away into Raine's eager arms. "Keep the brat quiet, will you?"

"Why, Paul?" she said, trying to maintain her composure. "Why are you doing this? You don't want to be a part of Caroline's life any more than

I want you to be. I don't want anything from you, not your money, not your name, *nothing*. Why don't you let me take Caroline and go home?"

His expression had seemed strained, but when he spoke, his voice was casual. "Out of my hands, babe. We're all pawns in the game. It's time you knew that."

As she let the curtain drift back into place, she heard footsteps, then knuckles on wood. A key turned in the lock, and the door opened.

"You decent?" Lucas Russell stepped across the threshold, a large grocery bag in his arms, a package of disposable diapers dangling from his free hand.

Immediately one of the thugs closed the door after Lucas. She heard the key turn in the lock.

"More decent than you," she snarled. "And keep your voice down. Caroline's asleep."

His blue eyes connected with hers. "Figured you and the kid would be getting hungry soon." Setting the packages on the desk in the corner of the room, he reached in and pulled out a lidded Starbucks cup. Gesturing to her with it, he said, "Got you some coffee, too, and a turkey sandwich."

"What about the baby?"

He nodded. "I bought a bottle and some powdered formula, but she's got a few teeth, so I tossed in some bananas and cereal. There's plastic spoons and bowls in the bag, too." When she sent him a *my, how thorough* glare, he said, "I have a couple of kids. It's been a few years, but I remember the drill."

Raising her chin, she crossed her arms tightly under her breasts. "Thanks for the groceries. Now get the hell out."

He shoved his hands in the back pockets of his jeans, and cut a look at the closed door. "I guess you're pretty mad, Ms. Preston, but you have to understand—"

"Oh, I understand, all right," she bit out, cutting him off. "Vaughn Corcoran dangled some money in front of your face, and you took it. I wouldn't care, except your lapse in ethics is very bad news for me and my child. So unless you mean to rectify that, get the hell out of my sight."

Flicking another quick look at the door, he stepped closer to her. Instantly she moved back, putting as much space between the two of them as the tiny room allowed.

On the bed, Caroline stirred, kicked her foot out from under the covers, then made a small sound in the back of her throat as she tugged on the pacifier in her mouth.

"The Corcorans are going to try and take my baby, aren't they?" Raine said, stabbing Lucas with her harshest glare. "Isn't that the plan?"

"I honestly don't know. I don't even know how they found out—"

"He's rich, powerful. He can do it." She paced away from him, then back again. "I'll be lucky if I get monthly visitation rights, by the time he's done smearing my reputation. I imagine he'll drum up an endless line of witnesses who will eagerly confirm how I threw myself at Paul with the express purpose of getting pregnant so I could tap into the Corcoran fortune."

A skeptical look came into his eyes, and he shot another quick look at the door. "You saying that's how it happened?"

"I told you to get out, now go!"

On the bed, Caroline stirred again, and Raine grimaced, admonishing herself for raising her voice. "Leave," she whispered harshly.

But Lucas didn't budge; instead, he continued gazing at her with that intense stare he had, as though, if he waited long enough, she'd just cave in and tell him the whole sordid story.

She didn't owe this kidnapping son of a bitch any explanations. He was free to make whatever assumptions about her he wanted; what in the hell did she care what he thought?

Lowering her arms to her sides, she paced away, then turned on her heel to glare at him.

Paul drugged and raped me! she wanted to scream. Fury bloomed inside her heart at how Georgie's boyfriend had taken advantage of her. What he'd done was despicable, and the fact he'd gotten away with it, reprehensible.

For the last nineteen months, she'd wanted to shout the accusation from the rooftops, find a way to prosecute Paul, make him pay emotionally, the way she had paid when she'd awakened and discovered what he'd done. She wanted people to know, to understand she hadn't done anything to bring this on. She had never attempted to seduce Paul Corcoran; in fact, just the opposite.

The very sight of him intimidated her, and she'd always tried to make herself small and unobtrusive whenever he was around.

For a while, though, right after the assault, she had questioned herself. *Had* she done something to encourage him? But the answer was no. Paul was a rapist, a slimy, creepy opportunist. She had done *nothing* to invite his attentions, and the fact he'd gotten away with it ate at her insides like a cancer.

An odd sort of look came into Lucas's eyes, a hardness that hadn't been there before. He shifted his stance and continued to watch her in silence.

She took in a deep breath, trying to force herself to remain calm. It had happened so long ago, and she'd been unconscious—she had no memory of the actual assault.

"I—I was staying with Georgie in San Francisco when she met him," she found herself saying. Oddly enough, just speaking the words out loud, telling someone, *anyone* what had happened, seemed to lighten her burden a little. "Paul was always making suggestive remarks to me, but I shrugged them off, thinking he was just being flirty. He's *like* that."

She crossed her arms over her stomach in a gesture of self-protection. "One day he came by to see Georgie, but she was working late. He asked if he could wait; I said sure. It was a warm evening, so I made iced tea. When I was in the bathroom, he put something in my drink. That's all I remember."

She turned away from Lucas then, shame and embarrassment burning her cheeks. Even so many months after the fact, the memory still had the power to anger and humiliate, as though it had happened just yesterday. "I really do think you should go now."

Lucas came up behind her, and she felt the heat of his body against her back. "You reported the assault to the police." Was that a question, or did he *know*?

"None of your damn business." She whirled on him, smacking her fists against his chest. "I told you what you wanted to know. Now go *away*."

His hands at his sides, he made no move to grab her or defend himself against her fists. Instead, his eyes focused hard on hers. She licked her lips and eased away from him, hugging herself protectively again.

At first she hadn't realized anything had happened. She'd awakened in the morning in her own bed, she'd showered, and begun to realize something wasn't right. She rethought the previous evening. When had Paul left? She didn't remember going to bed, falling asleep. As awareness crept into her brain, she cried out in shock and horror.

Georgie had driven her to the ER, and even though there was evidence of sexual activity, there was no evidence of rape, no bruising, no trauma. The arrogant son of a bitch hadn't even bothered to use a condom.

In spite of her lack of supporting evidence, she filed charges, and the police had talked to Paul. He admitted they'd had sex, but he insisted it was consensual.

Ha. What a joke. She'd never had consensual sex in her life. Intimacy was for other women; normal women. She'd shut that door a long time ago, too afraid to open it.

Whatever Paul had put in her drink was out of her system by the time she'd gone to the hospital. As a result, she couldn't prove a damn thing, and his father's lawyers made it very clear she'd be a fool to try. They'd ruin her reputation, paint her as a whore who'd seduced her best friend's boyfriend. Orphaned girl, bounced from one foster home to the next, troublemaker, promiscuous. By the time they were done with her, it was Raine who'd be in jail for date rape.

She didn't care, but they'd threatened to ruin Georgie, too, and that, she couldn't allow. So she'd dropped the charges, and closed her heart on men for good.

When she'd discovered six weeks after Paul's assault that she was pregnant, she'd been beside herself with pain and confusion. She was pregnant . . . *pregnant*, for God's sake! With Paul Corcoran's bastard child! A child of rape . . .

But it had been that thought that changed everything.

She began to feel sympathy for the baby, *her* baby. A reluctant kind of joy began to build within her. She was going to have a child, something she thought would never happen for her. Her own baby to raise, to love, to smother with all the affection she'd been denied.

Suddenly it no longer mattered how she'd conceived this child, it only mattered that her womb was no longer empty.

After long conversations with Georgie, many tears, and a few visits to a therapist, Raine decided to keep the baby, raise her, create a loving family of her own. Paul would never have to know.

Somebody tapped on the door. Over his shoulder, Lucas said, "Butt out. The lady and I are getting to know each other."

Outside, a man laughed and made a crude remark, then growled, "So don't take all frigging night."

Across the room, Caroline sat up, rubbing her eyes. She popped the pacifier from her mouth and flung it across the bed. "Ghat? Brf dem gha? Momma-ma-ma!" She grinned then, showing her four beautiful little teeth, as she began crawling toward Raine.

"She always wake up in a good mood?" Lucas asked.

"Yes," Raine said softly. "Always."

When Caroline reached the edge of the bed, she raised her chubby little arms and wiggled her fingers.

Bending, Raine lifted the baby, reveling in the weight of her child in her arms. Placing a kiss on the warm, damp cheek, she said, "Hungry?"

"Bfft!"

She turned to Lucas. "Go away now."

He gave another hasty glance at the door, then

stabbed her with a hard stare. "Drink the coffee. I had them make it extra strong. It'll keep you awake, alert."

"Why would I need—"

"Just do it." Moving to the door, he rapped on it twice. The key turned in the lock. Putting his index finger against his lips, gave her a nod, opened the door, and left.

Chapter Seventeen

A mantra is a prayer recited aloud. To invoke
peace and calm during times of great stress,
repeat the Heart-Calming mantra: *Gate gate
para gate para sum gate bodhi swaha.*

Georgiana Mundy's *Feng Shui for Lovers*

Ethan ended his conversation with his brother,
flicked his cell phone closed, and slid it into
the pocket of his jeans, all the while keeping his
eyes on Georgie.

She was exhausted . . . and beside herself with
justified outrage. Her beautiful eyes were rimmed
with red; stress and anger showed in the tight line
of her mouth. Her skin was pale, shocky. Though
she said not a word, accusation was clear to see on
her face.

"It's a six-hour drive north," he said. "We're
both tired and hungry. I think we should have
something to eat, then get some sleep. We can
leave just before dawn and be home by noon."

She raised her chin with exactly the air of defiance he'd expected. "I'm not tired. If you are, I can drive."

"It's not that, Georgie. You're just as worn out as I am. We both need a few hours' downtime—"

"Then I'll take Raine's car and go myself."

"Go where?"

She blinked at him as though the answer were so obvious as to make his question insulting. "I—I, well, back to San Francisco. Paul and Vaughn live in an enormous mansion in Pacific Heights. I'll go *there*, and—"

"And what?" he argued gently. "If you even get past the gates . . . there *are* gates, I assume? If you get anywhere near the front door, you'll do what? Huff and puff and blow his house down?"

"But if he has Raine and Caroline in there—"

"Regardless, he'll have you prosecuted for huffing and puffing without a license, and falsely accusing him of kidnapping."

She raised her hands in the air in a gesture of helpless frustration. "Well, it's better than just sitting here, watching the clock, wondering . . ."

Her words trailed off, lost some of their heat. She lowered her hands. She'd hit the argument wall, and they both knew it.

Closing the gap between them, he curled his fingers around her shoulders. "I know you're worried. But the Corcorans would be fools to hurt either of them. I don't know what they have planned, or why they took Raine and the kid, but no harm will come to them. I'm positive."

"You were also positive Lucas Russell was going to protect them!"

"Guilty as charged," he bit out. "And now I'm going to make it right. After I do, you never have to see me again. Deal?"

Her brows furrowed in a frown as she stared into his eyes.

"It's hard to sit and do nothing, Georgie, but—"

"Whatever." She stiffened. "I'm going to call the police—"

"Not an option. The orders were, no cops, and no FBI. Besides, I can't risk the authorities intervening and screwing things up."

Her doubled fists slammed into his chest as she glared up at him, a warrior goddess ready to do battle to avenge the ones she loved. "*You* can't risk it? A woman and a baby have been kidnapped! *Some*body has to do *some*thing!"

He closed his hands over hers, holding them prisoner against his chest. She squirmed, but he tightened his grip.

"Somebody *is* doing something, Georgie. Bringing in the local cops won't do any good since Corcoran and Lucas are long gone by now."

"Then who—"

"My brother Nate is a detective with the SFPD. He's going to do some checking, set up surveillance points, but keep it real low-key. Vaughn Corcoran is a very powerful man with political connections up the ying-yang. He's bound to have some law enforcement types in his pocket. Nate's doing all this on the QT, so word can't trickle up."

Her glittering eyes searched his. "Your brother? He's a good detective?"

"He's a great detective," Ethan answered without hesitation. "He'll come through for us." Tilting his head, he said, "And if you ever tell him I said that, I'll deny it."

She blinked and looked a little taken aback. "You don't like your brother?"

He shrugged, but didn't let go of her hands, still fisted against his chest. "I like him enough to take a bullet for him."

For a moment, her eyes flicked down to his side, then she met his gaze again. "Is that what happened?" she whispered. "You stepped in front of a bullet to save your brother?"

"Something like that," he said. "Listen, it's getting dark. I say we eat, sleep for a few hours, then hit the road about five."

For a moment, she looked like she wanted to pursue the matter, but instead closed her eyes. When she opened them again, she said, "All right. I don't like it, dammit, but all right."

He released one of her hands to brush her hair away from her face. Tipping her chin up, he sought her eyes once more. "I've got to make a few calls, talk to a few people who can help us. Could you make us something to eat? If you're too tired, we can call for delivery."

She shook her head. "I'm not hungry."

"You need to eat, whether you feel like it or not. You need the fuel. By the time we get back to Marin—"

"Marin?" Her eyes narrowed on him and she backed out of his embrace. "Why Marin? I told you, the Corcorans live in Pacific Heights."

He wasn't sure how much to tell her. While he didn't want to get her hopes up, he didn't want to frighten her any more than she already was, either. Hell. After what he'd put her through, he owed her the truth.

"My gut tells me Lucas's involvement in all this may not have been voluntary. I think he's planning something to get Raine and the baby out of danger. If he makes a run for it, I think he'll head for my house in Marin."

A myriad of emotions crossed Georgie's face, and he realized she'd begun to steel herself against whatever happened over the next few days. Watching her, he felt himself fall for her a little more, a little harder, a little more completely. She was tough and strong and smart.

But he'd fucked it up. Again. He'd finally gotten her to open up to him a little, trust him a little, and he'd blown it. No matter what his feelings for her were, she'd never return them, not now.

"If he does make a run for it," she said softly, "when will you know?"

"All I can say is that Raine and the baby are safe. I know your level of confidence in me is just about gutter-height right now, but I'm asking you to trust me, Georgie, this one last time. Between whatever Lucas is planning and what my brother is doing, Raine and the baby will be returned to you, unharmed. I'll stake my life on it."

Lucas played a slow game of solitaire at the small table in the room he shared with Honcho Espinoza, one of Paul Corcoran's two goons. Honcho's cohort, Drool, was a head shorter than the gargantuan Hispanic, and sported an overbite so severe, his speech was virtually incomprehensible.

Between them, Lucas thought, Honcho and Drool probably had a combined IQ equaling their individual chest measurements. They were muscle, paid to dance to Corcoran's tune and not care one way or the other about the melody. They looked like career criminals, and probably had rap sheets as long as his right leg.

Flicking over the next card, he eyed his options, placing the queen of hearts onto the king of clubs. He flipped another. The jack of diamonds. No place for it; he flipped again.

As for Junior Corcoran, Paul had seemed distracted and uncomfortable ever since they'd nabbed Raine and the baby. The baby. The way Corcoran looked at that kid, it was almost as though he hadn't known she existed until he and his thugs had burst into Raine's house and seen the playpen.

He turned over the last card. The joker. How in the hell had that gotten in the deck? He tossed it aside just as Honcho slammed the door open and stalked into the room. In his burly arms, he carried two grocery bags.

Dumping one of them out onto the twin bed closest to the door, he rummaged through the packages of sandwiches, Fritos, Chee·tos, and cellophane-wrapped junk food. Peeling back the paper from a gigantic burrito, he bit off a huge chunk. Past the bulge in his cheek, he snarled, "Hey, Russell. You can eat whatever you want, man, but keep your fucking paws off the Twinkies." From the second bag, he pulled a can of beer. Curling his meaty fingers around it, he popped the top with his thumb.

"Who's watching her door?" Lucas ventured, as he ripped open a bag of corn chips. "We spending the night here, or are we leaving soon?"

Honcho raised the aluminum can to his fleshy mouth and took several large swallows. Wiping his lips on the back of his hand, he said, "Drool's got it covered for now. Soon as it's real dark, we're gonna split. You be ready, amigo." His cold-eyed glare told Lucas that Honcho's calling him friend was simply a force of habit.

Food in hand, the hefty goon sank onto the edge of the mattress, which squeaked in protest at his weight. Locating the remote, he turned on the TV and began channel-surfing.

As Lucas picked up the cards and shuffled the deck, he absently popped a couple of chips in his mouth, enjoying the salty taste, reminding him it had been hours since he'd eaten.

How in the hell was he going to get a woman and a baby away from these guys? Maybe he should sneak off somewhere, call Ethan and set up an ambush, but that might go wrong and Raine or the kid would get hurt.

Dealing the cards out, he began to move them around, red to black, black to red. He crunched down on another mouthful of corn chips.

The dingy motel sat on the outskirts of Goleta, just a few miles north of Santa Barbara. Paul had apparently chosen it because the clientele seemed to be nil, they could park in front of their rooms, and come and go without the manager watching their every move.

The six of them were divided among three rooms, with two men in rooms on either side of Raine's. All the front doors faced the parking lot, and the only other exits were tiny windows above the tubs in the bathroom. Tiny being the significant word, since Caroline might have been able to fit through the window, but not Raine, and certainly not Lucas.

Even if he were to find a way to spirit her and the kid away, if the baby woke up during the process and cried, Lucas would undoubtedly be killed, leaving Raine to face three felons by herself.

Not an option.

He discounted Junior as much of threat. Paul was one of those glamour pusses—all looks, all attitude, sliding by on his old man's money and reputation, but a coward to the core. The fact he'd drugged a woman to have sex with her pretty much said it all.

And while Drool had a weapon, he was moronic and slow. Probably a small-time thug, petty crimes, misdemeanors, but without the killer instincts that seeped from every one of the Hispanic's pores.

Behind him, Honcho had settled on *Maury*, and seemed deeply interested in which of a pair of brothers had fathered some poor teenager's kid. The weepy young mother swore she'd been faithful to the older brother. Well, pretty sure anyway.

"She did it," Honcho mumbled past a mouthful of Twinkie. "Like, you can tell, man. She looks guilty as hell to me. Hey, Lucas. Don't you think this bitch looks guilty?"

Lucas spared a glance at the TV, where the large, pimple-faced teen was dabbing her eyes with a tissue.

"Yeah, I guess," he said as he checked his watch. "Give me the key, would you? I want to go visit my girlfriend, take her some Fritos. Maybe that'll make her a little more friendly."

Honcho snorted, then reached into the pocket of his stained white T-shirt, pulling out Raine's room key. Tossing it to Lucas, he warned, "Be back in five minutes, or I come looking for you, which I guarantee you would not want. Oh, and leave your cell phone and gun on the bed, *compañero*."

Shit, Lucas thought. "No problem," he said, scooping up a bag of corn chips.

As he let himself into Raine's room, he checked his watch again. Five minutes to form a plan for her escape. Five damn minutes.

It would just have to do.

Chapter Eighteen

To heighten your love life, place exactly three
or nine new plants in your bedroom. This vital-
izes the atmosphere, adding positive energy,
hope, and good cheer. And if those plants happen to have pink blossoms, then lie back and
prepare to be amazed!

Georgiana Mundy's *Feng Shui for Lovers*

Outside the kitchen window, a crescent moon
hung above the distant rooftops, a tipsy grin
among a thousand winking stars. Staring into the
velvet night, Georgie tried to cleanse her mind
of the pain she'd seen in Ethan's eyes when she'd
accused him of failing to protect Raine. He'd
clenched his jaw, refusing to defend himself, letting her vent her fury and fear on him.

She'd seen past his hazel eyes, deep into his
soul, and in that moment, she knew there was
nothing she could say to him, no accusation she
could levy that would punish him more than he
was punishing himself. Though she'd glimpsed

in Ethan's eyes what Lucas Russell's betrayal had cost him, she'd continued scolding him. Maybe something inside her had hoped if she yelled loud enough, it would drown out the sound of her own guilt at what she was doing to him.

Picking up the can opener, she twirled the handle idly in her hand. She knew Ethan better now, knew his moods; she'd witnessed his strengths, gotten a sense of his vulnerabilities. Though he could undoubtedly hold his own in a fistfight with five men, it had only taken a few harsh words from her to knock the wind out of him.

Even though she'd spoken from shock and worry, she wished she could call back those words. They'd struck him like barbed arrows through the heart; she'd seen in his eyes that they'd hit their mark. Hot guilt had replaced icy anger, and she felt her cheeks flush in shame.

Now that she'd put a little distance between Ethan and herself, she'd gained some perspective on what had happened; it hadn't been his fault. All he'd done, really, was put his faith in the wrong person. And he'd been unexpectedly betrayed.

That was something she understood right down to the atomic layer of her being.

His voice had shaken with determination as he'd promised to fix things, to make it all right. Though his expression had remained stony, she knew her words had wounded him, and she feared their poison would remain in his blood a long time.

Filling a large saucepan with cold water, she set it on the stove and turned up the heat, then went to the cupboard, where she pulled out a couple of red Fiesta ware soup bowls and set them on the table. By the time she'd added spoons, napkins, and tumblers, the water had come to a rolling boil. She tore open three cellophane packages and dumped the contents into the burbling water. After a quick stir, she put a lid on the pot and lowered the heat.

"Smells good," Ethan said from behind her. "What are we—"

"Top Ramen," she said. "It's almost done. Sit down."

As she turned toward him, he was staring at the pan, disappointment glazing his eyes. "Oh."

"Hey, you're lucky it's not a peanut butter and jelly sandwich and apple juice in a sippy cup, pal. The lettuce and meat were spoiled from sitting in the car all day."

"Georgie, I—"

"Let's not talk about it." She kept her tone soft, quiet. "For a while, let's just not talk about it, okay?"

"Look, I know today has been rough—"

He reached for her, but his cell phone buzzed in his pocket, diverting his attention. Flipping it open, he scowled, then looked at Georgie. "Sorry. I'd better take this." The phone to his ear, he said, "Yeah, Mom?"

Georgie cocked an interested ear in his direction as she poured soup into the two bowls. The kitchen windows steamed over, and the scent of salty chicken broth filled the air.

"I'm not in San Francisco right now, Mom," he said patiently, as he slid into one of the chairs at the table. "I can't come by until . . . no, not then. I'm in the middle of . . . yeah, that might work out, but if . . . uh-huh." He nodded a few times, then fisted his fingers around his spoon. "Maybe you should see a specialist. Obviously, the doctors you've been seeing . . . uh-huh. No, Andie can't, Mom. She just started an undercover assignment. Of course she didn't give you any details. It's *undercover*. No, Nate's busy being a newlywed."

He lowered his gaze and seemed to study his soup bowl. "I'll take care of . . . uh-huh . . . uh-huh. Look, I'll call you tomorrow and work out the details. We're just sitting down to eat, and . . . what? Yeah, I said we." He flashed a quick look at Georgie. "No, Mom, she's a client. Yes, *she* means the client is a woman. No, a *client*, Mom. I *know* Nate just got married. I was his best . . . no, Mom. It's not like that. I'm not seeing anyone. Listen, I have to go. You sure you're okay? Good. I'll call you tomorrow—"

Georgie slid into the seat across from Ethan's as he closed his eyes, rolled his lips together, and listened to whatever his mother was going on and on about; it didn't take a genius to figure out what that was.

He began to nod and lean forward a little like people do when they're hurrying to end a phone conversation. "I'll call you when I get back to town. Okay. Yeah. Me, too."

After he flipped the phone closed and set it back on the table, Georgie took a sip of soup, wondering which part of his conversation she should address first. Begin generally, she decided, then hone it down to specifics. "She just wants you to be happy."

He grunted, and sprinkled salt and pepper on the hot liquid in his bowl. "My mom hasn't got a clue what kind of life I lead, and I try very hard to keep it that way."

"Then why didn't you let your brother take care of your mom's problem?"

He shrugged, averted his eyes.

"Are you everyone's champion, Ethan?"

Flashing her a look, he said, "No," just like a petulant little boy. If there'd been a pebble on the ground in front of him, he'd have kicked it.

"I think you are, or you think you should be. Some people would call that kind of behavior controlling, but I think it's just because you feel you have to take care of everyone."

"I take care of myself," he groused. "That's it."

Georgie shook her head. "It's taken me a while, but I finally figured it out. I'll bet it's why you became a policeman, and why you're in the security business now. To take *care* of people, keep them safe. You were born to be a good guy. A hero—"

"I'm no hero, Georgie," he growled, his eyes snapping with sudden anger. "You certainly have evidence of *that*. Let's just eat and skip the psychobabble, all right?"

She should let it rest. They were tired, and the situation with Raine pressed down on both of them in painful proportions. But she couldn't let it rest, not now, not with her newfound knowledge of the way she felt about him.

"I don't want to pick any nits," she said slowly, swirling her spoon through the noodles in her bowl. "But you told me just this morning that I was *not* your client, yet I just heard you tell your mother I was. You also said you weren't seeing anyone. Now, if I were the type whose feelings got easily hurt . . ."

She shoved a glop of the savory noodles into her mouth, leaving the sentence for him to finish.

He scowled. "We are not talking about this right now."

She swallowed. "Okay. Let's talk about something else. Why don't you like your family?"

"I like my family about as much as anybody likes their family." He twirled some noodles around his spoon and lifted it to his mouth.

"Don't you like your brother's new wife?"

Around the bulge in his cheek, he admitted, "Tabitha's great."

"So it's your brother you don't like?"

"We have issues. Be quiet and eat. I need go get some sleep."

"Who's Andie?"

"My sister."

"She's a cop, too?"

He nodded.

"Working undercover must be very dangerous. Don't you worry about her?"

"All the time. But she's a police officer. She knows the risks."

"All of them?"

Setting his spoon down, his motions stilled, he looked into her eyes, and she knew she'd just crossed over into very dangerous territory. "What in the hell do you mean by that?"

She set her own spoon down and laid her hands in her lap. "Tell me about Cathy. Please."

He shook his head.

"I'm sorry for those things I said to you earlier. I know what happened wasn't your fault. I blamed you because I didn't know who else to blame." She lifted her gaze to his. "I know you did your best. Everything will be all right. I . . . I believe in you—"

"Don't," he snapped. "You have every right to be angry with me. I fucked up."

"You trusted this Lucas Russell guy. You must have had your reasons. How could you know he'd do . . . what he did?"

He blinked, squared his shoulders. "We are not discussing this right now. Not any of it."

Georgie took in a deep breath, nodded as though she were agreeing with him. Then, "I . . . care about you. And after my behavior earlier, I feel a sense of obligation to try and smooth things out. Please, Ethan. Tell me about Cathy. It's obvious that whatever happened with you and her has left you very wounded—"

"I'm not wounded." He laughed, too quickly, too easily. "Jesus, lady. Haven't you ever heard that no means no? I do not want to talk about Cathy. Besides, it was a long time ago. Just drop it, okay?"

She waited a moment, then said, "Earlier, you asked me to trust you, and I did—"

"But I—"

"Doesn't matter. You held up your end of the bargain. Believe me, I'm the last person to try and convince somebody to let down their guard, but Ethan, I see it in your eyes, whenever Cathy's name is mentioned. So much pain—"

"Stop it! Leave me and my pain alone, Georgie. This is *none* of your business." He shoved another bite into his mouth and stared into her eyes, challenging her to keep quiet.

Too bad for him she was lousy at heeding warnings.

"We *are* going to talk about this, Ethan, because whatever happened has become a barrier between us. I sat here just now and listened while you outright lied to your mother. You *are* seeing someone, and it's *me*. Yeah, I was pissed at you earlier, but I've moved on now and I've decided I don't want any barriers between us!"

Ethan crossed his arms over his chest. The muscle of his jaw worked as he studied the table.

"Oh, you're one of *those* guys, aren't you?" she

pressed. "The kind that, when he loses somebody he loves, keeps everybody at an arm's length, never allowing himself to love again because losing them hurts so much."

"That's not true," he bit out, stabbing her with those intense eyes.

"Well, try having *nobody*, and see how you like that!" she huffed. "Try bouncing from foster home to foster home for years and years and years, never landing anywhere for long, never forming bonds, and when you do, they yank you away and set you down somewhere else. Try having a childhood of Thanksgivings, Christmases, New Year's Eves alone. Bickering with somebody, *anybody* would be better than staring at the walls, all by yourself!"

He leaned toward her, his eyes glazed with fury. "You think being alone is bad, and sure, it can be. I'm sorry you suffered the way you did. I mean that. The ideal everyone wants is a happy family where times spent together are fun. But some families have so much baggage, so much conflict, so much *shit*, you're better off being alone! Families are not perfect. It depends on the *people* involved, their relationships, their history, external forces. Happiness is not a given, Georgie. It's not the default value."

Crossing her arms, she said, "All right. Granted. But I don't think that's true of you and your family."

"And you know *so much* about my family," he said dryly.

"I don't. But I know *you*, better than you think. And I've heard you on the phone to your brother and your mom. And I've heard the tone in your voice when you speak of your sister. I think you love them all just fine. Yeah, there's some stuff going on between you and Nate, but it's not so big you can't work it out."

"Thank you so much, Dr. I-Don't-Know-Crap."

She let her spoon fall to the table. "How'd we end up talking about your family? We were talking about Cathy!"

"No, we were *not* talking about Cathy. We were specifically—"

"I love you, Ethan!" she blurted, jumping to her feet. Her hands flat on the table, she leaned forward, glaring into his surprised, then suddenly guarded eyes. "I *love* you. I've felt it coming on for days now, like a virus you're hoping you can fight off. But I can't fight it off, and today I realized I don't want to. I've got a bad case of *you*, and I can't ignore the symptoms. I *love* you, you jerk! Now, what in the hell are you going to do about *that*?"

The words hung in the air between them. The kitchen grew quiet. A night bird squawked in the distance. A car drove by. A drop of water splashed from the faucet into the sink.

Ethan's eyes dulled as he set his mouth in a grim line across his face. "Don't love me, Georgie. Do yourself a favor and don't love me."

"Too late," she whispered. She reached down to stroke his cheek, but he bolted up, grabbing her shoulders, shoving her away. Behind him, his chair toppled noisily to the floor.

"For God's sake, *stop it!*" he choked. "You want to know about Cathy? Okay, fine. Here it is. Cathy didn't get sick, she wasn't in a car accident or a plane crash! I *killed* her. Do you hear me? Are you getting this, Georgie? *Cathy* loved me, too, and I killed her!"

Chapter Nineteen

Karma is the fate you've created for yourself
in this life as a result of your actions in past
lives. Also, what you do in this life will affect
what happens to you in future lives. In other
words, you create your own reality, whether
it's good . . . or not so good. If you have found
love to be elusive, you may, in effect, have only
yourself to blame. Strive to solve your problems in this life, or they will circle around to
torment you again.

Georgiana Mundy's *Feng Shui for Lovers*

I t was pathetic, the way Georgie was looking up
at him. Pity shone in her eyes. Pity he didn't
want, didn't need, and sure as hell didn't deserve.

Just looking at her made his chest hurt. He
wanted to shove her away, far away, out of his
sight and out of his mind.

He wanted to pull her close, bury his hands in
her glorious hair, feel her warm body pressed
against him. Lose himself in her.

He wished to hell he'd never met Georgiana Mundy. Then his world wouldn't have turned inside out, the ache in his heart he'd finally learned to ignore wouldn't have begun slicing him to pieces again, making him feel things he had no business feeling. When he was with Georgie, he wanted those things, those very things he didn't deserve to have.

Turning away from her, he started to leave the kitchen when he felt her fingers wrap around his wrist, halting his progress. Compassion shone in her eyes like candlelight, showing him the way to his own personal heaven.

"Please," she whispered, moving close to him. "Don't shut me out, Ethan. Share with me what happened. I want to know. I *need* to know."

He gazed down at her as his brain battled with his carefully submerged emotions.

Twisting his wrist, he captured her hand in his, tugging her through the door, down the shadowy hall, and into a dark bedroom. He didn't even know which one, he only knew that telling her what he had done could not stand the scrutiny of a bright kitchen light.

Besides, he didn't think he could bear to see the look in her eyes when she discovered what kind of man he was, what kind of man he *really* was.

In the darkness, he sat on the edge of the bed, feeling the mattress dip slightly under his weight. Without a word, Georgie eased down next to him.

The house was perfectly quiet now except for the rhythm of her breathing. As the small room filled with the scent of her floral soap, he inhaled deeply, letting the subtle fragrance calm him.

Releasing her hand, he leaned forward, placing his elbows on his knees. The wound in his side had begun to ache again; he ignored it.

"I was the detective in charge," he said. Beside him, Georgie inched a little closer. "We'd been after this guy for a couple of years. Drugs, mostly. Armed robbery. Human trafficking. Bad dude. We finally cornered him with the goods in a warehouse down on the docks. But before we had the scene secured, he'd grabbed a couple of hostages, two teenage girls who'd been riding bikes down by the waterfront. The procedure is, when hostages are involved, you've got to call for a negotiator."

"And they sent Cathy."

He nodded, blew out a harsh breath. "Yeah. They sent Cathy . . ."

"Hey, handsome," Cathy'd said when she stepped from behind the wheel of the silver metallic BMW that had been a birthday gift from her upper-crust father. In her white silk pantsuit, she looked like she was on her way to a society luncheon, not heading off to verbally wrangle with some low-life slimeball. "I hear you need a little help on this one."

Ethan had frowned into her blue eyes. Rays from the setting sun turned her cheeks a pale amber and brushed her blond hair with streaks of gold. "I didn't ask for you," he said. "Let me get someone else in here."

"Such a worrywart." Smiling, she tapped him on the chest. "It's my job, and I'm good at it, *and* my name was next on rotation. You just cover my ass, okay, good-lookin'?"

"Cathy, I—"

"Not your call, Inspector," she said, pulling her shoulder-length hair into a ponytail, fastening it with one of those elastic things. In the dying light, as she slipped into her Kevlar vest, his engagement ring sparkled on her left hand. "Let's do this. Tell me what we've got."

He stared down at her for a few more seconds. Blue and red lights flashed around them, bathing them both in fire and ice. In the distance, sirens blared, announcing the approach of more police units. Somewhere along the line, a bubble-headed TV newscaster had shown up and had to be hauled away to a safe distance outside the perimeter.

"This isn't good, Cath," he said. "Perp's holding two teen girls hostage. Access to weapons, and at least three armed men backing him up. If it goes bad, you'll—"

"What's his name? What'd he do? What does he want?"

Ethan shook his head in frustration, but finally allowed her to ignore his concerns for her safety. Inside his stomach, his guts twisted painfully.

"Charlie Wong," he said, his voice all business now. "Narcotics, mostly. Hasn't made any demands, but I'd imagine a free pass out of here would be high on his list."

She'd nodded, given him a wink, then gone out to do her job.

The hours dragged by, tensions mounted. At first, Wong wouldn't talk to her, but as time passed and he and his thugs grew restless, hungry, and worried, he finally caved.

With her cell phone to her ear, she said to Ethan, "He wants a van, a full gas tank, he takes the girls with him, and lets them go once he's sure he's not being followed." To Wong, she said, "No deal, Charlie. You release the hostages, then we'll talk again."

Flipping the phone closed, she met Ethan's eyes. "He wants a face-to-face, right now."

"It's not going to happen."

"Yes, it is. My call, Inspector. The girls are in bad shape, Ethan, you know what I'm saying? We've got to get them out of there."

"*Shit.*"

That was the last thing he'd ever said to Cathy. She'd taken that stupid-ass sentiment with her into eternity. Why couldn't it have been *I love you*? In the last six years, he'd asked himself that question a thousand times.

Next to him, Georgie eased a little closer, slid her arm around his back.

"She was good at her job," he said quietly. "Very good. I thought it would be okay. I didn't know the guy was determined to die. Suicide by cop, they call it. He knew there was no way out, didn't want prison. Decided to take as many cops with him as he could."

The warmth of Georgie's palm seeped through his shirt, reassuring him, silently encouraging him to continue.

"Wong exits the building," he said, reliving the scene—the uniforms moving quickly into position, the shouts ringing in his ears, the scream of sirens. The stench of tension and fear fills his nostrils. The goddamned fog is thick, getting thicker. His visibility's impaired. Under his breath, he spits out a vile curse.

"He's holding one of the girls in front of him. Kid's crying, terrified. Sharpshooters are in place now. We all have weapons drawn. Cathy's wearing her vest, but has no weapon. She reaches to pull the hostage away from Wong. The girl stumbles, falls to her knees, putting Cathy in the direct line of fire."

Cathy hadn't budged. She'd held her ground, keeping herself between Wong and the frightened teenager, giving the girl time to crawl to safety.

"A heavy mist has rolled in and I can't see Cathy very well. The scene isn't favorable for us, and I want to just get her out of there. I yell at her to step back so we can get a clear shot, but suddenly there's a barrage of fire from the warehouse. Wong goes nuts. Makes a grab for Cathy just as his cohorts burst from the door behind him. We return fire."

He stopped, licked his lips, trying to remember, desperate to forget.

"Cath . . . Cathy goes down," he whispered. "I

see her pitch forward and fall from the pier into the water. I go in after her. Damned water is like ice. I shout her name, but I hear nothing but foghorns, gunshots, sirens."

He'd splashed around in the water, calling for her over and over as cold salt water filled his mouth, his nose, stung his eyes.

"My hand . . . I feel . . . it's Cathy. She's face down. Face down in the water." He ran splayed fingers through his hair. "She's face down."

He thought he heard Georgie say she was sorry, but the buzz in his ears was too loud to tell.

"There are others in the water now, trying to get Cathy out. I'm giving her mouth-to-mouth, but . . ."

In between breaths, he yelled her name, begged her to come back to him.

But she was gone.

And all he could think was, he'd said *Shit*, when he should have said *I love you*.

What can a man do when he doesn't get a second chance to make things right? He was a man who fixed things. Where was his do-over? Where was Cathy's?

"Ethan," Georgie said gently, "it was the circumstances. You can't keep blaming yourself—"

"No?" he shouted, surging to his feet. In the dimly lit room, he could see her upturned face, her eyes wide in shock. She thought that was all there was, but wait until he dropped the big one on her.

"You don't understand, Georgie," he snarled.

The pain in his side burned like a son of a bitch. The words he was about to say lodged hard in his throat—the damning words that would push Georgie out of his reach forever. But he had to say them, she had to know. It was the only way she'd realize he wasn't the man she thought he was. "You don't *get* it, do you? When they did the autopsy, they found . . . they found . . . hell, it was *my* bullet that killed her, Georgie. *My* bullet. *Mine!*"

Scrubbing his face with his open palm, he paced the room. "I've gone over the scene a thousand times, maybe a million. I don't know how it happened. But it did. It fucking *did*."

He tightened his jaw, willing himself to stay calm, unemotional.

"She was going to be my wife, Georgie. I *loved* her, and I'm the one who killed her! How can I justify that? How can anyone? Huh? The bullet severed the carotid, lodged in one of the vertebrae in her neck. If it hadn't stuck there, I never would have known, always would have assumed. But it was *mine*. She was dead before . . . before I could—"

"Ethan," Georgie whispered, his name mere breath on her lips. Rising to her feet, she pressed her palms to his chest. "I'm so sorry. I'm so, so sorry."

"I'm no hero," he growled. "Don't love—"

"Shh," she hissed, putting her fingertips gently to his lips, silencing him. "Don't do this. It's okay, it's okay. C'mere. Come. It's okay."

He stood unbending, unyielding, as she wrapped her arms tightly around him. She whispered things in the dark, he had no idea what. His brain was still back there, under that pier, in that black water, his arms still held Cathy's lifeless body as he choked out her name.

Suddenly the strain was too much, and he bent his head, burying his face against Georgie's warm neck. His arms whipped around her, yanking her hard into him as he let himself succumb to her soft words and caresses.

Her silky hair was warm, and he reveled in the scent and sensation of it. Woman . . . soft woman . . . loving woman . . . Georgie. He needed this. His tortured soul needed this. Needed her. As wrong as it was, he just couldn't shove her away.

She pulled back a bit, lifting her head, and he felt her lips against his mouth.

The dam exploded. The emotions he'd suppressed for so long, the pain, the sorrow, burst from his chest. He thrust his fingers through her hair, arching her neck, kissing her violently. The kisses became hungrier, more urgent, more carnal. He couldn't stop, wouldn't, not until he'd consumed her. A fire burned inside him, scorching his guts, and only Georgie could soothe the wounds.

Thrusting his tongue into her mouth, he tasted her, slid his tongue along hers, turned their bodies until they fell onto the bed.

"Ethan," she panted against his open mouth as she began pulling at his clothes.

Unable to speak, he made a strangled cry at the back of his throat—the sound of a beast in heat. He tore at her clothing until she was naked. Blindly, wildly, he ran his hands over her body, cupping her breasts, devouring her nipples with tender nips and bites.

She squirmed beneath him, sliding her fingers through his hair, keeping his head against her breasts, urging him to feed himself on her passion.

Reaching down, he popped the buttons of his jeans, but her hand was there, tugging the fabric aside, gliding her fingers along his slick length. She moaned, whispered words of encouragement, then parted her legs to let him settle deeper into their embrace.

He nudged her knees wider apart until nothing stood between him and his goal. In one long thrust, he was inside her, pumping hard. The headboard slammed the wall in time with Georgie's gasping breaths. Inside his chest, his heart thundered against his ribs, but he bared his teeth, and thrust again, and again.

Her legs curled around his waist, holding him in place while she raised her hips off the bed in time with his ravaging thrusts. In his ear, she sighed his name again, and again, and again, caressing his heated flesh with her fingertips.

He stilled, fighting for breath, fighting to keep his brain separated from his actions. He didn't want to think, only wanted to feel. Only wanted Georgie's softness all around him, her sweetness.

He thrust again, and she cried out. Again, and she nearly screamed. Once more, and she tumbled, her body jerking, her cries of completion urging him on.

He came, hard, hot, fast, inside her, emptying himself, filling her. In that moment, he ceased to be a man, but became a mate, a primal creature bonded completely with his feminine opposite. They moved together as one, breathing in time, holding on tight, reveling in their wholeness.

Clenching his jaw, he pinched his eyes closed and fought to fill his lungs with air. Under him, Georgie had gone limp and languid, her gentle fingertips sliding up his back, along his shoulders, making little swirls as she eased them up his neck to caress his hair.

"Georgie," he whispered, resting his forehead on hers. "God. I didn't mean to . . . I'm sorry . . . that was—"

"Shhh," she panted softly. "It's okay . . . it's okay . . . don't be sorry. You're so good . . . you make me feel so good . . . don't ever be sorry . . ." Her fingers played with the damp ends of his hair as she seemed to relax beneath him.

I love you. I love you, Georgie. I wish I could tell you . . .

Unable to say the words, he rolled off her, then wrapped his arms around her waist, tugging her body close into his. He bent his head and placed a gentle kiss on her neck, hoping tenderness would be enough for her to know his feelings.

He felt her back move against his chest as she

inhaled a deep breath. She wiggled a little, nestling her sweet butt into his crotch. Sliding his leg over hers, he trapped her there and let himself enjoy the feel of her in his arms.

"I need to get something straight," she said, then placed a kiss on his forearm. "And it's not what you think." She bumped him with her butt, and he chuckled.

"Keep doing that, and something *will* be straight, and it *will* be what you think."

She settled closer. "Okay, think about this, then. Six years ago, a bullet from your gun found its way into the body of an on-duty hostage negotiator during a violent and confusing confrontation with a drug dealer and his gang, and you've been blaming yourself for it ever since."

He thought about it for a moment. "Granted," he said cautiously. "That's one way of putting it. Where are you going with this, Georgie?"

"Well, what if the situation had been reversed?"

"You mean, what if I had been the drug-dealing—"

"No." She wiggled free of his embrace, turned, and faced him. "What I'm saying is, what if Cathy had been the detective, and you had been the negotiator? What if the scene played out the same way, but instead of *you* shooting *her, she* shot *you*?" She searched his eyes as though seeking some long-lost truth. On a mere breath, she said, "What if you had been the one to die? Ethan, would you have wanted *her* to beat herself up forever and ever because of a horrible *accident*? An ironic and bizarre twist of fate?"

He blinked at her. At her bare waist, his fingers tightened. "Of course not. But that's not the way—"

"Maybe that's not the way it happened, but the fact remains, if the situation were reversed, and she was the one who accidentally shot and killed you, you'd want her to forgive herself, wouldn't you? Not blame herself for something that was nobody's fault? You'd want her to put it behind her, find someone else, be happy. Isn't that what you want for someone you love?"

His eyes burned. "You have no right—"

Her hand came up and she cupped his jaw. "I do. I really do. I do because I love you, and I hurt when I see the pain in your eyes."

"You have a little hurt in your eyes, too, you know."

In the darkness, he saw one brow arch. "Don't try and redirect the conversation, buster. It won't work."

"Fine. But you're hurt, and I see it. It makes me crazy. Makes me want to go after every person who's ever harmed you."

Her mouth found his in a gentle kiss. When she pulled away, she said, "See? Like I said, everybody's champion. But I'm flattered, nonetheless."

He swallowed, letting her words rumble through his brain. "Okay, we're both in pain. It's the price you pay for being human, I suppose."

"I disagree," she rushed. "I think the cost is

temporary and there is a limit, especially when the person paying the price was a victim. What do you say we make a deal?"

As he looked into her eyes, his heart wanted to shatter. How had he ever been so lucky to have found a woman like Georgie? Damn, she not only met his every move, challenged him on every level, she forced him to challenge himself. She wasn't going to let this go until she was damn good and ready.

"What kind of deal?"

She kissed him again, a slow, melting kiss that warmed his blood and fuzzed his brain. When their lips parted, she whispered, "Let it go now, Ethan. Let it go *now*, this minute. Never forget Cathy and what you had, but go *now*, out into the world, and be happy. It's what Cathy would want. You're being terribly unfair to her memory by not giving yourself a chance at happiness. She sounds like a strong woman. She's going to be really pissed at you when you see her again in the After-life."

Past the spears of pain and doubt in his heart, he said, "Yeah, she had quite a temper. Didn't take any shit off of anybody. Like someone else I know."

She shrugged, making her bare breasts rub against his chest. "I guess it's your curse to be attracted to smart, strong women."

Smiling into her eyes, he said, "Okay, if that's my part of the deal, what's yours?"

"Mine? Oh, well, that I . . . uh . . ."

"How about that you let your guard down a little? That you step out from behind that barrier you've built, and start trusting people. Not everyone is out to screw you over, Georgie."

"I've stepped. I mean, I told you I love you, didn't I?"

"Love and trust are two different things, Georgie. I'm a clueless male, and even I know that. Love usually implies trust, but in your case, it's an add-on, sort of like when you buy an electronic gizmo and the box says *batteries sold separately*."

Her brow creased in a worried frown. "All right. Deal. You put Cathy's death behind you, and I go buy some batteries."

Smiling at her, he said, "Deal. I guess we can work out the details later. Right now I'm starving. Can we heat up that soup?"

He helped her off the bed, then began retrieving her clothes from the floor where he'd tossed them in his haste to get her naked. Down the hall in the kitchen, his cell phone bleeped.

"I've got to get this," he said on his way out the door. Reaching the kitchen, he grabbed up the phone and flipped it open. "You got something for me, Nate? Anything on the Preston woman?"

He felt Georgie's presence behind him, turned to her, and slipped his arm around her waist. Her eyes were wide with worry, so he tugged her a little closer.

In his ear, his brother said, "No word on Ms. Preston, but there has been another, interesting development."

"Define interesting."

"Interesting meaning, I don't know if it's good or bad."

"If you aren't sure, then it's probably bad."

Nate blew out a harsh breath. "That's my take. Anyway, I thought you should know. Vaughn Corcoran had a weekend rendezvous scheduled with some woman, but he never showed up. He's been missing since Saturday, and nobody seems to know where in the hell he is."

Chapter Twenty

Visualization is a very powerful tool and can be used to attract anything you desire. Detailed visualization directs your subconscious mind, the *chi*, the universe, and your own belief system to manifest what you want. In going after your man, clearly see the initial circumstances of your meeting; visualize how your courtship will go; and see being in the arms of the man you love, forever and ever.

Georgiana Mundy's *Feng Shui for Lovers*

"Hey," Honcho growled as he punched Lucas in the shoulder, rousing him from his feigned sleep. "*Bastardo estúpido.* It's midnight. Time to go, man."

Sitting up on his bed, Lucas scratched the stubble on his jaw with his knuckles. By the dim light of the small table lamp on the nightstand, he watched his roommate tuck a .38 into the waistband of his pants.

"Time to go where?"

Honcho grabbed for his worn parka and shoved

his arms into it. "Drool and Corcoran are getting the chickie and her kid into the van. Time to split."

"Cool. Guess you can return my gun and my cell now." What the hell; it was worth a try.

"Right," Honcho snorted. "You may be working for Mr. Corcoran's *padré*, but you wasn't part of the original team. We're all going in the van, one big happy family. I keep your phone and your gun, and your car keys, until we've delivered the goods. *Then*"—he grinned, showing crooked yellow teeth—"you can have all your shit back."

Lucas pushed to his feet and followed Honcho out the door, apprehension churning away at his insides. Approaching the black delivery van, he took note that Drool was behind the wheel, while Paul Corcoran sat in the passenger seat, relaxing against the headrest, arms crossed over his chest, eyes closed.

Everybody was loose, casual. They obviously weren't expecting any kind of trouble. That might give him the edge he and Raine needed.

Behind the driver and passenger bucket seats in front, the van contained two rows of bench seats. As he slid across the cold vinyl behind Drool, Lucas shot a quick glance at Raine in the back row, the sleeping baby secured next to her in a sturdy car seat. Though Raine's gentle eyes were alive with fear, she held her jaw clenched tight, her mouth a determined line across her face. She gave him a subtle nod; she was ready.

If he was going to make a move, he needed to do it before they got on the road.

Pretending to fiddle with his safety restraints, he surreptitiously glanced around, checking his options. Honcho stood at the driver's-side window, giving Drool instructions on how to find the freeway. Corcoran still sat sprawled in his seat, eyes closed, not paying any attention to what was going on around him.

Lucas watched as Honcho finished talking to Drool, then walked around the front of the van. As the headlights flicked over the man's bloated body, the thug looked like a fat eel slithering through deep waters, black eyes alert, ready to go for the jugular.

When Honcho reached the open door on the passenger side of the van, he reached in, grabbed the handhold, and began hefting himself into the seat next to Lucas. For a moment, he was poised in midair—not in the van, not out of it. His center of gravity was off balance . . .

Lucas jerked to the right, bringing his elbow up, smacking Honcho's nose. He let out a yelp that was silenced when Lucas's fist slammed into the side of his head, sending him sprawling onto the parking lot's asphalt.

In a second, Lucas was through the open door, but Honcho was quick on the recovery and made a grab for Lucas's neck, wrapping thick fingers around his throat. With a sharp jerk, Lucas brought up his knee, connecting with Honcho's groin, making the thug gag and double over in pain.

Lucas grabbed for the .38 tucked in Honcho's waistband, but his fingers met only soft leather.

Shit. It must have fallen out during their scuffle. Somebody shouted, and he spun on his heel in time to see Drool and Corcoran exit the van and begin running toward him. Bending slightly, he readied himself to tackle whichever man came at him first.

But a blow from behind sent him to his knees as Honcho's boot connected with his kidneys. Gasping for air, he tried to stand, lashing out with his foot, landing a hard kick to his attacker's ribs, sending the man into a backward stumble. Out of the corner of his eye, he saw Drool take a step closer, a weapon in his hand, while Paul Corcoran hovered behind him, his eyes wide with confusion and fear.

Cowardly SOB.

Honcho recovered and stumbled to his feet, his eyes small and gleaming, his face bloody. At his sides, his fingers were outstretched, tense. He was going to kill Lucas with his bare hands. He took a step toward Lucas . . .

"Freeze! Drool, drop your weapon! Do it *now*!"

All eyes turned to Raine, who stood a couple of feet behind Honcho. In both her hands, she held the man's own gun aimed directly at Honcho's skull.

"I said drop it. *Now*!"

Drool grinned. "C'mon, lady. You ain't the type to shoot a man—"

Jamming the gun hard against the back of Honcho's neck, she snarled, "I wouldn't shoot a man, but I would shoot him."

"Drop the gun, asshole!" Honcho snarled at Drool.

Lucas reached over and snared the weapon from Drool's hand. "On the ground!" Lucas ordered. "All of you!"

Amid threats and curses, the three men slowly dropped to their knees, then onto their stomachs.

"You okay?" Lucas said to Raine.

"Y-yes." Though her reply was hesitant, the weapon in her hands never wavered as she held it on the men who'd kidnapped her.

"Give me Honcho's gun." When she complied, he said, "Get into the passenger seat."

Tucking Honcho's gun into his waistband, he quickly patted down the prone men, relieving Honcho of the knife hidden in his boot. "Get up," he ordered, motioning toward the room Raine had occupied. Locking them inside, he said, "Stay put, *comprenda*? First one of you I see in the rearview mirror, I blow his balls off."

From behind the closed door, Corcoran shouted, "You're a dead man, Russell! A fucking dead man!"

Running to the driver's side of the van, Lucas jumped in, slammed the door, and shoved it into reverse, backing like a shot away from the motel room door.

"You and the kid all right?" he panted.

Raine sent a quick look at the baby sleeping in the car seat at the back of the van. "We're good."

Thrusting the gearshift into first, he peeled out

of the parking lot and onto the sparsely trafficked boulevard, trying to put as much distance as he could between them and the motel. "It won't take them long to bust out of that room," he said, flicking a quick look over at Raine. "They have my car. We're going to have to ditch this van pretty soon." As he turned a corner, he said, "You were great. That was a gutsy move. I'd've never gotten away from those goons without your help. You saved my life."

Licking her lips, she nodded. "Well, I think you saved mine, so we're even."

Lucas turned off the brightly lit boulevard onto a dark residential street. A few blocks later, he turned again and parked the van behind a huge, overfilled Dumpster, where he turned off the headlights and stared into the rearview mirror. Nothing. No one on their tail. Safe for now.

"We ditch the van here," he said, turning off the ignition. "It's dark here, and pretty well hidden from the street. They could drive around for hours and not spot it."

She nodded, took in a deep breath. "Now what?"

"We walk away, find a secure location, and then I make a phone call. We'll, uh, we'll make better time if I carry the kid, if that's okay with you."

Raine looked into his eyes for a moment, then reached down and unbuckled her restraints. Silently, she made her way past the middle row of seats to the back where Caroline was still asleep.

By the time Lucas came around to the side door

and slid it open, Raine was waiting for him. Holding the baby close to her body, she searched his eyes once more, then gently placed the warm bundle in his arms.

"What happens after you make the phone call?" she said as she hopped out of the van.

He smiled and cradled Caroline close to his chest. "We wait for the cavalry to ride to the rescue. Let's go."

"There it is!" Georgie shouted, waving her hand at the windshield as her heart bumped along at twice its normal rate. "The Casa de Palmas Motel. Do you see number four, Ethan? Oh, oh, there it is! There it is! That one, on the corner!"

Next to her, Ethan guided the sedan into the motel's parking lot. "Try to stay calm, Georgie, or you're going to have a little Grasshopper heart attack—"

Before he could finish, she flung the car door open and began running toward the motel room. When she placed her open palm on the rough wood, she thought she saw movement behind the fish-eye peephole, then the door squeaked open to reveal a tall man, legs braced, a weapon in his right hand.

A second later, she felt Ethan at her back. "Lucas? Everything okay?"

The man named Lucas nodded as his sharp gaze darted past her, past Ethan, and out into the darkness. Apparently convinced they hadn't been followed, he opened the door wider, allowing them passage. Immediately he shut it again and slid the bolt home.

"Georgie?" Raine's voice came from behind the barrier of Lucas's body.

"Raine!" She pushed past the man, straight into her best friend's embrace. Their arms wrapped tightly around each other, they hugged and cried, saying nothing, just rocking back and forth. "Thank God you're all right," Georgie rasped, her throat choked with tears. "Caroline's okay?"

"She's not hurt," Raine said, her voice tight. Her palm curved around Georgie's cheek. "She's asleep. Slept through the whole thing. She's such a good baby."

Georgie smiled through her tears. "She is. She's just the *best* baby."

The two women smiled into each others' eyes, then laughed.

A moment later, Georgie became aware of Ethan's presence next to her. "I'm sorry to rush things, but we need to leave. If they find the van, they'll calculate how far you could have gotten on foot and search the radius."

Without a word, Lucas shoved his weapon into his waistband, went to the bed, and gently picked up the sleeping baby. "All packed," he said, sending a solemn smile to Raine.

Ethan snapped off the lights before opening the door a crack. Georgie's eyes never left his back as he took a moment to check outside. "We're clear. Georgie, you and Raine with the baby in the backseat. Hurry."

He kept watch while the women got settled into the plush leather seats, and Lucas placed Caroline between them.

"I'm sorry there was not time to grab the car seat. Scoot her up close to you," Lucas instructed, "then put your belt around both of you. You'll be okay."

Georgie watched the conversation with interest, catching the moment when Raine's and Lucas's eyes met and held. Was it her imagination, or did Raine's cheeks flush a little?

Lucas closed the door, and a second later, both men slid into their seats. Ethan pulled out of the parking lot, and they were on their way. But it wasn't until they reached the highway, zooming along under cover of dark, that Georgie finally let herself relax a little, finally let herself accept that the frantic nightmare was behind them.

The people she loved were safe. Her gaze went to Ethan. *All* the people she loved were safe.

She covered Raine's hand with her own. "Tell me more about when you first saw Paul." In the rearview mirror, her eyes connected with Ethan's.

Raine let her head fall back against the cushion. "I had just finished shopping at the farmers' market down on Cabrillo Boulevard. Caroline was in her stroller. And I looked up, and there was Paul, staring at me."

"Did he do anything?" Ethan asked.

"Well, no. That's why I wasn't sure at first that it was him. But, well, he looked at me, then he looked at Caroline, and he got this strange expression on his face. I panicked, turned the stroller around, hoping it wasn't really him. I hurried through the crowd as fast as I could, trying to lose him. When I got to my car, I didn't see him. I called Georgie as I drove home. When I got there, I locked us in. Then Georgie called to tell me to look out for Lucas, and then Lucas was at the door, and then . . ." With a weary sign, she said, "When I opened the door, somebody rushed past him—"

"Honcho," Lucas snarled. "It was that son of a bitch Honcho."

She nodded. "Yes, Honcho. He rushed past Lucas, and before I realized what he was going to do, he punched me, and after that, the next thing I remember is waking up to see Paul holding Caroline. It's something I never want to see ever again," she whispered. "Not as long as I live."

Ethan let Raine's words settle at the back of his brain. A scenario began to form inside his head, a scenario in which Lucas's actions may have been justified. He slid a look at his agent. "I remember warning you that if you fucked me over, I was going to beat the crap out of you. Am I going to have to make good on my promise?"

Lucas met Ethan's gaze. "If it'll make you feel better."

"It might. Start talking."

Lucas pursed his lips and nodded. "You know about my kids, right? My boys?"

"They live with your ex-wife in the Midwest somewhere."

"Yeah. Michigan. They're ten and twelve. They, uh, idolize me." His shoulder jerked in a quick shrug. "They shouldn't, but they do. They don't know about me, my past, why I was booted from the force. My ex-wife promised not say anything. She, you know, wanted to give them a good father as a role model."

"Okay," Ethan said. "Okay, so what happened? Corcoran found out about you? Threatened to tell your boys?"

"Yeah." He shifted in his seat, rubbed his face with his open hand. "He warned me that he'd discredit me in their eyes if I didn't help him."

"Jesus, Lucas. Why didn't you come to me?"

He snorted. "Are you kidding? After years of shit assignments, watching you watch me, I didn't want to do anything to destroy the credibility I'd finally earned. I . . . I thought I could handle Corcoran on my own."

Ethan bit down. Was he that big of a bastard? Had he been so hard on Lucas that when the man had gotten into real trouble, he hadn't felt he could come to Ethan for help? If that was true, then he was partly to blame for what had happened to Raine. In a more modulated tone, he said, "Go on."

"I made two files," Lucas said. "Gave you the real one, all the details on Georgie, Corcoran, Raine, and the kid."

Uh-oh. Ethan shot a quick look in the rear-view mirror, meeting Georgie's shocked eyes. *Oh, shit . . .*

"You knew about Raine and Caroline?" she accused, her eyes wide in astonishment. "You . . . I . . . *before* I told you? You *knew*?"

"Look, Georgie. I never meant to—"

"Stop." She held up her hands. "Just stop."

Crossing her arms over her stomach, she broke eye contact with him in the rearview mirror. The lights from a passing car illuminated her features, showing him clearly how hurt she was. He'd finally gotten her to open up to him, and now there was a new crime to lay at his feet.

Later, he decided. He'd talk to her later, get her to understand why he couldn't have let on how much he knew.

In the seat next to him, Lucas mumbled, "Oh. Uh, sorry."

"Forget it," Ethan said, glancing again into the rearview mirror, but Georgie refused to meet his gaze. He let out a harsh breath. "So what was in the file you gave Corcoran?"

"He wanted information on Georgie and Raine, so I gave it to him, but I left out the part about the kid." He shook his head. "Odd thing is, Corcoran Senior never said anything about a baby. I don't think he knew. I think he wanted the intel for some other reason."

"I agree," Raine offered, leaning forward a little. "He looked surprised when he saw Caroline. And he made a sort of joke when I woke up, about my not telling him he was a daddy. I really don't think he knew."

Ethan mulled this all over for a few minutes,

then said to Lucas, "When you first got to Raine's house, where was Paul? Was he there when you drove up?"

"I passed the van, but it was parked way down the street in front of somebody else's house. They must have followed Raine back from the market and were trying to figure out the best approach when I showed up . . . and walked them right through the front door." He blew out a heavy sigh, turned in his seat. Quietly, he said, "Sorry, Raine."

Though Ethan couldn't see her face, her voice was gentle, forgiving. "It's okay. You didn't know."

Georgie still wouldn't meet his gaze in the mirror. "So Raine opens the door and Honcho rushes in, pops her on the jaw. Then what?"

"Paul assumed I was working for his father, so he only confiscated my weapon and my cell. I was worried they were going to kill me or leave me behind, then Raine wouldn't have any protection. There were three of them, they were armed. I had no choice but to play along." Scrubbing his jaw with his knuckles, he said, "Paul wanted to carry the kid, but I insisted on holding her. Didn't want him or either of those other two idiots to do something stupid like drop her."

Raine let out a choked cry. In the rearview mirror, Ethan saw Georgie put her arm around Raine as she stroked the sleeping baby's hair.

"While Drool put Raine into the van," Lucas said, "Honcho yanked the baby seat out of Raine's car and I put the kid in it. Then Honcho drove my car to the motel. All I could do at that point was keep an eye on Raine and the kid, and wait for a lucky break."

"You should have come to me," Ethan growled. "If you hadn't gotten a break . . . shit, Lucas, when Corcoran first approached you, you should have come to me."

"Yeah, I know."

It was all water over the dam now, but when he stopped to think of how different the outcome might have been . . .

"What about your kids, your boys? Do you think Corcoran made good on his threat?"

"I don't think so." He tilted his head, lifted his shoulder in a quick shrug. "Doesn't matter anymore. It's time they knew the truth about me anyhow." A weary sorrow edged his words. "Secrets are strange things. You think they're neatly tucked away, hidden from the world, but they always find a way out. Always. Usually at the worst possible time, with the worst possible results. I figure it's time to just come clean. I love my boys. I owe them the truth. At least I won't have to suffer for years, wondering when the shit's going to hit the fan and they're going to find out about me, hate me for allowing them to think I was a good guy."

"You *are* a good guy," Raine corrected quietly.

Ethan wasn't happy Lucas hadn't come to him, but the upside was, he hadn't betrayed Paladin, or Georgie or Raine, or even himself.

"Okay," he muttered. "I won't kick the shit out

of you this time. But you're back on midnight surveillance until I say differently."

Out of the corner of his eye, he saw Lucas's mouth quirk in a stifled grin of relief. "I can live with that." A moment passed, then another. Then, "Thanks, Ethan."

Ethan checked his speed, and shot a quick glance at the rearview mirror.

"Georgie, when was the last time you saw Vaughn Corcoran?"

Her eyes met his in the glass. "Is this a question I need to answer?" she snipped. "Or is this one of those questions where you already *know* the answer and you just want to see if I'll—"

"I'm sorry, okay?" He flashed her a look, then returned his eyes to the road. "We can discuss that later. Besides, we have a deal, right?"

She glared at him.

"Georgie, I need to know when you last saw or had any contact with Corcoran."

"I haven't," she snapped. "I despise both him and his rotten-to-the-core son."

Lucas looked over at Ethan. "Why do you want to know whether she's seen Corcoran?"

"He's disappeared."

Raine leaned forward, curling her fingers over the back of Lucas's seat. "Why would a man like Vaughn Corcoran go into hiding?"

Ethan's gut tightened like it did when his instincts were trying to tell him something. "He wouldn't. Couldn't. Too many people on his payroll, too many people monitoring his whereabouts. He hasn't withdrawn any large amounts of money, and his cash machine cards haven't been used since Friday morning. Nobody can think of a reason for him to want to disappear."

"So," Georgie mused, "if he's not in hiding, where is he?"

Chapter Twenty-one

To encourage more people to help you, or to get more support out of the people already in your life, hang some pleasant-sounding metal wind chimes in the right, front area of your bedroom, home, or office.

Georgiana Mundy's *Feng Shui for Lovers*

A forest of redwoods stood guard on either side of the secured wrought-iron gate and all along the driveway, obscuring the house from view. Split-rail fences paralleled the wide pavement, showcasing roses of the billowing and rambling variety in glorious shades of apricot, yellow, and crimson. As Ethan's car rounded the final curve, Georgie took her first look at the house.

Her breath caught in her throat at the sight of the truly lovely place, and she started to comment on it—until she remembered how he'd deceived her, the conniving bastard.

"So," she said, "let me guess. This is a rental, right?"

Behind the wheel, Ethan's steady gaze met hers in the mirror.

"Time-share?" she ventured, putting as much sarcasm in her voice as she could. "You were in a coma and your mom chose it? You inherited it from your tasteful and gracious Aunt Gertrude?"

As the car came to a stop, she unbuckled her safety restraints and opened the door. Stepping out, she took in the two-story white stucco and adobe brick mansion, its clean lines and elegant charm glorified by the stunning blue sky overhead.

Situated on a cliff overlooking the Pacific, the estate seemed to be a cross between a Mediterranean villa and a country inn, with arched entryways accented with Spanish tiles, massive oak doors, and brown and burgundy trim.

It was absolutely gorgeous.

Lucas got out and opened Raine's door, taking the just-waking-up baby into his arms while Raine stretched her limbs. Flicking a glance back and forth between Georgie and Ethan, Lucas obviously noticed the tension between them. "Uh, you two go on ahead," he said. "I'll, uh, get the stuff from the trunk."

Crossing her arms under her breasts, Georgie faced the mansion. She tilted her head, pursed her lips. "Well, then, your purchasing agent has excellent taste in ashrams, Master."

"Wrong on all counts, Grasshopper." Ethan shoved his keys in his pocket and grabbed her arm to escort her toward the front door. "If you must know, I won it in a poker game."

"Ah. Makes sense," she said, trotting along beside him. "Given your nature, though, I was expecting something out of a horror movie . . . dark and stormy and all that. Maybe even a servant named Egor."

"That's Igor, and I had to let him go last week." He pressed a numbered keypad next to the hand-carved oak door. "His hump wouldn't fit through the threshold."

Something clicked, something buzzed, and the latch hissed. He entered the foyer, his fingers still curled around Georgie's arm. "Hi, honey, I'm home!" he yelled.

A shrill, "Wooo-hoooo! Up here!" echoed from the top of the staircase. Ethan was involved with someone? And he'd made love to Georgie without ever saying a word?

For a moment, she thought her heart was going to sink to the highly polished red tile floor, until she turned to see a woman come bouncing down the stairs. She had a head of thick, spiked white hair, slightly creased, too-tanned skin, and a speed-bump bosom. Dressed in a tie-dye tunic, black leggings, and white Nikes, her only jewelry was an array of six studs in each ear, trailing in rainbow gems from ruby at the top, to amethyst at the lobe. A pink iPod hung from a strap around her neck. "I was so happy when you called and said you were bringing home a *girl*," she announced, turning her beaming smile first on Ethan, then Georgie, then back to Ethan. "Like, it's about damn time, Darling."

When she reached the bottom of the wide oak staircase, her blue eyes glittered with what appeared to be mischief, as she tugged the earpieces out of her ears and held out her hand to Georgie. "Moxie Bigelow, honey. The Darlings' housekeeper, not to mention gourmet chef, personal secretary, emotional rock, and all-around gal Friday, at your service."

Georgie almost laughed out loud. She *loved* how the woman called him Darling.

As Georgie took Moxie's outstretched hand in a ferociously sincere grip, the housekeeper's eyes flitted from Georgie's toes to the top of her head, then back down again. "You are even prettier in person than you are on TV! Got all your cookbooks, hon. Tried to feng shui the Darling here, but you know how stubborn these macho types can be." Releasing Georgie's hand, she leaned toward Ethan, whispering loudly, "Marry her, you big dumb lug. She'll give you *gorgeous* babies—"

"Moxie," Ethan said dryly. "Enough, okay? You're beginning to sound like my mother." Though his words could have been interpreted as irritation, the tender look in his eyes gave him away.

Moxie put her hand on a tilted hip. "I *like* your mother, and when it comes to your future, the woman has a *point*." Returning her scrutiny to Georgie, she cocked her head, narrowing one eye. "You only planning on staying for a few days, hon, or has Mr. Marin County's Most Eligible

Bachelor finally figured out he needs a woman of his own around here?"

"We already discussed all this on the phone, Moxie," Ethan said. "You know why she's here. Are the rooms ready? Did you get baby stuff and food for the kid?"

The woman straightened her spine and raised her hand. For a moment, Georgie was certain she was going to salute. Instead, she tapped her orange-glossed lips with her index finger. "Ready rooms? Check. Groceries in the fridge? Check. Crib? They delivered it about an hour ago, along with diapers and clothes for the baby, and things for both the ladies. Check, check, check, and check."

Georgie's eyes widened in surprise. "You got a crib, diapers, baby clothes . . . I . . . how on earth did you—"

"I'm good, sweet thing," Moxie said lightly. "Been at it since the Darling called me." Casting a glance at Ethan, she drawled, "I so deserve a big fat raise for this."

Ethan snorted. "We'll discuss it when I've eaten, gotten some sleep, and had my head examined for ever hiring you in the first place."

"Well, then again, money ain't everything," Moxie stated, sending him a meaningful look. Then she smiled in a dreamy kind of way. "A *baby*. In this house. *Never* thought I'd see that happen. Can't wait to get my hands on her. Nothing like droolly baby kisses. Ten months old, is she?"

Georgie nodded.

Moxie rolled her eyes. "Dear God, such a sweet age. She and your friend still out in the car?"

Georgie nodded again. "They're coming."

As she almost danced toward the front door, Moxie cast a wicked glance at Ethan. "Say, Darling, you bring that hunky Lucas Russell with you?"

"He'll be along."

Moxie grinned at Georgie. "Always wanted to get my hands on that one. But I'm a Scorpio. Prob'ly wear the man out!" She winked, then turned and walked down the steps and into the circular drive.

Georgie shook her head, her jaw slack. "I cannot believe such a fun, sparkling, energetic, fabulous, out-there creature works for *you*. She's wonderful. And the way she orders you around. It's, well, it's admirable! Where on earth did you find her?"

Ethan scowled down at her, his hazel eyes narrow and calculating. "Don't think I let just *anybody* order me around, Grasshopper. Moxie and I go way back." Bending his head, he brushed her lips with a soft kiss. "Were you able to get some sleep in the car?"

"No, and no kisses for you, pal," she huffed, shoving him away. "You have a lot of explaining to do, but I'm just too tired to listen to it all right now. Let's just say I'm mad at you, and leave it at that."

Behind them, Moxie stepped through the door, a bright-eyed Caroline clinging tightly to the housekeeper's neck. Raine and Lucas followed more slowly.

"Jee!" Caroline shouted when she saw Georgie. "Bha ghat mom-ma-ma-ma Jee! Jee!"

"Yes, it's me." Georgie laughed, leaning up to kiss the baby's soft mouth. Caroline made a loud smack against Georgie's lips, then looked around, babbling incoherent baby observations on the décor.

"Why don't I take this bundle of sugar upstairs and give her a bath, and a change of diaper, if my nose doesn't deceive me?"

Raine laughed and raised her arms to Caroline. "Please don't bother. I can—"

"No bother, hon! You just relax and let me take care of the little princess here." She bustled past the group and headed up the stairs. "When you're ready, come on up and I'll show you your room and the nursery. Got a spot for you, too, Mr. Hunky Agent Man." Over her shoulder, she gave Lucas a come-hither look.

Lucas grinned. "Lead the way, Miss Moxie. I'm kind of beat, though. You'll have to do all the work."

"Don't tease me like that," the housekeeper called down from the top of the stairs. "Might just take you up on it, Mr. Man."

As Moxie and the baby disappeared down the hall, a large white cat uncurled itself from the landing and blinked yellow eyes down at Georgie. Stretching, it turned and followed the sound of the housekeeper's voice as she chatted to Caroline.

"You have a cat?" Georgie said to Ethan.

Casual shrug. "Came with the house."

Raine moved to the foot of the stairs. "I guess I'll go on up and help Moxie with Caroline's bath, then get cleaned up myself. Maybe try to get some sleep." With her hand on the banister, she looked at Ethan. "Thanks for rescuing us."

Georgie watched as his eyes grew dark, serious. "I'm sorry you were put through all that. But you'll be safe here. I promise."

Raine smiled and climbed the stairs, Lucas right behind her.

Turning to Ethan, Georgie said, "What time is it?"

He checked his watch. "Eight-thirty."

"I have to call Ozzie, beg off on the Monday taping, but I won't be able to get out of it tomorrow."

"I don't want you going anywhere until I find out where Vaughn Corcoran is. You're safe here, there's no reason to—"

"Sorry," she interrupted. "But it would throw Ozzie and KALM into utter chaos if I didn't do the taping tomorrow."

Though he looked disgruntled about it, he made no further comment. Grabbing her hand, he began tugging her toward the staircase. "Moxie?" he yelled up the stairs.

"Yes, Darling?" came the echoing reply from somewhere on the vast second floor.

"Did you put the stuff you got for Georgie in my room?"

"Yes, Darling."

Georgie just about choked. "Well, that was damn presumptuous of you—"

"Shut up. I'm exhausted, but I won't sleep a wink unless you're next to me."

"I'm mad at you, *remember*?"

"Like you'd ever let me forget it," he mumbled.

Halting, he pulled her toward him. Gently grasping a hank of her hair, he held her head as he placed a kiss on her open mouth. By the time he let her go, she had not only forgotten why she was mad at him, she'd forgotten what planet she lived on.

Tuesday morning, Ethan found himself pacing the set, watching Georgie as she checked her list of ingredients for the show's taping. Her brow furrowing in concentration, she moved from the stove to the refrigerator, checklist in hand, mumbling to herself and making little notes in pencil. Iona trotted along behind everywhere she went, pins in her mouth, a tape measure around her neck.

With her hair loose around her shoulders, and her eyes laughing at him the way they always did, Georgie looked this morning as she had always looked to him—pretty and sweet and sexy. Now that he knew her so much better, he would throw in words like smart, savvy, compassionate, tender, tough, loyal . . . and *his*.

Last night, they'd slept a little, made love a lot, and he'd fallen more deeply in love with her. When she was sated, putty in his arms, he said,

"I'm sorry about deceiving you, Grasshopper. I couldn't tell you I knew about Raine and the baby. I kept thinking I'd made enough headway that you'd trust me enough to confide in me."

Snuggling closer, she slid her arm over his chest. "I wanted to tell you everything. I was so tired of carrying the burden of truth all by myself, but I didn't know if you were working for Corcoran."

He arched a brow and looked down at her. "Still mad at me?"

"Hell, yes," she snorted.

Smiling, he placed a kiss on the top of her head. "Good. Just so we understand each other."

He figured it would always be that way between them; she was too smart and independent to take things at face value. She would always keep her guard up, ask questions until she heard the answer she wanted. Some men hated that, but he liked knowing she was capable of thinking on her feet, that she didn't take crap from anyone, and that she stood up for herself and for those she loved. He knew he was intimidating, and would run right over a weaker woman. Some men liked that. He didn't. He wanted a woman who could go toe-to-toe with him; he wanted a woman he could respect.

He wanted Georgie. Crossing his arms over his chest, he leaned against a partition and let his gaze roam over her body. From the top of her luxurious dark hair to the tips of her pretty pink shoes, she was *exactly* what he wanted.

She must have felt him looking at her, because she raised her eyes to him and smiled. "I've been thinking."

"Hmm. Thought I heard something rattling in here."

She made a face, then said, "You want everyone to think you're distant, uncaring, but that's not true. You're kindhearted and sweet."

"Just the kind of reputation a police officer wants to have," he drawled. "Really puts the fear of God into the bad guys."

Georgie picked up a spoon, wiped it with the edge of her apron. "Whatever you say, Detective. Hey, have you talked to Ozzie yet?"

"Couldn't find him. They said at the front desk he hadn't come in yet."

Her brows lowered. "That's strange. He's always here for my tapings, and always early. Like a mother hen checking to see if the barnyard is in order."

"Yeah? Well, where do you think he is, then?"

At that moment, the director yelled for everyone to take their places. "On my way," Georgie said, setting the spoon on the counter. "No audience today, Ethan, so we should be done in an hour or two."

He looked on while Georgie went through her paces, smiling for the camera, giving hints, tips, and advice on how to feng shui your home to make it more romantic. What in the hell for? he wondered. Anyplace you could stretch out and have sex was plenty romantic. Must be a woman thing.

As the show began to wrap up, he felt his cell phone vibrate inside his pocket. Checking the readout, he moved out of the set's microphone range, pressed the button, and put the phone to his ear. "Yeah, Nate. What's up?"

At the other end of the connection, Ethan could hear sirens, voices, someone shouting orders. "Well," Nate said, "I've got kind of a bad news, badder news situation here I thought you should know about."

Ethan lowered his head, cupping his hand over his right ear while he listened intently. "Yeah?"

"Yeah. A couple of hours ago, we got a call. Neighbors complained of a foul smell coming from the house next door. Turned out to be one very deceased Vaughn Corcoran."

Ethan pulled in a breath. "Jesus Christ, Vaughn Corcoran's *dead*? The ME nail the cause?"

"Looks like heart failure. Somebody stuck a knife through it."

The little hairs on the back of Ethan's neck began to prickle, then his gut tightened. "Well, if that's the bad news, then what's the badder news?"

"That would be the crime scene."

"What do you mean?" he said slowly.

"What I mean is, Vaughn Corcoran was stabbed to death in Georgiana Mundy's bedroom."

Ethan's jaw dropped. "No . . . fucking . . . way."

"Fucking way. Now the only question is, do

you want to bring her with you, or do I need to send a uniform to pick her up?"

Caroline had been so fussy, it had taken Raine an hour to get the baby down for her nap. She'd taken a bottle, but was so wound up from crawling around, exploring the big house, and petting the soft white kitty, she cried whenever Raine tried to put her in the crib. Finally, Caroline's long lashes rested against her chubby cheeks, her pouty little mouth went slack, and she drifted off to baby dreamland.

The crib Moxie had acquired was magnificent, from its hand-carved oak headboard of fairies frolicking through a forest, to the soft sheets and bumper pad printed with gray and pink kittens pouncing and prancing and dancing.

Bending over the rail, Raine placed a kiss on her baby's cool cheek. "Sleep tight, my angel."

With one last look, she eased out of the room, closing the door behind her. As tired as Caroline was, with the combination of a bottle and a hearty lunch of mashed bananas and rice cereal, she'd probably sleep like a rock for at least three hours.

The nursery was accessible through a connecting bathroom, so as she returned to her own room, she glanced at the clock. It was nearly one.

Ethan and Georgie were gone and weren't expected back until at least four. She knew Lucas was across the hall, in his room. Moxie was working out in the garden. Caroline was asleep.

Even though she was nervous, she had a decision to make. A choice, really. Ever since she'd met Lucas, something inside her had been urging her to take a second look at this one, not dismiss him as quickly as she had the others, maybe even be a little bold.

She sat on the edge of her bed, resting her elbows on her knees.

She'd never considered herself particularly proactive, but maybe that needed to change. There was something she wanted, something she had been thinking about for a long time now, but didn't know how to get. It all came down to trust—who could she trust to help her do this thing she wanted to do?

Everything inside her promised that Lucas Russell was the right man at the right time with the right moves.

Her cheeks suddenly felt too hot for her body. Rushing to the bathroom, she splashed cold water on her face and tried to quiet her racing heart.

Raising her head, she looked at herself in the mirror. Really, it was now or never. *Don't chicken out, Raine. Even if he laughs at you, at least you took the step, made the move, were bold.* Hell, she'd held a gun on a group of thugs without breaking a sweat, but this, she was nervous about?

She clenched her jaw and lifted her head, squared her shoulders. *Yeah, okay. It's time. Let's do this thing.*

The changes of clothes Moxie had provided were practical and attractive, and fit fairly well considering the housekeeper had only had Ethan's description of her and hadn't known her size. However, nothing in the high-end department store bags could be construed as sexy, alluring, or seductive.

But Lucas was, after all, a man, and bare skin would probably work just as well.

Quickly shucking off her clothes, she reached for the silky blue robe hanging from the back of her door. Wrapping it around her naked body, she took one last check in the mirror.

She pinched her cheeks, fluffed her hair. Moistening her lips, she smiled weakly at her reflection. Okay, not a siren, but not half bad, either.

With her ears buzzing, her heart hammering, and her knees quaking, she approached Lucas's door and knocked once. Hearing nothing, she turned the knob and eased the door open.

The drapes were drawn against the bright afternoon sun, casting the room in a soft amber light. Lucas sat on the bed, his back against the headboard, an open book on his lap. Except for the pair of faded denims he wore, he was naked. His neck crooked a little, his eyes were closed.

She turned to go.

"Raine?" he rasped, his deep voice rough with sleep. "Is everything all right?"

Swallowing the gigantic lump in her throat, she closed the bedroom door and made her way toward the bed. When she reached it, she stopped.

"Raine?"

She licked her lips. "Are you married?" she whispered.

"Uh, no. Not anymore." His blue eyes clouded with confusion.

"Are you engaged?"

"No. Raine, why—"

"Are you involved with someone in a relationship that could be in any way considered committed?"

"No. Look, Raine—"

"So, you're free?"

He cleared his throat, then rubbed his hand over his face as though trying to make some sense of all this. "I'm free," he said.

Her eyes traveled over his handsome face, across his broad shoulders. His bare chest was covered with a slight dusting of blond hair, and his abs were taut. As he set the book aside, his rounded biceps bulged, and his pecs flexed. Yes, she thought. Yes, he was definitely the man for the job.

"Okay, then," she mumbled. Loosening the tie on her robe, she let it slip from her shoulders and slide down her back until it fell in a silky puddle of fabric at her feet. "In that case, would you please make love to me?"

For long seconds, the only sound in the room was their breathing. His had changed, and it now seemed as though he was working for every breath. Finally, he said, "Raine, I . . . that's the sweetest proposition I've ever had. And, um, the most unusual."

Sliding out of bed, he reached for her robe and wrapped it around her, covering her body. "You're tired, emotionally drained, confused. You don't want this, Raine. Maybe you should go back to your room now."

"But I do want this. I want to make love with you. I've never, I mean, I . . . well, for a long time—"

"You don't have to explain," he murmured. She felt his hand caress her hair and she realized she wanted so much more of him than even just this. "I think you should choose a better man for this than me."

She turned to him, defiantly shoving her robe away, pressing her naked breasts against his chest. "I can't think of a *better* man."

"Dear God, Raine," he choked, wrapping his arms around her, holding her close. "You deserve so much better than a man like me. I don't know what to say . . ."

She slipped her arms around his neck, letting the heat of his body warm her. Against her stomach, she felt his erection, and for the first time in her life, she wasn't afraid. This was Lucas, after all. The man *she* chose, the man *she* wanted . . .

He lowered his head, found her mouth, kissed her. A moment later, she pulled back, searching his eyes.

"I know you did a file on me," she whispered. "How . . . how much do you know about me?"

A mix of compassion and anger filled his eyes. "Everything. I'm sorry."

"Not your doing. Not your fault."

"Even so," he said softly. His thumb caressed

her cheek. "Even so. And then what that bastard Corcoran did to you. I can't believe how well you've come through that. I swear I don't think I've ever met a woman I've admired so much as you. Jesus, Raine, you're incredible."

"To be honest," she said, laying her head against his chest, glad Lucas was taking this slowly, allowing her some time, "when I think about what Paul did, I'm just glad I don't remember it."

Lucas bent, sliding his arm under her knees. In a moment, she was lying on the bed, facing him, wrapped tightly in his embrace. Burrowing her face into his shoulder, she smiled. This was good, this was right. She wanted this . . .

He was quiet for a moment, then said, "If you'd feel comfortable sharing it with me, I mean, if you'd like to talk about it, I'd like to hear what happened. I know the basics, but I'm curious as hell about what he said when you confronted him. What kind of rationale did the bastard have for doing what he did to you?"

Reaching up, she let her fingers stroll through his hair, caress his neck, his shoulders. He bent his head and kissed her forehead, then the tip of her nose, then settled in for a deep, luxurious kiss on her mouth. His hand eased up to cup her breast, slide over her taut nipple. It felt so incredibly good.

She suddenly wished she'd met Lucas two years ago, instead of Paul. But then she wouldn't have Caroline.

"He . . . Paul actually acted insulted," she stumbled as Lucas nibbled on her neck. "When I accused him of rape, he sort of laughed, shrugged it off, and said none of the others had complained. I sensed that he really didn't think it was a big deal, and didn't even really consider it rape, since the victim wasn't aware of what was happening."

Lucas lifted his head and scowled down at her. "Wait. He said *no one else* had complained?"

She nodded. "Yes."

"Huh." He looked thoughtful for a moment. "Well, isn't that interesting. I wonder who 'no one else' is?"

After that, he returned his attention to her mouth, her breasts, slid his hand down her thigh. After that, they didn't talk for a long, long time.

Chapter Twenty-two

Death destroys the balance of energy in a
house. Do not build your new home on, or near,
a graveyard or butcher shop. And if someone
dies inside your house, it is especially unfortunate if they *do* so downstairs.

Georgiana Mundy's *Feng Shui for Lovers*

Shocked and confused, Georgie arrived with
Ethan, to see the street in front of her house
clogged with police cars, aid vehicles, and a coro-
ner's van, as well as a gaggle of TV, radio, and news-
paper reporters. She'd never attended a crime
scene before, but even so, this one seemed rather
quiet, subdued somehow, and she wondered if it
was always this way.

Her neighbors, people she'd known for years,
stood in small huddles, murmuring among themselves, speculating, casting curious gazes at each
other, and at all the goings-on.

And why wouldn't they? If what Ethan said
was true, a man who was basically her employer,

head of a billion-dollar multimedia empire, and possibly California's next political powerhouse— not to mention the fact he was her ex-boyfriend's father—had been found in her house, in her *bedroom*, with a nine-inch butcher knife embedded between his shoulder blades.

Once the news leaked—and it always leaked— that Paul Corcoran had fathered a child by Georgie's best friend, and that Georgie hated both the Corcorans, there would be no doubt in the eyes of the world that Georgie had had more than enough motive for murder.

This was just the kind of setup the media loved. Famous people . . . sex, lies, explosive emotions . . . murder. It would make national, probably even international news, and until the police identified the killer, she sure didn't need a detective to explain to her that she was suspect number one.

As she stood by the open door of Ethan's car, staring up at her own house and the activity going on around and inside it, she felt as though someone had punched her right between the eyes, and she just hadn't collapsed to the ground yet.

Ethan slid his arm around her waist. Was it a show of moral support, or did she look like she was going to hit the ground, face first? "You hanging in there?"

"I'm hanging," she murmured, hoping that wasn't an unfortunate choice of words.

"Nate wants to talk to you. Just be honest, okay?" She blinked a couple of thousand times, then shoved his arm away. "Be honest?" she repeated. "Be *honest*? You don't think . . . I mean, you can't believe that I had *anything* to do with—"

"Ms. Mundy?"

She shifted toward the voice. "Yes?"

"I'm Inspector Darling. Nate Darling. Hey, Ethan."

The two men studied each other for a moment, then shook hands. "Hey," Ethan said.

Nate released his brother's hand, then shoved both his hands in his pockets. "I need to take your statement, Ms. Mundy." When he smiled, his grin was boyish, charming, disarming.

She flicked a sour look at Ethan as if to say, *Ah, the congenial, affable, nice brother,* then said to Nate, "Sure."

Nate Darling was as tall as Ethan, and as good-looking, but instead of Ethan's dark hair and hazel eyes, Nate was blond, his eyes brown. He wore gold wire-rimmed glasses—which somehow managed to make him look even hunkier.

Standing side by side in exquisitely tailored suits, Ethan and Nate made a stunning pair— masculine, rugged, intense. They looked like two movie stars on a break from shooting an action scene, and Georgie imagined that, whenever they entered a room together, feminine hearts actually fluttered.

"Can I go inside?" She glanced up at her house, wondering what the police were doing to the energy of her personal space, how devastating this was going to be to her carefully orchestrated feng shui, and whether the murder had damaged it beyond any cures she could use. She was probably going to have to call in a feng shui grand master to help her overcome the devastation.

"Not yet," Nate said. "Ms. Mundy, what kind of relationship did you have with Vaughn Corcoran?"

She hated him. "I hated him. I mean, I'm sorry he's dead and everything, but I hated him."

"Where were you on Saturday?"

"I picked her up early," Ethan interjected. "We drove to Napa together."

Nate shifted his attention to Ethan. "When you picked her up, *early*, did you go into her bedroom?"

The question hung in the air between them for a moment. "No." To Georgie, he said, "You were in such a huff when we left, did you remember to lock your front door?"

Had she? Thinking back, she was so flustered that Ethan had demanded he drive her to Napa, she'd slammed the door closed, but had it locked properly?

"I—I think so," she said softly. "It's a new lock. Maybe it didn't close all the way. I don't know for sure."

"Anybody else have a key to your house?"

"No. I hadn't had time to give the new key to anyone." She shook her head as though that might rattle the answer loose. "I just don't know."

Nate adjusted his glasses. "The ME places prelim TOD sometime between late Friday night and noon on Saturday." He looked at her, as though waiting for her to blurt out a confession.

"Well, obviously he had to have been killed after I left!" she snapped. "I mean, I *do* get a little messy sometimes, but I *really* think I would have noticed a dead man lying across my bed with a knife in his back! *Very* poor feng shui."

Nate's eyes narrowed. "You left him lying across your bed?"

"Nate," Ethan said harshly. "I was *in* the house Saturday morning—"

"But you didn't go in the bedroom."

"No, but I find it hard to believe that Georgie could have stabbed a man to death, then just left him there while she went away for the weekend. That would make her either a textbook sociopath, an Academy Award–winning actress, or she had a blue-ribbon case of PMS that rendered her both temporarily insane *and* amnesic."

"I don't get PMS!" she snapped.

He eyed her. "Right."

Ethan turned to Nate and the two men glared at each other.

"What time did you leave on Saturday?" Nate asked.

"Around nine-thirty."

"And her behavior at that time was . . ."

"Agitated, argumentative, snotty, huffy, pushy, *pissy*. In other words, normal."

Georgie gasped, then she smacked his arm

with her open palm. When he looked down at her, his eyes held a smile. With a snort, she averted her gaze.

Nate rolled his lips together, avoiding eye contact with either of them. He cleared his throat as though he were fighting a laugh, then said to Georgie, "I want to know everything you did Friday night until Ethan picked you up on Saturday."

"I didn't do anything special," she said. "I came home from the studio about six on Friday. Had dinner, worked on the computer for a while. Went to bed. No phone calls, no visitors. Got up Saturday morning to get ready for the drive to Napa, when Ethan showed up."

Ethan started to say something, but the chiming of his cell phone interrupted him. "Hang on," he said, checking the readout. "It's Lucas." Putting the phone to his ear, he said, "Yeah?"

Georgie watched as he listened for a moment, then his head slowly came up and his eyes found hers. "Uh-huh. Yeah, that *is* interesting. Thanks."

Flipping the phone closed, he returned it to his pocket. "Georgie, did Paul ever indicate that Raine wasn't the only woman he drugged and raped?"

"What?" she choked, taken completely off guard by the question. "He did that to *other* women besides Raine? Why, that . . . that . . ."

Ethan's eyes glittered with tightly restrained anger. "Lucas said Raine told him Paul made a remark that nobody else ever complained about being assaulted, which tells me Raine wasn't his only victim."

Georgie let that information roll around inside her head for a moment. "Well, that would give somebody a reason to kill Paul, but not Vaughn."

"And since Georgie supposedly wasn't home," Nate said, eyeing her meaningfully, "how did Corcoran's body end up in her bedroom?"

Ethan directed his attention to the house. Without looking at anyone in particular, he said, "I want to see the crime scene. Let's go."

After settling Georgie on the couch in her living room—under the watchful eye of a uniformed officer—Ethan stood in the threshold of Georgie's bedroom. Staving off a knee-jerk cringe, he reached into his breast pocket and pulled out a flat tin of Vicks, twisting off the cap, applying a glop of the ointment to his handkerchief, which he then held over his nose. Nothing like a little Vicks up the nasal passages to stave off the stench of death.

He glanced around the room. "Georgie didn't do this," he said flatly. "She's simply not capable of murder, let alone . . . this."

Nate scowled over the edge of his own white handkerchief. "They say love is blind."

"They also say you're a dick."

Behind his glasses, Nate's brown eyes glittered. "So, slap my ass and call me Edna. Ethan's in love. Hey, I'll be your best man, and you won't even have to get on your knees and beg."

Ignoring Nate's obvious attempt to find out about his relationship with Georgie, he shifted his focus to the crime scene.

The body of Vaughn Corcoran lay sprawled face down on the floor at the foot of Georgie's neatly made bed, in a pool of his own black blood—the knife that killed him still protruding from his back.

"No signs of a struggle," Nate murmured absently, glancing around the room. "Must have caught him by surprise . . ."

"So he either knew and trusted the killer, or didn't know the perp was behind him."

"The ME said there's only the one stab wound. No overkill, no multiple points of entry. Didn't see any defensive wounds on Corcoran's arms or hands. Perp stabs him, he falls, bleeds out. Pretty cut-and-dried, no pun intended."

"Georgie did not do this, Nate."

"So you've said. They're about ready to transport to the morgue. You want to take a closer look before they zip him up?"

The room had already been photographed and dusted for prints. Even so, Ethan moved cautiously toward the body, careful not to disturb any possible evidence.

Crouching, he looked at the knife, the wound, and the position in which the corpse lay. Vaughn Corcoran was not a big man. In life, he'd stood maybe five-six, five-seven and weighed in at probably one-forty, one-forty-five. A woman of Georgie's height and strength could conceivably have killed him with one hard, well-aimed thrust.

Ethan rose to his feet, taking in the small room,

neat in every other way except for the corpse sprawled awkwardly on the bloody Oriental rug.

Movement over his head caught Ethan's attention. Above the middle of her bed, she'd hung a mobile of about twenty long chandelier-type crystals. In the slight air current near the ceiling, the crystals slowly spun and glittered as they cast tiny rainbows onto the coverlet below. Most everything in the room, from the wallpaper, to the bedspread, to the vase of flowers on the dresser, to the bathrobe hanging on the back of the door, was some shade of dark or light pink. Oddly, it wasn't overpowering, just pretty. Feminine. Probably very feng shui.

Stepping out into the hallway, he lowered the kerchief and said to Nate, "Who called it in?"

"Dispatch said he claimed to be a neighbor reporting a foul smell coming from this house; didn't give a name. It was a cell phone and caller ID was blocked. We questioned everyone within nose range, but they all denied making the call."

"The body isn't that ripe. I didn't smell anything until I got up here."

"So somebody wanted this body found sooner rather than later. Maybe he didn't know Georgie had gone away for the weekend, or maybe he did, and didn't want her walking in on a dead body in her bedroom."

Ethan caught his brother's gaze. "So you believe Georgie's story."

"I'm inclined to believe her, sure," Nate said, shoving his hands into his pockets. "This crime scene just doesn't add up, and the timing is suspicious. But I've got to follow the evidence, Ethan. You know that. I'll have more when forensics is finished and the autopsy report comes in. I'll be very happy when we can eliminate Georgie as a possibility." He looked Ethan in the eye. "Honest."

Ethan felt the tense muscles in the back of his neck relax a little. "Okay, let's try a few scenarios on for size. Let's start with the fact Raine Preston may not have been Paul Corcoran's only rape victim."

Nate cocked his head, then nodded absently. "Makes sense. A guy like that, not too bright, something works once, it'll work twice, especially if the women are too confused or intimidated to report it." He jutted out his lower lip. "That would make for some mighty pissed-off, frustrated, powerless women."

"Exactly. But what if . . . and this is a big what-if . . . what if there's one who's maybe a bit of an opportunist? Figures she can make some money off this situation."

"You're talking blackmail."

Ethan nodded. "Indeed I am. Maybe she hits up old Paul, maybe she goes directly to the Bank of Papa Vaughn. He gives her buckets of money, and in return she keeps her mouth shut and doesn't ruin his political plans."

"But how could he be sure the money would keep her quiet forever?"

"He couldn't. My guess is, if this scenario plays out, Corcoran got tired of paying, or was worried the woman was a loose cannon. He wants to finish it once and for all."

"Sounds good," Nate said, "with the possible exception that we have absolutely no evidence, and nothing to go on but what-ifs."

Ethan ran his fingers through his hair, then scrubbed his jaw with his knuckles. "Yeah, but these what-ifs feel right. Well, almost right. I still can't figure out why the murder took place in Georgie's house. Unless . . ."

He let the ideas bump up against each other in his brain for a moment. "Unless . . ." he said slowly, "unless Corcoran didn't know who was blackmailing him and *assumed* it was Georgie or Raine."

Nate paced away from the window, then back again. "He comes here, maybe to talk, more likely threaten. He rings the bell. Nothing. Doesn't know she's left for the weekend. He tries the front door. It's open. He walks in, thinking she's still in bed, goes to the bedroom. Wham."

"And if he thought it was Raine, he'd already sent his goons to go find her, bring her back, have a talk with her." He slapped his forehead. "Shit. And here I was thinking all along it was about the kid, but now I'm not so sure. According to what both Raine and Lucas said, I don't think Vaughn or Paul even knew about the baby. It was about blackmail . . . it was always about blackmail."

"So who killed Corcoran? Was the killer already in the house, or did he follow Vaughn inside, see his opportunity, and take it?"

Outside, someone was yelling, making a hell of a racket. Ethan and Nate shot a look at each other, then moved into the living room.

Georgie was standing now, her eyes wide in alarm. Her fingertips rested against her lips while three officers stood at the door, trying to keep Paul Corcoran from bullying his way in.

"Dad?" he screamed. "I want to see him! Let me see him! Let me by, assholes. My tax dollars pay your fucking salaries! Let me by! Dad? Dad!" His red, swollen eyes turned to Georgie. "You bitch! You goddamned bitch! You'll pay, I swear to God, you'll pay!"

Ethan blew out a long breath. "Oh, goody. It's Junior Corcoran. Hmm. I wonder who inherits Daddy's empire now that the old man is dead?"

Chapter Twenty-three

When doing affirmations, it is better to ask for "the perfect guy for me" rather than ask for "Joe Mann" by name. You might *think* you want hunky Joe, but maybe he's all wrong for you. Since we always get what we wish for, let the Powers That Be do their thing and deliver the man who is perfect for you. Then, if it's still Joe, you'll know. Sure, it's a leap of faith, but isn't everything?

Georgiana Mundy's *Feng Shui for Lovers*

Paul Corcoran slammed down his father's phone, slumped in his father's chair behind his father's desk in his father's office, and thought about life, how it tossed you a few curves when you least expected it.

The stench of the holding cell at the precinct still clung to his nostrils. It had probably been a mistake to show up at Georgie's house last night, but when he'd heard she'd murdered his father . . . well, he'd had to see for himself. Of course, if he'd shown a little restraint and stayed away, he wouldn't have been arrested for kidnapping, but Dad's lawyers had bailed him out quickly enough. It was something he'd grown to rely on over the years. Besides, with the spin the overpaid shysters would put on it, he'd never be convicted— after all, he'd only wanted to see the child Raine Preston had withheld from him.

So Raine had a kid. His kid. Huh. Go figure. He was a *father*, not that he cared. Except, well, the brat looked just like him, and that was cool in a way. He'd known the minute he'd laid eyes on her, not to mention the fact he could read a calendar and knew how to count. Yeah, his kid, all right. Jesus.

He let his gaze meander around his father's office—maybe his office now, if the board voted him in. Nah. Never happen. What he knew about running a multimedia empire you could fit into a shot glass.

Tilting the chair back, he stretched his legs in front of him, propping them up on the desk, crossing them at the ankles. He thought of Georgie. Georgie, who'd killed his father. Georgie, who'd ruined everything.

He'd sort of loved her once. Even thought about asking her to marry him. After all, she was hot-looking, and famous. Would've made a good wife for the son of a future governor of California.

But, hot as she was, she'd never let him sample the goods, so he'd done her friend instead. Admittedly, a bad judgment call on his part. Bad planning, too. Georgie would never have married him after finding out about that. Ah, well. Live and learn.

He scratched his jaw, then picked up a piece of paper from the desk and crumpled it into a tight ball. Taking aim, he tossed it into the leather trash container in the corner. Right in. Nothing but net. Heh. Two points.

Yeah, all this was his now, but it didn't mean a whole hell of a lot. His old man had never approved of him, never figured him for having any brains, thought he was all eye candy and empty calories. His mother must not have liked him very much, either. She'd run off when he was three. Who knew where she was these days?

Despite his obvious misgivings about Paul, Vaughn had always granted him a huge allowance, and never questioned how he spent it. But according to the lawyer he'd talked to a few minutes ago, the gravy train was about to derail.

Sly old bastard. According to Vaughn's lawyer, the old man had left Paul one million bucks, and instructions on how to turn it into one billion. Yeah, right. Hell, a million bucks would barely cover fuel for his cars. As for turning it into one billion? Thirty-five years of age was way too late in life for a playboy to learn how to make a living.

Of course, he could always contest the will, but that would take time and money. And he had neither.

He'd always had a temper, but now red-hot

toxic fury oozed through his system, burning holes in his life, turning his future to ash.

Georgie had sent his nifty little gravy train straight off a cliff. Somebody should make her pay for that. Somebody really should.

A single tap on the office door, and it opened to reveal Dumb and Dumber.

"Close the door, Honcho," he snarled, his mood worsening as the reality of the penniless decades ahead began to sink in. "What'd you find out?"

"It's confirmed, compadre," the thug said shutting the door behind him, then dropping into an overstuffed leather chair. Drool stayed by the door, his arms dangling at his sides like a stringless puppet.

"She's in Marin," Honcho said, "with that security guy your old man—"

"My *father*," Paul snapped. "Not my 'old man,' my father!"

"Honcho didn't mean no disrespect, Mr. Corcoran," Drool mumbled, then shoved his hands in the back pockets of his baggy jeans.

"Shut up, you idiot." He glared at Drool, then returned his attention to Honcho. "Tell me more."

"It's no secret, man. It's like you heard the cops talking at the bitch's house." He sprawled back in his chair, let his arms hang over the sides. "She's in sort of a custody kind of thing while they figure out whether she whacked your old, eh, Mr. Corcoran. Darling used to be a cop, some big-shot detective. Word on the street is, something bad goes down, and he retires right after. But he still has clout."

"Who in the hell else could have killed him?" Paul yelled. Honcho and Drool both shrugged and averted their eyes. "She *did* it. Her house, her bedroom. He told me himself that she was probably the one blackmailing him, *and* that he was going to put an end to it."

But somehow, it was Georgie who'd ended it, and now Paul's future was very much in question.

"She needs to pay," he mumbled to no one in particular. "I want her to pay. You hear me? You *understand*?"

Honcho grinned and Drool chuckled.

"Yeah," Honcho said. "I think you still got some time left on the meter, especially since the Santa Barbara deal went bad. What do you want us to do?"

Paul tented his fingers in front of his mouth. "So this detective's place is in Marin?"

"Yeah."

"How do we get in?"

"Well, the front's out. I hear the place is gated, the house has all kinds of security and shit, so—"

Honcho started in his chair, and Drool flinched when Paul flung his feet off of the desk and jumped up, slamming his palms on the desk. "Wrong answer, asshole! I asked you how we get in!" He wanted Georgie's hide, and he would *have* it.

Drool swallowed and took a cautious step back,

but Honcho simply shrugged. "As it so happens, amigo, there is a way."

Georgie awoke on Wednesday morning with her bare arms and legs tangled with Ethan's. Easing her body closer, she pressed her breasts against his bare chest, raised her left leg until the sensitive flesh of her inner thigh grazed his groin. If that didn't rouse him—so to speak—he must be totally zonked. Though he didn't wake up, he made some kind of throaty male grouchy *hrmph*-ing noise, and settled his head deeper into his pillow; the arm around her waist tightened.

They were alike on all the levels that counted. She'd seen many of his flaws, and none were so bad she couldn't cope, and even though he thought she was *pissy*, when he said the word, when he looked at her, the expression in his eyes was soft, tender, almost as though . . .

Did he love her? she wondered. He'd had plenty of chances to say it, or at least hint at it. Maybe he loved her, and just hadn't found the right time to tell her. Things had been pretty hectic. Or perhaps he was never going to tell her because he'd decided to ignore the feeling until it went away.

She thought he'd made some headway when he'd finally told her about Cathy's death. But even though they'd made a deal—which had been *his* idea, no less—maybe he would stay closed, grief-stricken, and guilty forever, never let himself love again. Or maybe he simply didn't love Georgie enough to put Cathy behind him.

Cathy was a hard act to follow. Ethan had loved—and lost—an incredible woman, and Georgie felt torn between admiration and respect for her, and a shameful tinge of jealousy.

Gazing at Ethan's handsome face, she analyzed each separate detail, matching his features with his personality. She lifted her hand and trailed her finger slowly down his nose to the tip. His nose was perfect—long, somewhat thin, but with a small bump near the top that indicated he possessed an iron will, and let nothing stand in the way of getting what he went after.

She wondered what it would be like to be the object of that kind of intense desire, and whether he pursued women with the same single-minded determination that he pursued everything else.

Her thumb grazed his cheekbone. He had power cheekbones, the kind that were high and classically chiseled. All Ethan had to do was walk into a room, and he was immediately in charge.

His lips were slightly full and curved, the cleft above his upper lip deep and wide, signaling he had a sense of humor, was extremely sensual, and a woman would be wise to put him in control of her body.

"Like what you see?" he drawled, his eyes still closed. A smile crept slowly over his mouth. A second later, Georgie caught the glint of hazel green as he opened one lid a fraction. "It's not fair to take advantage of a man while he's in the throes of an erotic dream."

She smiled sleepily at him. *I love you. Can't you see it? Don't you know? I can't say it again, not out loud, not until I know how you feel. Do you love me back, Ethan? Will you ever love me back . . . ?*

Suddenly embarrassed at how needy she'd let herself feel, she shoved herself out of his arms and sat up, pulling the sheet around her quickly cooling body. Crossing her arms over her breasts, she stared at the room at nothing in particular.

Out of the corner of her eye, she saw his brow furrow in confusion. "What?" he said, sitting up next to her. "Georgie? What's going—"

"Your bedroom's all wrong," she rasped. Swallowing, she steadied herself and guided her thoughts away from the words she really wanted to say. He could love her or love her not; it didn't matter. But she was not going to turn needy over him. She was *not.* "Um, wrong colors, wrong furniture, wrong placement. I'm surprised you're as healthy as you are, given the negative *chi* that permeates this house."

"Dear God," he said dryly. "What could I have been thinking?"

"Never mind," she groused. "I'll have Moxie help me with the cures."

"The cures?"

"The, uh, fixes. They're called cures. To your bedroom, to your house. The cures will stabilize your life force, your prosperity, and your frigging *happiness.*" She hadn't meant to snap out that last part, it just sort of forced its way past her resolve.

"Okay," he said, watching her warily. "But what if I think my *chi* is fine right where it is?"

"It's not. If it were . . ."

She jerked her body around to face him. His eyes were guarded, but his mouth curved at one end. He was laughing at her! Fighting hard not to snap at him again, she said, "As I see it, I'm going to be stuck in this place for some time to come."

"Yes, you are in my custody until the police figure out who killed Corcoran. It may take years." His eyes smiled into hers. "Maybe decades."

"Well, in that case, I'm *redecorating*. You can afford it. Since I can't go into the station to work, I can't leave town, I can't go back to my house because it's a *crime scene*—" Her voice broke over that one. "And I can't prove I didn't kill Vaughn, I need to find something I *can* do!"

"Don't hide my remote control," he quipped. "That's all I ask. I have to go into the city and meet with Nate today. Ask Moxie for anything you need. I know the last few days have been tough, so if feng shuiing the hell out of my house will help you cope, knock yourself out, Grasshopper. I'm leaving Lucas here to keep an eye on things. You'll be perfectly safe."

"Sure, I'm safe," she drawled. "As safe as anyone can be who's under suspicion for murder."

"You didn't do it."

"I know!" Okay, so she was stretched a little

thin. Maybe a day alone with nothing but the sun, the sea, and her own thoughts would help her decompress.

He chucked her chin with his knuckle and grinned at her . . . and there it was again, that warm something reflecting in his eyes that she could have sworn was love. But when he spoke, all he said was, "The SFPD and I will find out who killed Corcoran. In the meantime, decorate your little heart out. I'll be home in time for dinner."

"Ethan?"

"Mm-hmm," he murmured as he leaned forward to place a kiss on the back of her neck.

"Have you, um, have you ever considered telling Nate what you told me about Cath—"

"No," he warned in a low voice. "My brother and I don't have that kind of relationship."

She inhaled, then turned to look at him. "Maybe we could expand our deal to include other people, like maybe your brother."

"It's not gonna happen. Drop it, Georgie."

Lowering her lashes, she studied the sheet crumpled around her body. "I'll drop it, after I say just one more thing." She lifted her hand, pointing her index finger into the air.

He sighed, deep, long, loud. "*What* one more thing?"

"Well, you have to start trusting Nate sometime. You made a deal with me; maybe you could make one with him, too."

Tossing the covers off his body, he stood and began walking naked to the bathroom, allowing her a glimpse of the angry red wound slashing across his rib cage.

"Does it still hurt? Where you got shot? Where you took that bullet for your brother, as you put it?" She cocked her head and blinked innocently at him.

He stopped, his arms dangling at his sides. For a moment he remained silent, then he turned to meet her gaze. "Don't leave the estate grounds. You're well protected here, so *stay* here. Are we clear on this?"

"Yes, Master," she said sarcastically, crossing her fingers under the sheet. "Very clear."

After a somewhat wary-looking Ethan kissed Georgie good-bye, she stayed in bed awhile, thinking about him and how she would fix up his house, especially the bedroom. No matter what the future brought, making the place a peaceful, properly feng shui'd home would be her gift to him.

Everything in the bedroom—and in the whole house, from what she'd seen so far—was masculine. Hard-edged black lacquer pieces, too-bright lighting, and not a hint of tenderness or romance, or the earth or the elements anywhere. The place screamed, *Bachelor pad! Single and staying that way!*

Silly man.

Her gaze fell on his pillow and she knew she couldn't resist. In the time-honored way of women in love, she rolled over and smooshed her face into its softness, breathing deeply, sighing his name. His scent, clean and musky, filled her senses. Then she wrapped her arms around the pillow as if it were his body and hugged it, inhaling, cuddling, smiling.

Mmm. Ethan's pillow. If men only knew what their pillows went through in the arms of the women who loved them . . .

Finally releasing it, she pushed her covers off and padded to the window that overlooked the usually blue Pacific. Today, however, thick gray fingers of fog crawled toward the shore far below, turning the water a gloomy steel-green. Time to get a move on. Quickly showering, she dressed in jeans, a pullover sweater, and sandals.

Leaving Ethan's bedroom, she walked silently down the long hallway. All was quiet, so she assumed Lucas, Raine, and the baby were still asleep.

Downstairs, she passed from room to room on her way to the kitchen, making mental notes of the ghastly problems in decorating she'd need to correct. While everything was tastefully done, it was obvious a decorator had furnished the place, and not Ethan, and certainly not a woman who loved him. It was a place to live, not a home. By the time she was done with it, he'd never want to leave.

Neither would she.

The huge corner kitchen had wraparound windows that faced west, and even though the property was surrounded by tall trees, she spotted a gate in the distance that probably led down to the beach. Perfect. Rocks and pebbles smoothed and shaped by ocean currents, gnarled driftwood made fluid and soft-edged by sand and salt and sea, would provide a great addition to Ethan's bedroom, and invite the magnificent Pacific right into his personal space. Fabulous *chi.*

"Mornin', honey."

Georgie jumped and turned around. Moxie stood in the wide kitchen doorway, holding the magnificent yellow-eyed white cat.

"Back at ya," Georgie said. "Your cat's gorgeous."

Moxie set the fluffy white bundle on the floor. Tail shooting for the sky, the feline padded over to a food dish by the back door and began taking delicate bites of the fishy concoction in the bowl.

"She is beautiful," Moxie agreed, as she shuffled in worn slippers over to the coffeemaker. "But she's not mine. Belongs to the Darling."

Georgie cocked her head. "He told me she came with the house. I figured he was joking, though, and that she belonged to you."

Moxie let out a hearty laugh. "Nope. Truth is, he found her as a kitten. Named her Violet because she was so shy. She'd been tossed in a trash dump, all scrawny and starving. Brought her home. Spent a fortune in vet's fees. Insisted on feeding her himself."

"*Ethan?*"

Moxie wiped her hands on the brilliant red tunic top she wore over white leggings, then smiled at Georgie. "He's like that. Loves animals and kids. Hides it real good, though, doesn't he? The man's always taking in strays." She arched a thin brow and sent Georgie a meaningful look. "Like me."

As the heady aroma of fresh-brewed coffee filled the kitchen, Georgie said, "You take in strays, too?"

Reaching for a couple of coffee mugs from the cabinet next to the stainless steel refrigerator, Moxie said, "No. Meaning I am a stray. Eight years ago, my ex beat the living shit out of me. I was nearly dead. Cops show up and my Darling gives me first aid till the paramedics arrive. He was still a detective then. Before he left the force and got all rich. Went with me to the hospital."

"Oh, Moxie. I'm so sorry."

Moxie lifted a shoulder, ran her fingers through her spikes of white hair. "The ex was a real charmer, but then, so was I. All drugged up, bag of bones, no skills, no job. Darling came to the hospital every day. Don't know what he saw in me. Such a mess I was back then. Said he had a job for me, but I had to stay clean. Made me promise. I still had enough brain cells left to take him up on his offer, and I've never looked back."

Leaning her hip against the shiny black marble counter, Georgie said, "He's very special."

"He's a man puts his money where his mouth is. Lots of the help he's had over the years have been like me, specially once the money started rolling in." Moxie's eyes grew serious. "We had a gardener on the place, up until a few months ago. Murdered by some lunatic. Darling took it upon himself to track the killer, even defying his own brother to nab the perp. Closed the case, but he ended up with a bullet in his side."

Georgie nodded absently, thinking about Ethan's

refusal to discuss the details of how he'd come to take that bullet. He didn't think of himself as a hero; she couldn't think of him any other way.

"I'm in love with him," she said, raising her head to gauge Moxie's reaction.

"I know." A quiet grin spread across the housekeeper's features. "He's in love with you, too."

Georgie's heartbeat quickened and her blood warmed as hope flooded her system like a soft spring rain. "He hasn't . . . did he say something to you?"

Her smile broadened. "No, but he loves you all the same. Apparently, he hasn't finished analyzing it to death yet." She rolled her expressive eyes. "My Darling, he's big on analyzing, but he always manages to come up with the right answer."

There wasn't much Georgie could say to that, so instead she said, "Look, I, um, I told him I was going to do a little redecorating, so I should get started." Speculating on Ethan's feelings for her were counterproductive. Unless and until he told her how he felt, she was only setting herself up for heartbreak. Gesturing out the window, she said, "Does that gate back there lead down to the beach?"

"Sure does. Got a cipher lock on it on the other side. Once you go through it, you need the code to get back in." Glancing at the coffeemaker, she said, "Why don't I give you a complete tour of the house and grounds, then you can get going on your redecorating?"

"Sounds fantastic."

By the time Moxie had given Georgie a room-by-room analysis of the house, and they'd strolled through the extensive gardens, then had a bite of lunch, it was closing in on one in the afternoon. Raine and Lucas had come downstairs to say hello, then disappeared somewhere outside, taking Caroline with them in the stroller.

Back in the kitchen, Georgie said, "That cipher lock code, twelve-twenty-five, right?"

"Right," Moxie agreed. "Once you go through the gate, there are steps carved right into the rock. It's steep, but doable. Nice cove at the bottom with a pretty little beach. Rocks on either side keep it safe and private. The original owners used to have big parties and people would dock their boats and climb the stairs to the terrace. There's even a pier that runs out past the breakers."

"Well, I just want to collect some driftwood and beach rocks for Ethan's bedroom."

Moxie tilted her head. "So you'll need some-thing to carry it all in," she said, her eyes bright with enthusiasm.

Shuffling over to a tall cupboard, she rum-maged inside for a minute, then pulled out a large canvas sack with handles. "This should do the trick." On the counter, the coffeemaker burbled and popped with a fresh pot. "It's still chilly out there. Let me pour you a cup to take with you."

Outside, the canvas tote in one hand, a mug of steaming coffee in the other, Georgie was met once more by the cool afternoon air. She smiled to herself, ready to enjoy a little time alone.

After Moxie's extensive, detailed, and enthusiastic tour, her mind was filled with ideas for transforming Ethan's house. Yes, this was just what she needed.

Mist blew through the bars of the wrought-iron gate to curl around the redwoods, flower beds, small pines, and lush ferns that surrounded the house. The hinges squeaked as she pulled the gate wide enough to walk through; immediately, it snapped shut behind her.

Taking a sip of coffee, she gazed out across the Pacific—or as much as she could see of it through the blanket of fog. Moxie was right. The natural curve of the coastline and cliffs created an inlet, a small cove, and private beach that was inaccessible except by boat. At the north end of the inlet, a narrow dock jutted far out into the water.

She began descending the wide steps, inhaling deeply of the briny air, letting the soft mist cool her cheeks. Tossing her head, she smiled, feeling like a healthy young animal out in the world.

As she continued on down, the sound of the surf grew louder until she finally reached the bottom of the path and stepped onto the sandy beach. The mist was thinner here, allowing her to see the small waves that crashed and tumbled over each other as they raced onto the hard sand, then retreated, leaving only a thin sheet of salty foam in their wake.

Overhead, seagulls whirled and argued, while a weak sun tried to break through the clouds.

As she strolled toward the pier, she thought she caught a glimpse of red in the mist near what must be the end of the dock. Narrowing her eyes, she tried to make it out, but the fog over the water was too dense.

Spotting a pretty seashell near her feet, she bent and picked it up, enjoying the feel of the gritty grains of sand on her fingers.

"Well, I'll be damned."

The man's voice came from behind her. As she whirled to face it, the coffee mug flew from her hand and the coffee splashed out, instantly absorbed into the wet sand as though it had never been.

Panic choked her. She felt like she was in one of those nightmares where you want to scream, but can't. Her heart slammed against her ribs so hard, her whole body jerked. Fear thickened her brain as she simply stared at Paul Corcoran. Behind him, two men leered at her, making her feel queasy.

Reaching for her arm, Paul yanked her close to his chest, tightening his grip until she wanted to cry out. But she didn't.

"Here we were, trying to figure out a way past that gate up there, and what do you think? The very lady I came to see comes trotting on down the steps, right into my lap."

"W-what are you doing here?" she managed on a voice too breathy and thin.

Paul's usually even features morphed into something ugly, something hateful, and her legs nearly went out from under her. His grip tightened even more and she thought she'd cry out, but just then he shoved her, and she fell hard into one of the other men's barrel chest. She tried to push herself away from him, but his thick fingers encircled both her wrists in an iron grip.

"Georgie? Is that you down there? Who's with you?"

Raine! It was Raine, calling to her from the top of the cliff!

Quickly pulling in a deep breath, she screamed, *"It's Paul! Tell Ethan—"*

Her head snapped to the side as the flat of Paul's hand met her cheek in a vicious slap.

"Shut up!" he shouted, looking around frantically, then up at the cliff where Raine was screaming Georgie's name. "Honcho," he ordered, gesturing to Georgie. "Get her into the boat. We've got to get the hell out of here!"

Chapter Twenty-four

Stay in the present, in the *now*. If you drag energy from the past with you into the future, like, hello! Don't expect anything to change! You want a new man in your life? Then let go of the old one(s). Release all that negative energy by forgiving—forgive whoever hurt you, but most of all, forgive yourself. The only person all that old hate, anger, and guilt will impact is you.

Georgiana Mundy's *Feng Shui for Lovers*

"I understand the police spoke with you this morning." Ethan studied the station manager's face. Ozzie Horton was as easy to read as a kindergarten coloring book. He avoided direct eye contact, blinked rapidly and constantly, stuttered, hemmed and hawed, and sat poised on the edge of his desk chair, ready to scurry to the door if Ethan said boo. "You told them you don't know anything about the murder."

Horton nodded several hundred times, as though he were watching a hyperactive kid on a pogo stick. He still refused to meet Ethan's gaze. "That's what I told them."

"But you do know about the murder, don't you." It wasn't a question.

The station manager lowered his head and rolled his lips inward, as though he were fighting to keep words from escaping from his mouth.

Settling back in his chair, Ethan studied the man, then said quietly, "Where were you, Mr. Horton, when Vaughn Corcoran was murdered?"

He swallowed, licked his lips, then swallowed again. "Home. I was at home. My partner, Phillip, and our son Josh can verify that."

"Would Phillip or Josh lie to protect you?"

Horton flicked a hurt look up at Ethan. "No. No, no. I would never ask them to do such a thing. Especially not Josh. What kind of lesson would that be for a six-year-old? No, we had a dinner party Friday night that went on until the wee hours. Lots of our friends were there. Saturday morning, Phillip and I took Josh to the park."

Ethan made a few notes in his pad, then set it down on the desk. Gauging Horton's nervous expression, he said, "But it's obvious that's not all to the story. Why don't you tell me the rest?"

Tiny beads of sweat began to pop on Horton's forehead and his eyes seemed to glass over. On the desk in front of him, his fingers shook as he twisted them together, first one way, then the other.

"I—I don't know what to do!" he blurted. Finally looking Ethan in the eye, he stumbled, "I care v-very much about Georgie. But if I say anything, someone else I care very much for might get into trouble!"

"The truth is what it is, Mr. Horton." He leaned forward. "Are you aware of what Paul Corcoran did to Georgie's friend Raine?"

Horton nodded. "Yes. Yes, yes. I found out a few months ago." Genuine compassion filled his eyes. "Absolutely *despicable*."

"You caused the trouble on the set, messed up the spices. You put the oil of rosemary in the ice cubes, didn't you?"

His gaze shot to Ethan's, but he didn't deny the accusations. "I had to. I'm sorry. Sorry and ashamed." He fiddled with the ring on his left hand, turning the gold band around and around. "Mr. Corcoran's dead now, so I guess none of it matters anymore. He—he wanted to hassle Georgie, he said. He thought she might be blackmailing him over what Paul had done to her friend. He threatened that if I didn't help him, he would see to it that Josh was taken away from Phillip and me." His brows snapped together as panic thickened his voice. "I was terrified he'd make good on it! He was a hateful man!"

"So why'd you hire me?"

"I had to make it look like I was trying to get to the bottom of things—and keep suspicion off myself." He smiled weakly. "Guess I should have hired one of your less competent competitors."

Instead of agreeing, Ethan said, "But Georgie wasn't the one blackmailing Corcoran, was she?"

"I *told* him it wasn't her," he rushed. "Couldn't

be. Georgie's just not like that. She's too up front. I—I thought maybe it was her friend Raine doing it." He shook his head slowly, whispering, "I discovered the truth the day after Mr. Corcoran was killed."

Watching Horton carefully, Ethan said, "And the truth was, Paul had drugged and raped another woman at KALM, hadn't he? And she confided in you. And you're worried it was she who killed Vaughn Corcoran."

He wrung his hands together; his normally rosy cheeks were pale, his voice quavered. "Mr. Corcoran told me he was going to confront Georgie and put an end to it once and for all. I was terrified, I tell you! I didn't know what he meant by that, put an end to it once and for all. And . . . and then when they found him there, in her house, dead, I—I . . . got so confused!"

"But you knew someone else had a motive, and you began to suspect *her* of the murder."

"Yes. She's been acting strangely since Mr. Corcoran's death, very tense, nervous. Jumps like a cat whenever you so much as say her name. She's always lived on the edge. I think now she's maybe gone over. I don't want to believe she's capable, but . . ." He shook his head. "I should have come forward. I—I just didn't want anybody else to get hurt!"

Ethan stood. "Let's take a walk, okay, Mr. Horton? Get this whole thing straightened out?"

A few moments later, they stood outside her door. Ozzie knocked, went in first. When he stepped aside and she saw Ethan, her eyes grew large and wary.

"Listen to me, hon," Horton said gently. "Ethan here would like to speak to you for a few minutes, okay? I think . . . I think you should. You know what I'm saying?"

She dropped the container of pins she was holding as her gaze met Ethan's. Yeah. It was there, all right. In her eyes.

"I'm going to call someone," Ethan said. "A detective. He'll take your official statement. In the meantime, I think maybe you'd like to contact a lawyer."

For a moment, Iona just stared at him. In the depths of her eyes, fear and indecision clearly warred with self-preservation as she seemed to gauge whether she should make a run for it. Finally, her eyes quieted, her shoulders relaxed, and she slumped into the wooden chair by the wardrobe rack. Closing her black-lined lids, she let her head fall with a dull thump against the wall behind her.

"Yeah," she whispered to the air. "That would prob'ly be a real good idea."

Georgie sat very still on the cushioned vinyl seat in the back of the speedboat as the man they called Drool guided it slowly through the choppy waves. The wind off the surface of the water whipped her hair around her face and into her mouth, and she wished she could tie it back, but Honcho had bound her hands.

She stared down at her wrists. *I will be patient. I will wait for my chance. It will come. I will be ready.*

The words became her silent mantra as she lifted her gaze to search the water for nearby boats that might come to her rescue. So far, she'd seen several fishing trawlers and sailboats at a distance, but none had been close enough that she could call to them. Even if she tried, before she could make a sound, Honcho would either shove her to the bottom of the boat and out of sight—or overboard, where, without the use of her arms, she'd drown.

Nothing that had happened in Georgie's life had ever prepared her for being kidnapped. She had no training, no frame of reference, no plan— other than what she'd seen in movies or read in books. Not knowing what the men intended to do with her now that they had her contorted her brain, obscured her thinking. She needed a clear head, so she took in deep, calming breaths, all the while affirming she was strong, capable, and safe.

As the boat cut through the steady roll of waves, she shut her eyes and envisioned Ethan, sending him telepathic messages . . .

I'm here. I'm alive. Please find me. I love you.

I will be patient. I will wait for my chance. It will come. I will be ready.

I'm here. Find me. Please find me, Ethan. I love you.

She'd lost one sandal back at the beach, her mouth hurt where Paul had hit her, and the dense fog wrapping around her like an icy cloak chilled and stiffened her muscles. The smell of diesel fuel mixed with briny ocean air unsettled her stomach as the boat chugged through the water, hugging the coastline, carrying her farther and farther away from the people she loved.

Her eyes fell on Paul, sprawled in the seat next to Drool at the front of the boat. Stupid, arrogant son of a bitch. How dare he? How *dare* he!

Anger fueling her resolve, she yelled at his back, "Take me to shore, Paul! You already have charges against you . . . don't make things worse. Let me go!"

Paul swiveled his chair around to face her. He leaned forward, his elbows on his knees, a skeptical sneer on his face. Raising his voice above the roar of the engine, he shouted, "You think I care what happens to me? For Christ's sake, Georgie, I've basically been disinherited. That means no money!" He threw his hands up, and shrugged in a gesture of helplessness. "And since it's all your fault—"

"What are you talking about?" she choked against the wind. "How is this my fault?"

"If you hadn't murdered my father, I'd still be fat, dumb, and happy! Oh, and rich!"

"I didn't kill your father! Is that what you think?" She stared at him, everything finally clicking into place. "Paul, I did *not* kill Vaughn! I thought *you* killed him!"

"Even I'm not stupid enough to bite the hand that feeds me!" he screamed, baring his perfectly white teeth. "*You* killed him. *You* ruined my life, and for that, sugar tits, you are going to pay with everything you've got!"

Ethan and Nate watched in silence as the uniformed officers led Iona away, her wrists cuffed behind her back. Not that she'd give anybody any trouble; she'd been grateful to confess, relieved it was over. He'd seen it a lot. When decent people did something heinous, they simply couldn't live with the guilt and generally spilled their guts the first chance they got.

As they'd sat in Horton's office—a nervous-looking young attorney by her side—Iona had cried through the whole deposition.

"Mr. C-Corcoran came to the studio real early on Saturday morning just after we finished taping a show for Iggy. Corcoran was in an ugly mood. I overheard him saying something about Georgie, and I got worried, so when he left the studio, I followed him." She wiped the tears from her eyes, blew her nose. "He drove to Georgie's house."

Nate stood by Horton's office window, his arms crossed over his chest. "What happened after you arrived at Ms. Mundy's?"

She lifted one shoulder, tossed her head back, sniffed. "I—I watched him ring her doorbell, then she let him in. At least, I thought she did, but the door must not have been locked. Anyway, he went in, and I crept inside after him. Heard him searching the house, yelling for her. 'I know it's you, bitch!' he shouted. Then he lowered his voice and sort of growled like an animal, 'I'm going to kill you myself, and I'm going to enjoy it.'"

Pausing for a moment, Iona ran her tongue over her lips and swallowed.

"I didn't realize Georgie wasn't home. I thought she was hiding in the closet or something. So I snuck into the kitchen and grabbed a knife. When I went through her bedroom door, his . . . Mr. Corcoran's back was to me. He was furious, really screaming now. 'Wait until I get my hands on you!' he said. 'I'm only sorry it was your gutless little friend Paul raped, and not *you*!'"

Iona bowed her head as tears slid down her cheeks to splash unheeded on the table. "How could he s-say such a thing? Such an evil, heartless man. I was so *angry* that he thought what Paul had done was okay, and that he even wished it on another woman!" She raised her head and looked directly into Ethan's eyes. "Paul had used and humiliated me, and this man didn't even care! I wanted to hit him, pound him with my fists, but the knife was in my hand . . . I rushed at him, and when I struck him, it just sort of . . . went in. He fell." She gave a weak, sad laugh. "I . . . he didn't even know it was me."

Ethan watched as her lawyer spoke softly into her ear. Iona's shoulders drooped and she nodded, letting out a long breath. It was over now. She probably hadn't slept or eaten since it happened. But with her conscience finally clear, she could relax.

"Were you the one who phoned the police?" Nate asked.

She nodded absently. "Yeah. When I realized Georgie wasn't even there, I ran away. Later, when I got to thinking about it, I didn't want her to come home and find . . . well, you know . . . the body. So I called the cops." Raising her head, she sought Ethan's eyes once more. "I didn't understand until Mr. Corcoran started yelling, that he thought Georgie was the one who was blackmailing him. But it was me. I—I didn't mean to kill him, but I can't be sorry he's dead! I wouldn't have let Georgie be charged. I would never have let that happen. I would have come forward. I *swear*."

Ethan met her watery gaze. "I believe you, Iona."

As the elevator doors closed on the sobbing young woman in handcuffs, Ethan said to Nate, "Whose fingerprints were on the knife?"

"Georgie's. But it was from her kitchen, so that was a given. There was a second set of partials. I imagine they'll match Iona's."

"I imagine so."

Silence stretched between the two men, but for the first time in over twenty years, Ethan didn't feel awkward about it. It was more like two old friends who didn't need to speak, who felt comfortable just standing next to each other, absorbed in their own thoughts, yet still connected on a gut-deep level.

Nate seemed to be waiting for something, so Ethan ventured casually, "How's Tabitha? You . . ." —he shrugged—"happy?"

Nate shoved his glasses up on his nose and grinned. "Yeah."

"So, being married's good?"

Nate's smile went a little sappy. "Yeah."

Ethan pushed the elevator button, turning over the idea in his mind. Maybe Georgie had been on the right track. Maybe it was time . . .

As they waited in silence, he mulled over what to do next. The cowardly thing would be for Ethan to keep quiet and never tell Nate about Cathy. After all, if he never said anything, he would never have to face his brother's condemnation.

But there had been enough fences strung between them over the years. Maybe Georgie was right, maybe it was time to tear them away. Besides, he missed his brother, the way they'd been when they were kids, like in that old photo he had on his desk. He wanted that relationship back again—if it wasn't too late—and if making things right took letting Nate inside his darkest secret, his most monumental failure, maybe it was worth the risk.

"Listen, Nate," he said, his head down, his hands in his pockets. "There's something I've been meaning to tell you. Uh, wanting to tell you, actually. Something about me you should know."

A bell dinged, and the elevator doors slid open. As the men stepped inside, Nate pushed the button for the first floor. "Okay. You have my undivided attention for the next thirty-one floors."

Ethan felt the ground beneath him fall away as the elevator began its descent. He was riding on thin air, and the metaphor wasn't lost on him.

"Six years ago," he began, "before you moved

back to San Francisco, I, uh, I almost got married. Her name was Cathy. She was a PD negotiator. Long story short, we were working a hostage situation . . . shots were fired. She, uh, she died."

Next to him, Nate was silent for a moment. Then, quietly, he said, "Jesus, Ethan. I'm sorry. I had no idea—"

"There's more," he said flatly. Though Nate fell silent again, Ethan could feel his brother's eyes on him. "During the autopsy . . . look, the bottom line is, Cathy got caught in the crossfire and it was, uh, it was my bullet that killed her."

There. It was out. No regrets. Let the chips fall where they may.

In silence, the elevator plummeted past the twenty-fifth floor, twentieth, fifteenth as the two brothers simply stood next to each other.

As the elevator car began to slow, Nate spoke. "Before I met Tabby, I'm not sure I would have understood . . . I . . . well, to lose her now . . ." Ethan felt his brother's hand grip his shoulder. "You doing all right?"

Ethan cleared his throat. "Getting there." And thanks to Georgie, he was.

Nate dropped his hand. "Look, you need anything—"

"Yeah."

"Want to talk—"

"Yeah, okay."

"I can, you know, do that."

Ethan nodded. "Good."

Nate nodded. "Yeah, good."

Both men shrugged.

The elevator slowed to a stop and a bell pinged, but as the doors slid apart, Ethan stepped in front of Nate, blocking his exit.

"Look, uh, thanks," he said. "For understanding. Not condemning. I, uh . . . well, just thanks, that's all. After all the shit between us, I don't have any right to expect—"

"Hey," Nate interrupted. He adjusted his glasses while a slow, serious smile crept over his lips. "As a very fine and honorable man once said to me . . . you're my brother."

Ethan grinned at Nate in a conspiratorial way, as he had when they'd been boys and they'd both been caught with their hands in any number of cookie jars.

When Nate grinned back, Ethan felt as if the weight of the world had just been lifted from his shoulders. It had been a long time coming, and now that it was here, it felt good. It felt damn good.

Inside his jacket pocket, his cell phone vibrated at the same time he heard Nate's chime. They chuckled at each other as they each answered their phones.

A moment later, their smiles vanished. Nate's head came up, his gaze locked with Ethan's. Without so much as a word between them, they turned, and together, ran like hell for the door.

Chapter Twenty-five

When you finally find the man of your dreams, squeeze him, tease him, please him, but above all, never let him go. They say good men are hard to find. They are right.

Georgiana Mundy's *Feng Shui for Lovers*

"**F**ound it." Ethan tapped the image on the dashboard computer screen. "I *knew* that son of a bitch had to own a boat. Even Paul Corcoran isn't stupid enough to kidnap a woman in a rental."

"Yeah," Nate drawled, "in the off-season he probably uses it to putt-putt around the shallow end of the gene pool."

Ignoring his brother's debatable wit, Ethan said, "Look, see?" He tapped the screen again. "There's a 2006 Checkmate Bowrider with a three-hundred-horsepower MerCruiser engine registered under the name CorCorp, one of Corcoran's holding companies. It's kept in a slip at the Alta Vista Yacht Club."

In the passenger seat, Nate leaned forward and narrowed his gaze on the data. "Alta Vista, huh? Very private, very exclusive, very expensive. From the beach in Marin, that's about twenty coastal miles." He eased back into his seat. "But Raine said she didn't see the boat because of the fog. We don't have visual confirmation it was a Bowrider that took Georgie."

"It's it, though. Has to be."

Inside Ethan's head, reality, conjecture, and reason meshed to form an image of what had happened—and anticipate what might happen next.

It was the next part that had his gut twisting like a ball of snakes.

Hours had passed since he'd gotten the call that Paul Corcoran had nabbed Georgie. During that time, he and Nate had interviewed some of Corcoran's employees, made phone calls, and driven to places Paul might have taken her. Nothing.

Afternoon had begun melting into evening. Soon it would be dark, and still no sign of her, or the men who'd abducted her. Nearly half a day had passed during which time anything could have happened to the woman he loved.

If he let himself think of what Corcoran and his thugs might have done, might be doing to her even now, it would drive him crazy; he wouldn't be able to focus. She was in the hands of an admitted rapist who believed she'd murdered his father, not to mention two felons who made their living hurting . . .

"You okay, Ethan?"

He blinked away the images and nodded at his brother. "Yeah. Just lost in thought for a second."

"We'll find her," Nate said. "From what I've seen of Georgie, she's tough. She'll make it through."

Sucking in a deep breath, Ethan gave his brother a sharp nod. Until this was over, he had to set aside his personal feelings so his brain could analyze, evaluate, conclude. Georgie deserved nothing less than every ounce of brainpower he owned if he was to get her back—but damn, it was easier said than done.

Tell Ethan—she'd shouted the words at Raine.

Tell Ethan what? Tell Ethan not to worry? Tell Ethan which way we went? Tell Ethan I love him?

If she thought she was going to die, which of those things would she say?

But he knew. He already knew.

"Okay," he said. "They've grabbed Georgie, gotten her into the boat. Now what? Where do they go? And how fast? If they clip along at too high a rate of speed, they risk attracting the attention of the Harbor Patrol, so they're going to take it slow. Seventeen, maybe twenty knots."

Nate snorted. "It's after seven now. Even if Corcoran used his dick as a rudder and his ears as oars, they still could've made Alta Vista by two or three."

Ethan stared over at Nate. "Great. Now I'm going to have that image stuck in my head for days."

With a wiggle of his brows and a flash of white teeth, Nate said, "Not my problem."

Ignoring his brother for the moment, Ethan leaned back behind the wheel, turning the calculations and logic over and over in his brain. "It's been like pea soup off the coast all day. Very low viz. My bet is, they've been dinking around all afternoon, hiding in the mist, waiting for nightfall so they can dock. Either they left a car inside the marina lot or nearby."

Nate adjusted his glasses, then pulled out his cell and punched in some numbers. Putting the phone to his ear, he said, "So using your logic, they haven't hit land yet. It'll be pitch-dark in less than an hour, so . . . Yeah, hi. I need the number for the Alta Vista Marina? Great, can you connect me, please?"

Ethan shut down the computer and cranked the engine, listening to Nate's conversation.

". . . it's not? You're sure? What's the slip number? Yeah, thanks. Look, we'll be there in fifteen. If he docks before we get there, call me immediately. Yeah, Inspector Darling. Uh-huh. Don't go there, pal," he growled. He gave the guard his cell phone number, ended the call, and shoved the phone into his jacket pocket. "I'm changing my name."

"Yeah, gets old. What'd he say?"

"You were right, big brother. According to the logbook, Paul Corcoran and two guests took the boat out early this morning, but have not returned."

"What about his car? Did he leave it in the lot?"

"Yes, it's an SUV, and it's still there."

Ethan mulled it over. "If they douse their running lights, they probably think they can nav right into the slip unnoticed. If they're lucky, there won't be a lot of people around, it's a foggy night, they spirit Georgie off the boat and into the SUV, then drive away without anybody being the wiser."

"But where do they go from there?"

"Nowhere. Because we're going to be there to stop them."

By the time they reached the marina, it was dark. Nate flashed his badge at the guard, who let them pass without comment.

"Slip D-2," Nate said. Gesturing, he added, "I think it's down that way."

Even though it was a weeknight, the parking lot was moderately full. Couples strolled from their cars or up from the dock to the clubhouse restaurant for an expensive dinner, fine wine, quiet conversation.

As the two men made their way through the mist, down the dock toward Slip D-2, Ethan heard the sound of a speedboat in the distance, slowly chugging toward them through the fog.

He touched Nate's arm. "Hear it?" Reaching under his jacket, he eased the .38 from the holster snuggly strapped to his shoulder, as his brother made a grunting sound and did the same.

A man and a woman, tightly wrapped around each other, began walking onto the dock, but Nate flashed his badge and quietly asked them to return to the restaurant. Wide-eyed and apologetic, they rushed away, glancing nervously over their shoulders.

As the boat came closer, Ethan thought his heart would burst in his chest. What if this wasn't Corcoran after all? What if he'd guessed wrong and this was just some guy returning from an all-day fishing trip? What if . . . so many things, none of them good.

Crouching, he took cover behind a clump of pilings, then eased himself up so he could see over the top. Beside him, his brother did the same.

The motor went silent as the bow of the boat materialized through the mist. Momentum carried it quietly right into Slip D–2. It made a thumping noise as it smacked into the bumper on the side of the dock.

Ethan swallowed, and the sound reverberated in his ears like a gunshot.

He felt Nate move away and behind him, farther into the shadows. A moment later, he heard his brother on his cell, calling for backup.

The man Lucas had described as Honcho threw a line around a dock cleat, while the other thug, probably Drool, shut off the engine. No one spoke as Paul stood, bracing his legs to keep from falling out of the rocking boat.

Ethan's gaze fell on Georgie, sitting at the stern, and he thought he'd go nuts with relief. At first, his blood boiled with rage, then chilled, forming icicles sharp enough to pierce his veins.

They could have killed her, dumped her body

anywhere in the bay. Though he hadn't dared let himself voice it to Nate, the thought had been there all the same, eating away at his brain. Her hands were bound in front of her, but from what he could see, she was all right. She was alive— and he was going to make damn sure she stayed that way.

Paul reached down and yanked Georgie to her feet. Her body fell against his, and she struggled to push herself away.

"Keep that mouth of yours shut," he warned. "If I tape it, somebody might notice, but if you make one single tiny little sound, I'll kill you right here, right now. Remember, I have nothing to lose . . ."

Through the darkness and the mist, Ethan couldn't see her eyes clearly, but if he knew Georgie, there'd be fury in them.

And fear.

The thought sickened him. When this was over, he'd make sure she was never afraid of anything ever again. If it took the rest of his life, he'd make sure.

Honcho and Drool jumped onto the dock, then turned to help Georgie from the boat. As soon as Paul's feet touched the pier, he grabbed Georgie's arm. "Remember what I said, sugar tits."

Just then, the door to the restaurant at the end of the marina burst open, and a group of people spilled out onto the upper dock. Light from the interior splashed across the scene, illuminating Paul and his grip on Georgie's arm.

Paul and his goons stood frozen, uncertain what to do. And in that moment, everything changed.

Georgie whirled, lashing out at Paul with her foot. She connected with the back of his knee, and he stumbled. With her bound hands, she formed a fist, slamming into his face, sending him backward into the speedboat, where he lay stunned and motionless.

"Fire!" she screamed. "Help! Fire, fire! Over here! Fire!"

As one, Ethan and Nate rounded the pilings.

"Police!" Nate shouted. "Hands in the air! Now!"

Honcho bared his teeth and grabbed for Georgie. His arm around her throat, he yanked her against his chest. "Back off or I break her neck!" With his free hand, he reached behind him and pulled out a revolver, placing it against her jaw.

Nobody moved. In the distance, the sound of sirens screaming toward the marina made the crowd of civilians break into confused chatter. Quickly, they backed away to the safety of the restaurant.

"There's nowhere for you to run, Honcho!" Ethan shouted. "Give it up. Let her go. No need to make this worse than it already is!"

"I can take him," Nate said under his breath. The revolver in his hands was aimed directly at Honcho's head. "Say when."

Behind Honcho, Drool looked like he might make a move, then thought better of it, put his hands in the air, and sat on the dock.

"Honcho!" Ethan yelled. "Drop your god-damned weapon and let her go!"

In a rush, that night came back to him—a sickening flashback he'd hoped never to witness again. The lights, the sirens, the desperate man holding a woman Ethan loved hostage.

He felt his palms grow slick and he was afraid he'd drop his weapon. Beads of sweat formed on his brow, on the back of his neck, trickled down his spine. Cold sweat. Deadly cold. His stomach soured and his muscles cramped. Not again . . . he would not let this happen again . . .

His gaze shifted to Georgie. Honcho's arm was around her throat, nearly choking her. The gun pressed to her jaw made her mouth flatten in pain, but there was no pain in her eyes. No anger. No fear. What he did see there shocked him to the core.

Trust. Complete and total trust.

Georgie, who had rarely trusted anyone in her life, trusted him with that very life.

"*Georgie,*" he whispered, and she smiled at him.

"*I love you,*" she mouthed. "*Go for it.*"

Somebody shouted, somebody screamed, somebody ran. Sirens blared, people yelled. A shot shattered the night, then another.

Honcho cursed, slammed Georgie in the side of the head with his fist, then shoved her toward the edge of the dock. She stumbled, seemed to try and catch her balance, but toppled over the edge and into the water.

Ethan bolted around the pilings, running like hell toward where she'd fallen. Through the mist, he saw Honcho take aim. He vaguely registered a shout behind him, then an explosion. Honcho's somber expression changed to surprise, and his weapon fell from his fingers. As Ethan dove for the water, Honcho's lifeless body crumpled to the dock.

Shock numbed him as he went deep and the cold sea closed over his head. He kicked and shot for the surface.

How much time had passed? She'd been punched, stunned. Her hands were tied. She wouldn't be able to swim.

"*Georgie!*" he shouted, his mouth and nostrils filled with salty water. Déjà vu hit him, sickened him, and still he kept calling her name.

He swam under the dock, but it was too dark to see. Then somebody else was beside him in the water.

"Did you find her?" his brother shouted.

"No!" Ethan slapped at the water, twisted, stopped, listened. "Georgie!"

"Eth-Ethan!" came the broken cry. Silence. She'd gone under again.

"Somebody get some lights down here!" Nate yelled as Ethan turned toward the sound of Georgie's voice.

He went under again. His arms outstretched, he tried to grab hold of her. He stayed under, kicking, reaching, praying until his lungs nearly burst. Shooting for the surface, he gulped more air, then went down again.

His fingers splayed, he reached and grabbed and clawed and clutched, and this time, he connected.

Grasping a fistful of her shirt, he shot once more for the surface, pulling her to him, holding her close, lifting her shoulders out of the water.

She gasped once, choked, then . . . nothing.

"No!" he rasped, his voice hoarse from the shouting and the salt water. Pressing his shaking fingers against her neck, he checked for a pulse. Couldn't find it. He moved his fingers, searching, searching, desperate to find her heartbeat.

There. There it was. Like a butterfly on his fingertips.

He took in a lungful of air, pressed his mouth to hers, and breathed his life into her. And again. And again.

Finally, she moved, shifted in his grasp. He felt her arms slide over his head, her bound hands holding him captive.

Somewhere in the distance, in a world outside his own, he heard his brother shouting for paramedics.

"Georgie," Ethan breathed. "You okay?"

His vision blurred, but it wasn't the chill Pacific stinging his eyes.

"You found me," she said weakly. "I knew you'd come. We had a deal. I didn't forget."

"Yeah," he choked. "We had a deal."

He couldn't say anything more, so he only held her close, letting the frigid water buoy him up while they waited to be hoisted out of the water.

"You were gutsy," he finally managed. "Smart, to yell fire." He stroked her hair away from her face. "Grasshopper, I . . . you have to know . . . I should have told you before . . ."

She raised her face and pressed a cold, salty kiss on his mouth, halting his bungled confession of love. "I know, Master," she whispered. "I know."

Epilogue

So what happens if you feng shui your world, and you still don't meet the man of your dreams? Keep at it, of course! Continue with your affirmations, your positive visualizations, keep your mind open, and follow your heart. Feng shui works; don't give up on it, and it won't give up on you!

Georgiana Darling's *Feng Shui for Newlyweds*

Six months later . . .

"E than?" Georgie shouted. "I'm up here!" She tossed the ivory silk dress over her head, smoothing it down her hips. Glancing quickly at the bed, she bit her lip.

A moment later, Ethan appeared in the doorway, smiled at her, then immediately scowled. "You moved my bed again."

"*Our* bed. You don't want to get sick, do you? Or die in your sleep?"

He crossed his arms over his chest. "Listen, Mrs. Darling. Since we got married, you've moved that bed three times, scattered or replaced the furniture in the living room four times, and put little red tassels on every electronic gadget in the house."

"*Cures*," she said, as she hunted in the enormous walk-in closet for the shoes that matched her dress. "Red offsets the negative *chi* of all those harmful electrode thingies. Ah, there they are," she muttered, spying the pair of heels.

As she bent to slip the shoes on, he came up behind her, wrapping his arms around her waist, then sliding his hands lower, splaying his fingers across her abdomen.

"I like your baby bump," he said, then kissed the back of her neck.

"All that unprotected sex was bound to lead to an increase in the population," she said dryly. "You need to get a hobby."

"I have one," he said, and nuzzled her neck again.

Straightening, she leaned back against his hard chest and placed her hands over his. "Not much of a baby bump yet," she said. "Catch me again in six months, and you won't even be able to get your arms around me."

"I'll always be able to get my arms around you, Grasshopper," he promised softly. "What time do we have to be there?"

She snuggled against him, happier than she'd ever imagined she could be. She'd married the man of her dreams, and was pregnant with their first child—the first of many, she hoped. Though Paul hadn't spent a day in jail because of the rapes, he and Drool had been convicted of kidnapping and assault; they'd both be in prison a long, long time.

As for Iona, while she had been convicted of manslaughter, her case was under appeal, and Georgie and Ethan were doing all they could to try and get her a new trial.

"The wedding's at two," she said, "but I told Raine we'd be there at one. Lucas's sons flew in last night, so I promised we'd watch Caroline and the boys until the ceremony starts."

Ethan grunted, then kissed the back of her neck again. Nudging her toward the bed, he said, "Sit."

"We don't have time—"

"Not for that," he interrupted.

She sat and looked up at him, and her heart fluttered just like it did every time she saw him, or thought of him, or kissed him, or thought of him, or slept with him, or thought of him . . .

"I have a wedding present for you," he said, digging into his pocket. He pulled out a small black velvet box, then crouched in front of her and placed it in her hand. "I hope you like it."

She blinked in confusion. "But today is Lucas and Raine's wedding day, not ours. And you already gave me a wonderful wedding present." She patted her tummy. "Something I've always wanted."

His hazel eyes gleamed. "I know. But I saw

this, and thought of you, and wanted you to have it. I think it'll go perfectly with your outfit."

His grin told her there was something ... unusual about this gift. Something special and secret between them, and her heart fluttered all over again.

Holding the little box in her palm, she slowly opened the lid. "Oh, Ethan!" she choked, tears of surprise and joy filling her eyes. "It's perfect. I *love* it. Put it on me."

Lifting the chain out of the box, she admired the little gold grasshopper, its arms and legs bent in a jaunty dance, its tiny top hat set at a rakish angle, a happy grin on its itty-bitty face. In its gloved hand, it carried a walking stick with a small diamond for a knob.

As she stood, Ethan took the necklace from her, unclasped it, and slipped it around her neck, fastening it in back.

His fingers were warm on her skin, and she laughed, letting her happy tears flow freely.

He cupped his palms around her shoulders, turning her to face him. "Like it?" he asked, hope and love shining in the depths of his eyes.

She pressed her lips together and nodded, afraid to speak. God, pregnancy had made her so emotional! Or maybe it was her incredible love for Ethan that had her bursting into tears of joy over the silliest things.

Raising her gaze to meet his, her voice choked with emotion, she whispered, "I love you so much."

His eyes grew serious as his hands slid up to cup her face. Bending his head, he placed a lingering kiss on her mouth.

"And please to remember, Grasshopper, I love you." Then, with a calculating look in his eye, he murmured tenderly, "Are you *sure* we don't have time?"

Next month, don't miss these exciting new love stories only from Avon Books

The Wicked Ways of a Duke by Laura Lee Guhrke

An Avon Romantic Treasure

Prudence Bosworth never dreamed that she'd inherit a fortune, but now that she has, she wants only one man: Rhys De Winter, the Duke of St. Cyres. But Rhys is far from perfect, and Prudence must show that their love is worth giving up his wicked ways.

Hello, Doggy! by Elaine Fox

An Avon Contemporary Romance

Keenan James thought he had all the answers when it came to women. After all, if he can handle a dog that only responds to "Barbra Streisand," he can handle a relationship. But psychologist Tory Hoffstra has him all turned around. Now he just needs to figure out if it's her ideas that drive him wild...or the woman herself?

A Seduction in Scarlet by Sara Bennett

An Avon Romance

Portia, Lady Ellerslie, is willing to risk it all for a night of passion. Even if it means entering a scandalous new world, finally having a chance to be with the man she loves is worth it. But what will happen when her secret is found out?

One Night With You by Sophie Jordan

An Avon Romance

Lady Jane Guthrie had been through a lot, and no one was more deserving of freedom than she. But after meeting Seth Rutledge, Earl of St. Claire, he shows her that one night will never be enough...and he won't rest until he's won her heart.

Visit www.AuthorTracker.com for exclusive information on your favorite HarperCollins authors.

Available wherever books are sold or please call 1-800-331-3761 to order.

REL 1207

Avon Romantic Treasures

Unforgettable, enthralling love stories, sparkling with passion and adventure from Romance's bestselling authors

AND THEN HE KISSED HER   *by Laura Lee Guhrke*
978-0-06-114360-1/$6.99 US/$9.99 Can

CLAIMING THE COURTESAN   *by Anna Campbell*
978-0-06-123491-0/$6.99 US/$9.99 Can

THE DUKE'S INDISCRETION   *by Adele Ashworth*
978-0-06-112857-8/$6.99 US/$9.99 Can

THE VISCOUNT IN HER BEDROOM   *by Gayle Callen*
978-0-06-078413-3/$6.99 US/$9.99 Can

HOW TO ENGAGE AN EARL   *by Kathryn Caskie*
978-0-06-112484-6/$6.99 US/$9.99 Can

BEWITCHING THE HIGHLANDER   *by Lois Greiman*
978-0-06-119134-3/$6.99 US/$9.99 Can

JUST WICKED ENOUGH   *by Lorraine Heath*
978-0-06-112970-4/$6.99 US/$9.99 Can

THE SCOTTISH COMPANION   *by Karen Ranney*
978-0-06-125237-2/$6.99 US/$9.99 Can

IN MY WILDEST FANTASIES   *by Julianne MacLean*
978-0-06-081949-1/$6.99 US/$9.99 Can

UNTOUCHED   *by Anna Campbell*
978-0-06-123492-7/$6.99 US/$9.99 Can

Visit www.AuthorTracker.com for exclusive
information on your favorite HarperCollins authors.   RT 0907

Available wherever books are sold or please call 1-800-331-3761 to order.

DISCOVER ROMANCE *at its*

SIZZLING HOT BEST FROM AVON BOOKS

Passions of the Ghost   by Sara Mackenzie
978-0-06-079582-5/$5.99 US/$7.99 Can

Love in the Fast Lane   by Jenna McKnight
978-06-084347-2/$5.99 US/$7.99 Can

Beware of Doug   by Elaine Fox
978-0-06-117568-8/$5.99 US/$7.99 Can

Arousing Suspicions   by Marianne Stillings
978-0-06-085009-8/$5.99 US/$7.99 Can

Be Still My Vampire Heart   by Kerrelyn Sparks
978-0-06-111844-9/$5.99 US/$7.99 Can

One Night With a Goddess   by Judi McCoy
978-0-06-077460-8/$5.99 US/$7.99 Can

At the Edge   by Cait London
978-0-06-114050-1/$5.99 US/$7.99 Can

When She Was Bad   by Cindy Kirk
978-0-06-084790-6/$5.99 US/$7.99 Can

The Forever Summer   by Suzanne Macpherson
978-0-06-116126-1/$5.99 US/$7.99 Can

Dead Girls Are Easy   by Terri Garey
978-0-06-113615-3/$5.99 US/$7.99 Can

CRO 0707

Visit www.AuthorTracker.com for exclusive
information on your favorite HarperCollins authors.

Available wherever books are sold
or please call 1-800-331-3761 to order.

AVON

978-0-06-124086-7
$13.95 ($17.50 Can.)

978-0-06-082481-5
$13.95 ($17.50 Can.)

978-0-06-087608-1
$13.95 ($16.50 Can.)

978-0-06-114874-3
$13.95 ($16.50 Can.)

978-0-06-082972-8
$13.95 ($17.50 Can.)

978-0-06-123221-3
$13.95 ($17.50 Can.)

Visit www.AuthorTracker.com for exclusive
information on your favorite HarperCollins authors.

Available wherever books are sold, or call 1-800-331-3761 to order.

ATP 1207